Happy Father's Day to our
beloved Dad and Grandpa!!!

We couldn't have picked
a better man for the job!

We love you —

Les, Sandy, Samuel & Natalie

(1997)

END
OF THE
DRIVE

BANTAM BOOKS BY LOUIS L'AMOUR
Ask your bookseller for the books you have missed.

NOVELS
Bendigo Shafter
Borden Chantry
Brionne
The Broken Gun
The Burning Hills
The Californios
Callaghen
Catlow
Chancy
The Cherokee Trail
Comstock Lode
Conagher
Crossfire Trail
Dark Canyon
Down the Long Hills
The Empty Land
Fair Blows the Wind
Fallon
The Ferguson Rifle
The First Fast Draw
Flint
Guns of the
  Timberlands
Hanging Woman Creek
The Haunted Mesa
Heller With a Gun
The High Graders
High Lonesome
Hondo
How the West Was
  Won
The Iron Marshal
The Key-Lock Man
Kid Rodelo
Kilkenny
Killoe
Kilrone
Kiowa Trail
Last of the Breed
Last Stand at Papago
  Wells
The Lonesome Gods
The Man Called Noon
The Man From
  Skibbereen
The Man From the
  Broken Hills
Matagorda
Milo Talon

The Mountain Valley
  War
North to the Rails
Over on the Dry Side
Passin' Through
The Proving Trail
The Quick and the
  Dead
Radigan
Reilly's Luck
The Rider of Lost Creek
Rivers West
The Shadow Riders
Shalako
Showdown at Yellow
  Butte
Silver Canyon
Sitka
Son of a Wanted Man
Taggart
The Tall Stranger
To Tame a Land
Tucker
Under the Sweetwater
  Rim
Utah Blaine
The Walking Drum
Westward the Tide
Where the Long Grass
  Blows

SHORT-STORY COLLECTIONS
Bowdrie
Bowdrie's Law
Buckskin Run
Dutchman's Flat
End of the Drive
The Hills of Homicide
Law of the Desert Born
Long Ride Home
Lonigan
Night Over the
  Solomons
The Outlaws of
  Mesquite
The Rider of the Ruby
  Hills
Riding for the Brand
The Strong Shall Live
The Trail to Crazy Man

Valley of the Sun
War Party
West From Singapore
West of Dodge
Yondering

SACKETT TITLES
Sackett's Land
To the Far Blue
  Mountains
The Warrior's Path
Jubal Sackett
Ride the River
The Daybreakers
Sackett
Lando
Mojave Crossing
Mustang Man
The Lonely Men
Galloway
Treasure Mountain
Lonely on the
  Mountain
Ride the Dark Trail
The Sackett Brand
The Sky-Liners

THE HOPALONG CASSIDY
  NOVELS
The Riders of the High
  Rock
The Rustlers of West
  Fork
The Trail to Seven Pines
Trouble Shooter

NONFICTION
Education of a
  Wandering Man
Frontier
The Sackett Companion:
  A Personal Guide to
  the Sackett Novels
A Trail of Memories:
  The Quotations of
  Louis L'Amour,
  compiled by
  Angelique L'Amour

POETRY
Smoke From This Altar

END OF THE THE DRIVE

LOUIS L'AMOUR

BANTAM BOOKS
NEW YORK   TORONTO   LONDON   SYDNEY   AUCKLAND

END OF THE DRIVE

A Bantam Book/June 1997

Library of Congress Cataloging-in-Publication Data
L'Amour, Louis, 1908–1988.
End of the drive / Louis L'Amour.
p.   cm.
Contents: Caprock rancher—Elisha comes to Red Horse—
Desperate men—The courting of Griselda—End of the drive—The
lonesome gods—Rustler roundup—The skull and the arrow.
ISBN 0-553-10648-1
1. Frontier and pioneer life—West (U.S.)—Fiction. 2. West
(U.S.)—Social life and customs—Fiction. 3. Western stories.
I. Title.
PS3523.A446E47   1997
813'.52—dc21   96-36872
                                    CIP

Published simultaneously in the United States and Canada

Bantam Books are published by Bantam Books, a division of Bantam
Doubleday Dell Publishing Group, Inc. Its trademark, consisting of the
words "Bantam Books" and the portrayal of a rooster, is Registered in U.S.
Patent and Trademark Office and in other countries. Marca Registrada.
Bantam Books, 1540 Broadway, New York, New York 10036.

PRINTED IN THE UNITED STATES OF AMERICA

BVG   10 9 8 7 6 5 4 3 2 1

CONTENTS

Caprock Rancher / 1

Elisha Comes to Red Horse / 16

Desperate Men / 36

The Courting of Griselda / 55

End of the Drive / 69

The Lonesome Gods / 84

Rustler Roundup / 93

The Skull and the Arrow / 240

Afterword / 245

END
OF THE
DRIVE

END
OF THE
DRIVE

CAPROCK RANCHER

When I rode up to the buffalo wallow, Pa was lying there with his leg broke and his horse gone.

Out there on the prairie there wasn't much to make splints with, and Pa was bad hurt. It had seemed to me the most important things for a man to know was how to ride a horse and use a gun, but now neither one was going to do much good.

Earlier in the day Pa and me had had a mean argument, and it wasn't the first. Here I was, man-grown and seventeen, and Pa still after me about the company I kept. He was forever harping on Doc Sites and Kid Reese and their like . . . said they were no-goods. As if he was one to talk, a man who'd never had money nor schooling, nor any better than a worn-out coat on his back. Anyway, Doc and Kid Reese weren't about to be farmers or starving on a short-grass cow ranch.

Pa, he'd been at me again because I'd be dogged if I was going to waste my life away on what little we could make, and told him so . . . then I rode off to be an outlaw. For the first two miles I was good and mad, and for the third mile I was growling some, but I'd made most of ten miles before my good sense got the better of me and I started back to help Pa. He had a far piece to go, and he was a lone man packing twenty thousand dollars through some mighty rough country.

It was midafternoon of a mighty hot day when I came up to that buffalo wallow, and Pa had been lying there four, five hours. His canteen had been on his saddle and the horse had taken off, so I got down and gave him a swallow or two from mine.

All that argument was forgotten. Times like that a man is best off doing one thing at a time and not worrying around too much.

"Thanks, boy." Pa returned the canteen to me. "Looks like I played hob."

"That gray never did have a lick of sense," I said, and then I told it to him. "You got a busted leg, but your jaw's in good shape. So you set back an' argue with me whilst I set that bone."

"You just forget about me. All that money is in those saddlebags, and less than a third of it ours. You forget me and hunt down that horse."

That twenty thousand dollars was from a steer herd we'd taken to Kansas and sold, and folks back home were a-sweating until we got back with the money. Cash money was hard to come by those times, and most of this would go to mighty poor folks who hadn't seen a hard dollar since who flung the chunk.

"You got a broke leg. We'll take care of that first."

Nothing was growing around but short grass and some knee-high mesquite, but I got Pa's leg set and cut mesquite with my bowie and splinted up best I knew how. All that time he set there a-looking at me with pain in his eyes and never let out a whimper, but the sweat stood out on both our faces, you can bet.

If you were ever seventeen years old and standing in a

buffalo wallow one hundred and fifty miles from home, and your pa with a broke leg, you know how I felt. And only one horse between us.

With my help he got straddle of that horse and we started off with two things in mind. To get to a creek where there was water, and to find that fool horse.

Judging by the tracks, that gray had taken off like wolves was after him, but after half a mile he began to slow up and look back expecting to be chased. Then on, he got the smell of water and just sort of ambled, taking a bite of grass or mesquite beans now and again. Pa, he sat up in the leather and never said I, yes, or no. This time it was up to me and both us knew it.

The sun was beyond the hill and color was in the evening sky when we saw those other tracks. They came in from the southeast and they were the tracks of three shod horses . . . and they caught Pa's horse.

This was just across the border from Indian Territory and while honest men crossed it, but aside from the Indians, few honest men lived there. To be a Deputy U.S. Marshal in Indian Territory was like standing yourself up in the business end of a shooting gallery. Every outlaw in the country spent time there, and we knew if those had been good men who caught up Pa's horse, or even a decent kind of outlaw, they'd backtrack to find the rider. In those years folks were helpful to one another, and to be afoot in a country like that was about the worst that could happen. It left a man with mighty few possibilities.

These men had caught up Pa's horse and checked the saddlebags, and they didn't come looking for Pa.

"Son,"—Pa could read those tracks as well as me— "don't you get any notions. You ain't about to go up against three men, not with me in this condition."

"Ain't nothing to worry about. Those boys are friends of mine. One of them is Kid Reese and another is Doc

Sites. Why, I'd know those horse tracks if I saw them in Gilead. This time of night they won't go far and we'll have your horse and money in no time."

Pa, he just sat up there on my horse and he said nothing at all for a while, and then he said, "Ed, you reckon those boys would give back twenty thousand dollars?"

It gave me an uneasy feeling, him saying that. Pa set no store by either of them, but they were good boys. Free and easy, that's sure, but they were friends of mine. When Pa and me moved into that Texas country they'd let me take up with them. We-all were usually up to no good, but that was what you'd expect from three youngsters caught somewheres between being boys and being men. It's true we were always talking of standing up a stagecoach or robbing a bank, but that was mostly talk. Taking money from a friend . . . well, they weren't that kind.

It was not much of a creek. Stars were in the sky when we fetched up to it, and it wasn't more than two, three feet wide and maybe four, five inches deep, but it was wet water, lined with willows and cottonwoods and grass aplenty. When I helped Pa off the horse, I bedded him down and filled the canteen for him.

"You set quiet," I said, "I'll go fetch your horse."

"Don't be a fool, Edwin," Pa said. "You say those boys are your friends, but there's a sight of money in those saddlebags . . . not many who value friendship that high."

Pa never called me Edwin unless he was downright serious. That money was important for reasons beyond what it could buy. Pa was always holding on about the value of a good name, and for the first time I was faced up to what it could mean. Pa was a respected man, but if we showed up without that money a lot of folks were going to remember that I'd been swaggering it around town with Doc Sites, Kid Reese, and that outfit. Some of them were going to say things about us losing the money, and Pa would take the blame as well as me.

We Tuckers never had much but an honest reputation. We were never able to get ahead. A while back we lived in Missouri, and that was the year Pa had his first good crop, and the year the grasshoppers ate him out. Two years of bad drought followed and we lost the place. We settled in Texas then and worked like dogs, and when we got our first trail herd together the Comanches came down and burned us out in the light of the moon. They burned us out, drove off our cows, and killed Uncle Bud.

They killed Uncle Bud and they'd taken his scalp. Pa, he rode after them but he never got back with any cows. Somewhere along the way he found Bud's scalp, which we buried out where the body was.

This herd we had just sold in Kansas was our first since then, and the first thing Pa had to show for twenty years of hard work . . . and the first many of our neighbors had to show. If we'd got through to the ranch with that money we'd have had an edge on the future.

I guess it was my fault. While we were separated that morning the gray shied and threw him, and had I been where I should have been I'd have dropped a loop over that gray's neck and he wouldn't have gone anywhere at all. It was lucky I'd quit sulking and started back; I'd been mad but I wasn't ready to strike on my own yet. I was figuring on hooking up with Kid Reese and Doc before I did anything permanent.

Those boys were friends of mine, but something was gnawing at me. What were they doing away off up here at a time like this?

Leaving Pa alongside the creek with his pistol to hand,

I mounted up and started along the creek in the direction those tracks had taken. About a half mile from where I'd left Pa, I smelled smoke.

They were camped on a grassy bench alongside the creek and under some big old cottonwoods. They had a fire going and I could see the firelight on their faces, and hear the murmur of voices. There was a third man at the fire whom I had never seen before, but I knew who he was from his description. It was Bob Heseltine.

How many stories had they told me about the doings of Bob Heseltine? To those boys he was big as all outdoors, and according to them he was the best rider, the best shot, and the most fearless man who ever came down the pike. Bob Heseltine, they told me confidentially, had held up the Garston Bank . . . he had killed Sheriff Baker in a stand-up gun battle, and he had backed down two—not one but two—Texas Rangers. And all they could talk about was all they were going to do when Bob Heseltine got back. And here he was.

He was a mite shorter than me but wide in the shoulder, the hide of his face like tanned leather. He had deep-set blue eyes and he wore two guns tied down and sized up like a mighty mean man. Why, I'd heard more stories about him than about Clay Allison or Jim Courtright or Wild Bill Hickok.

Pa's horse was there and still saddled, but the saddlebags lay on the ground near the fire and they had the money out on a blanket where they could count it. They were going to be disappointed when they found that was our money, and belonging to folks back home. It isn't often a man finds twenty thousand dollars riding around on a lost horse.

"Hi!"

They were all so set on that money that when I hailed

them they came up with their guns drawn. They stood there blinking their eyes at me like owls in a hailstorm.

"It's all right, Bob," Reese said. "This here is Ed Tucker, the one we were tellin' of. Ed, what in blazes are you doin' out here?"

"I see you found Pa's horse," I said, "and our money."

Doc's lips sort of thinned down and Heseltine's head turned real slow to look at me again. Kid Reese, he looked everywhere but at me. Right then I began to wonder about those boys.

Firelight flickered on their faces, on the flanks of the horses, on the gold and silver spread on the blanket, and off their rifle barrels, setting against their saddles. It was so quiet a body could hear the cottonwood leaves brushing their pale green palms one agin the other, and out there beyond the light the creek water chuckled and whispered around rocks or something in the stream.

"I'm afraid you've got this all wrong, boy," Heseltine said. "I don't know you and I don't know whose horse this is. We found this money, and finders is keepers."

"Now wait a minute . . . Doc here, he knows Pa's horse. So does Reese. They saw it many times down Texas way."

Heseltine turned his head to look at them. "Is that true? Do you know this horse?"

Doc Sites looked at the ground and he looked away at the creek and he shook his head. Kid Reese, he said, "It don't look like any horse I ever saw before, Bob. It's just a lost horse, that's all."

Seemed like a long time I sat there, looking at the firelight on that money. I'd never seen that much money before but it didn't look like money to me, it looked like Pa sweating over his fields back in Missouri, and like all the work we'd done, by day and night, rounding up those cattle and putting brands on them. It looked like all those folks around us who shared the drive with us . . . that money was there for them.

"Stop your foolin'," I said, "Pa's back in the brush with a broke leg, broke when this horse throwed him. I got to get back there with this horse and that money."

"You can have the horse. Take it an' welcome," Heseltine said quietly, "but the money stays here, and you're leavin' unless you want to try to do something about it . . ."

All three of them were facing me now, and Heseltine was all squared around to make his fight. Doc had a rifle in his hand and Kid Reese stood there with his thumbs in his belt, just a-grinning at me. They would do whatever Bob Heseltine had said, and he'd told me what to do.

"I figured we were friends." It sounded mighty weak and they could see I was backing down. The three of them stood there looking at me and making me feel mighty small.

"We could take him in with us," Sites said, "he's a good kid. He'll do what you tell him, Bob."

That made me kind of mad. Here I'd been ready to ride off and leave Pa, and they expected me to do what somebody told me.

"Half the money is mine," Heseltine said. "If you boys want to split your half with him, to hell with you. He's your friend."

A stick fell into the fire and sparks lifted into the night. Bob Heseltine was looking straight at me, and I knew what he was thinking. He was thinking he could kill me and wondering if he should.

Pa, he used to tell me when a man is holding the wrong cards he shouldn't try to buck the game. It's better to throw in your hand and wait on another deal.

Only thing that had me worried was whether I could get out of there alive.

"Looks like you got me euchred," I said then, and I started backing to my horse. There was a minute or two when it looked like Heseltine might shoot, but he just looked at me and turned away.

Kid Reese whispered, "You ain't gonna let him go? He'll have the law on us."

"For what?" Heseltine asked. "For finding money?"

Time to time, riding alone and thinking like a body does, I'd imagined myself in positions like this, and each time I'd known what to do. Right off I told them, and then I shot it out with them and always came off a winner. It beats all what a man's imagination will do for him, and how different it is when he faces up to something like that. Right then I felt mighty puny . . . backed down by those three, and me in the right.

Going back down the trail I kept telling myself I'd have shot it out if it hadn't been for Pa, but deep down I wasn't so sure. If I was killed, Pa would be left to die. Maybe I was thinking of that and maybe I was just scared.

Yet I couldn't recall being exactly scared . . . only that I was in the middle of something I'd be better out of.

Pa was sitting up with his back to a tree when I rode up. He had the coffee pot on, for that had been among the stuff I left beside him when I shucked my gear at the camp. Pa was sitting up but he looked poorly. His face was gray and tight-drawn.

"Three of them?" He studied the situation awhile. "That's our money, boy. We were trusted with it."

We drank our coffee, and neither of us talked much,

but it gave me time to sort of get things settled down inside me. A man doesn't always know what to do when things happen quick-like and when for the first time he's faced up with gun trouble and no way accustomed to it. But this was showing me a few things and one of them was that Pa had been right about Doc and Reese.

When it came right down to it those two shaped up like a couple of two-by-twice tinhorns. Neither of them had nerve enough to talk up to Bob Heseltine . . . but neither had I.

"I got to go back," I said, "I got to go back and make my fight. Else I'll always think I was scared."

"You and me, Ed," Pa said, "we've had our troubles but you never showed anything but sand. There's scared smart and then there's scared stupid. I think that you did the right thing." Pa reached for a stick lying among the branches of a fallen tree, and he had out his bowie. "We're going back, boy, but we're going together."

We'd taken our time. Pa had a pipe after his coffee and while he smoked he worked on a crutch. My mouth was all dry inside and my stomach was queasy, but once we decided to go back I felt a whole lot better. It was like I'd left something unfinished back there that just had to be done.

And I kept thinking of Sites, not willing to face up to it, and Reese, who was supposed to be my friend, wanting to kill me.

"You did right, Ed," Pa told me, speaking around his pipe stem. "You did the smart thing. They will think you were scared off."

"That Heseltine . . . they say he's killed a dozen men. He's robbed banks and he's got a mean reputation."

"I like to see a mean man," Pa said. "Most of them don't cut much figger."

Pa had finished working out his crutch. It wasn't

much, just a forked stick trimmed down a mite so he could use the fork to hold under his armpit. I helped him to the horse, and once he got a foot in the stirrup and a hand on the horn he was in that saddle. Meanwhile I smothered our fire. Nobody wants to turn fire loose in grass or timber unless he's a fool.

"A bank robber don't shape up to me," Pa said. "When he goes into a bank with a gun, he don't figure to get shot at. If he expected it he'd never take the first step. He threatens men with folks depending on them and steals money he's too lazy to work for.

"The James boys swaggered it mighty big until a bunch of home folks up at Northfield shot their ears off, and the Dalton gang got the same thing in Coffeyville. The McCarty boys tried it in Colorado, and all those bold outlaws were shot down by a few quiet men who left their glass-polishing or law books to do it."

Well, all those outlaws had seemed mighty exciting until Pa put it thataway, but what he said was true. Pa was a little man himself, only weighed a hundred and thirty pounds, though he had the strongest hands I ever did see. Strong hands from plowing, shoeing horses, and wrassling steers.

Close to midnight we fetched up to their fire.

"Help me down, Ed," Pa said, whispering. "I want to be on the ground."

We walked up to the fire, our boots making small sounds in the grass. Pa was carrying my Colt in his right hand, and I carried a shell under the hammer of my Henry rifle. Those boys weren't much account at keeping watch; they were setting around a blanket playing cards for our money.

"You boys are wasting time," Pa told them. "You're playing with money that don't belong to you."

Pa had that crutch under his left shoulder, but he held

that Colt in one big hand and it pointed like a finger at Heseltine.

"Hear you're a killing man," Pa said to him, "but you size up to me like a no-account, yellow-bellied loafer."

"You got the drop," Heseltine said. "You got a loud mouth when you got the drop."

"The drop? You figure we're in some kind of dime novel? Ed, you keep an eye on those others. If either of them make a move, shoot both of them and after they're laying on the ground, shoot them again!"

Deliberately Pa lowered the muzzle until it pointed into the grass beside his foot. "Now, Ed tells me you're a fast hand with a gun," Pa said, and he limped forward three steps, his eyes locked on Heseltine's, "but I think you're a back-shooting tinhorn."

Heseltine looked at Pa standing there on one leg and a crutch, and he looked at that old pistol. He looked at Pa again and he drew a long breath and held it. Then he let his breath go and stood there with his hands hanging.

"Nobody's got the drop now, Heseltine." Pa spoke quietly but his pale eyes blazed in the firelight. "I'm not going back without that money. And if you try to stop me either you're gonna die or both of us are gonna die!"

Sweat was all over Bob Heseltine's face, and it was a cool evening. He wanted to go for his gun the worst way, but he had another want that beat that one all hollow. He wanted to live.

Kid Reese and Doc Sites stood there looking at the big man and they couldn't believe it, and I'm sure I couldn't. A body didn't need to read minds to guess what they were thinking, because here was a poor old gray-haired caprock rancher on one leg with his gun muzzle down calling the bluff of a gunman said to be among the fastest—although, come to think of it, I never heard it said by anyone but Doc or Reese.

Out of the corner of my eye I could see Pa standing there; for a little man he looked mighty big, and I suddenly found myself thinking about how it was that my pa had come back with Uncle Bud's scalp. No Comanche warrior ever left a trophy like that beside the trail. Surely no Comanche warrior would ever let a trophy like that go without a fight to the death. It seemed all Bob Heseltine had to do to die was lay hand on his guns.

Pa's pistol swung up. "You had your chance. Now unbuckle your gun belt and step back."

Heseltine did what he was told and I went forward and gathered his guns. Then I picked up all that money and stuffed it in the saddlebags, and I went through their pockets checking for more.

"Time you learned a lesson, Edwin," Pa said to me. "Time you learned that it's what's inside a man that matters, not how fast he can draw a gun."

Pa backed off a few careful steps and without looking at me, he said, "Ed, you and him are going to fight. He needs a whoppin' and you're going to give it to him, do you hear?"

Pa gestured with the Colt. "You others stay out of this . . . it's a fair fight, between the two of them."

Well, I looked over at Heseltine; he was six or seven years older than me an' he outweighed me by more than a few pounds. I thought of that story where he killed the sheriff, and then I remembered that he'd just backed down to a crippled-up old man who'd been armed with little more than a fiery force of will and my old Colt.

I put down my gun.

Heseltine took off his calfskin jacket and spat on his hands, looking over at me. "Why, you weak-kneed little whelp, I'll—!"

Another thing Pa taught me: If you're going to fight . . . fight. Talk about it after.

Lifting my left fist I fetched him a clout in the mouth with my right, and right then I saw that a mean man could bleed.

He came at me swinging with both hands. He was strong, and he figured to put the sign on me. He moved well, better than me, but he hadn't put in all those years of hard work that I had.

He walloped me alongside the jaw and it shook me some, but not like I figured it would. He hit me again and I saw a kind of surprised look come into his eyes, and I knew he'd hit me as hard as he could so I fetched him right where he'd been putting all that whiskey. He grunted, and I spread out my legs and began whopping him with both fists . . . and in that regard I take after Pa. I've got big hands.

He went down to his knees and I picked him up by the collar and looked him over to find a place that wasn't bloody where I could fetch him again, but the fight was all out of him and Pa said, "Let him go, Ed. Just drop him."

Seemed like he would go down easier if I fetched him a clout and I did, and then I walked back to get my gun, blowing on my sore fists.

Pa looked over at Doc Sites and Kid Reese who were staring at Heseltine like it was a bad dream. "You two can keep your guns," he said. "This is Indian country, and I just hope you come after us.

"Whatever you do," he added, "don't ever come back home. There will be too many who'd like a shot at you."

Neither of us felt like camping that night with home so far away, so we rode on with the north star behind us. Pa's leg must have been giving him what for, but he was in a good mood, and my fists were sore and my knuckles split, but I felt like riding on through the night.

"You know, Pa, Carlson's been wanting to sell out.

He's got water and about three hundred head, and with what we've got we could buy him out and have margin to work on. I figure we could swing it."

"Together, we could," Pa said.

We rode south, taking our time, under a Comanche moon.

ELISHA COMES
TO RED HORSE

There is a new church in the town of Red Horse. A clean white church of board and bat with a stained-glass window, a tall pointed steeple, and a bell that we've been told came all the way from Youngstown, Ohio. Nearby is a comfortable parsonage, a two-story house with a garreted roof, and fancy gingerbread under the eaves.

Just down the hill from the church and across from the tailings of what was once the King James Mine is a carefully kept cemetery of white headstones and neatly fitted crosses. It is surrounded by a spiked iron fence six feet high, and the gate is always fastened with a heavy lock. We open it up only for funerals and when the groundskeeper makes his rounds. Outsiders standing at the barred gate may find that a bit odd . . . but the people of Red Horse wouldn't have it any other way.

Visitors come from as far away as Virginia City to see our church, and on Sundays when we pass the collection, why, quite a few of those strangers ante up with the rest of us. Now Red Horse has seen its times of boom and bust and our history is as rough as any other town in the West, but our new church has certainly become the pride of the county.

And it is all thanks to the man that we called Brother Elisha.

He was six feet five inches tall and he came into town a few years ago riding the afternoon stage. He wore a black broadcloth frock coat and carried a small valise. He stepped down from the stage, swept off his tall black hat, spread his arms, and lifted his eyes to the snowcapped ridges beyond the town. When he had won every eye on the street he said, "I come to bring deliverance, and eternal life!"

And then he crossed the street to the hotel, leaving the sound of his magnificent voice echoing against the false-fronted, unpainted buildings of our street.

In our town we've had our share of the odd ones, and many of the finest and best, but this was something new in Red Horse.

"A sky pilot, Marshal." Ralston spat into the dust. "We got ourselves another durned sky pilot!"

"It's a cinch he's no cattleman," I said, "and he doesn't size up like a drummer."

"We've got a sky pilot," Brace grumbled, "and one preacher ought to balance off six saloons, so we sure don't need another."

"I say he's a gambler," Brennen argued. "That was just a grandstand play. Red Horse attracts gamblers like manure attracts flies. First time he gets in a game he'll cold deck you in the most sanctified way you ever did see!"

.   .   .

At daybreak the stranger walked up the mountain. Years ago lightning had struck the base of the ridge, and before rain put out the fire it burned its way up the mountain in a wide avenue. Strangely, nothing had ever again grown on that slope. Truth to tell, we'd had some mighty dry years after that, and nothing much had grown anywhere.

The Utes were superstitious about it. They said the lightning had put a curse on the mountain, but we folks in Red Horse put no faith in that. Or not much.

It was almighty steep to the top of that ridge, and every step the stranger took was in plain sight of the town, but he walked out on that spring morning and strode down the street and up the mountain. Those long legs of his took him up like he was walking a graded road, and when he got to the flat rock atop the butte he turned back toward the town and lifted his arms to the heavens.

"He's prayin'," Ralston said, studying him through Brennen's glass. "He's sure enough prayin'!"

"I maintain he's a gambler," Brennen insisted. "Why can't he do his praying in church like other folks. Ask the reverend and see what he says."

Right then the reverend came out of the Emporium with a small sack of groceries under his arm, and noting the size of the sack, I felt like ducking into Brennen's Saloon. When prosperity and good weather come to Red Horse, we're inclined to forget our preacher and sort of stave off the doctor bills, too. Only in times of drought or low-grade ore do we attend church regular and support the preacher as we ought.

"What do you make of him, Preacher?" Brace asked.

The reverend squinted his eyes at the tiny figure high upon the hill. "There are many roads to grace," he said, "perhaps he has found his."

"If he's a preacher, why don't he pray in church?" Brennen protested.

"The groves were God's first temples," the reverend quoted. "There's no need to pray in church. A prayer offered up anywhere is heard by the Lord."

Ralston went into the hotel, and we followed him in to see what name the man had used. It was written plain as print: *Brother Elisha, Damascus.*

We stood back and looked at each other. We'd never had anybody in Red Horse from Damascus. We'd never had anybody from farther away than Denver except maybe a drummer who claimed he'd been to St. Louis . . . but we never believed him.

It was nightfall before Brother Elisha came down off the mountain, and he went at once to the hotel. Next day Brace came up to Brennen and me. "You know, I was talking to Sampson. He says he's never even seen Brother Elisha yet."

"What of it?" Brennen says. "I still say he's a gambler."

"If he don't eat at Sampson's," Brace paused for emphasis, "where does he eat?"

We stared at each other. Most of us had our homes and wives to cook for us, some of the others batched it, but stoppers-by or ones who didn't favor their own cooking, they ate at Sampson's. There just wasn't anywhere else to eat.

"There he goes now," Brennen said, "looking sanctimonious as a dog caught in his own hen coop."

"Now see here!" Ralston protested. "Don't be talking that way, Brennen. After all, we don't know *who* he might be!"

Brother Elisha passed us by like a pay-car passes a tramp, and turning at the corner he started up the moun-

tain. It was a good two miles up that mountain and the
man climbed two thousand feet or more, with no switch-
backs or twist-arounds, but he walked right up it. I
wouldn't say that was a steep climb, but it wasn't exactly
a promenade, either.

Brace scratched his jaw. "Maybe the man's broke," he
suggested. "We can't let a man of God starve right here
amongst us. What would the folks in Virginia City say?"

"Who says he's a man of God?" Brennen was always
irreverent. "Just because he wears a black suit and goes
up a mountain to pray?"

"It won't do," Brace insisted, "to have it said a
preacher starved right here in Red Horse."

"The reverend," I suggested, "might offer some point-
ers on that."

They ignored me, looking mighty stiff and self-
important.

"We could take up a collection," Ralston suggested.

Brother Elisha had sure stirred up a sight of conversa-
tion around town, but nobody knew anything because he
hadn't said two words to anybody. The boys at the hotel,
who have a way of knowing such things, said he hadn't
nothing in his valise but two shirts, some underwear, and
a Bible.

That night there was rain. It was soft, pleasant spring
rain, the kind we call a growing rain, and it broke a two-
year dry spell. Whenever we get a rain like that we know
that spring has surely come, for they are warm rains and
they melt the snow from the mountains and start the
seeds germinating again. The snow gone from the ridges
is the first thing we notice after such a rain, but next
morning it wasn't only the snow, for something else had
happened. Up that long-dead hillside where Brother Elisha walked, there was a faint mist of green, like the first
sign of growing grass.

Brace came out, then Ralston and some others, and we stood looking up the mountain. No question about it, the grass was growing where no grass had grown in years. We stared up at it with a kind of awe and wondering.

"It's him!" Brace spoke in a low, shocked voice. "Brother Elisha has done this."

"Have you gone off your head?" Brennen demanded irritably. "This is just the first good growing weather we've had since the fire. The last few years there's been little rain and that late, and the ground has been cold right into the summer."

"You believe what you want," Ralston said. "We know what we can see. The Utes knew that hillside was accursed, but now he's walked on it, the curse is lifted. He said he would bring life, and he has."

It was all over town. Several times folks tried to get into talk with Brother Elisha, but he merely lifted a hand as if blessing them and went his way. But each time he came down from the mountain, his cheeks were flushed with joy and his eyes were glazed like he'd been looking into the eternity of heaven.

All this time nothing was heard from Reverend Sanderson, so what he thought about Brother Elisha, nobody knew. Here and there we began to hear talk that he was the new Messiah, but nobody seemed to pay much mind to that talk. Only it made a man right uneasy . . . how was one expected to act toward a Messiah?

In Red Horse we weren't used to distinguished visitors. It was out of the way, back in the hills, off the main roads east and west. Nobody ever came to Red Horse, unless they were coming to Red Horse.

Brennen had stopped talking. One time after he'd said something sarcastic it looked like he might be mobbed, so he kept his mouth shut, and I was just as satisfied, although it didn't seem to me that he'd changed his opinion of Brother Elisha. He always was a stubborn cuss.

Now personally, I didn't cater to this Messiah talk. There was a time or two when I had the sneaking idea that maybe Brennen knew what he was talking about, but I sure enough didn't say it out loud. Most people in Red Horse were kind of proud of Brother Elisha even when he made them uncomfortable. Mostly I'm a man likes a hand of poker now and again, and I'm not shy about a bottle, although not likely to get all liquored up. On the other hand, I rarely miss a Sunday at meeting unless the fishing is awful good, and I contribute. Maybe not as much as I could, but I contribute.

The reverend was an understanding sort of man, but about this here Brother Elisha, I wasn't sure. So I shied away from him on the street, but come Sunday I was in church. Only a half dozen were there. That was the day Brother Elisha held his first meeting.

There must've been three hundred people out there on that green mountainside when Brother Elisha called his flock together. Nobody knew how the word got around, but suddenly everybody was talking about it and most of them went out of curiosity.

By all accounts Brother Elisha turned out to be a Hell-and-damnation preacher with fire and thunder in his voice, and even there in the meeting house while the reverend talked we could hear those mighty tones rolling up against the rock walls of the mountains and sounding in the canyons as Brother Elisha called on the Lord to forgive the sinners on the Great Day coming.

Following Sunday I was in church again, but there was nobody there but old Ansel Greene's widow who mumbled to herself and never knew which side was up . . . except about money. The old woman had it, but hadn't spent enough to fill a coffee can since old Ansel passed on.

Just the two of us were there, and the reverend looked mighty down in the mouth, but nonetheless he got up in the pulpit and looked down at those rows of empty seats and announced a hymn.

Now I am one of these here folks who don't sing. Usually when hymns are sung I hang onto a hymnal with both hands and shape the words and rock my head to the tune, but I don't let any sound come out. But this time there was no chance of that. It was up to me to sing or get off the spot, and I sang. The surprise came when right behind me a rich baritone rolled out, and when I turned to look, it was Brennen.

Unless you knew Brennen this wouldn't mean much. Once an Orangeman, Brennen was an avowed and argumentative atheist. Nothing he liked better than an argument about the Bible, and he knew more about it than most preachers, but he scoffed at it. Since the reverend had been in town his one great desire had been to get Brennen into church, but Brennen just laughed at him, although like all of us he both liked and respected the reverend.

So here was Brennen, giving voice there back of me, and I doubt if the reverend would have been as pleased had the church been packed. Brennen sang, no nonsense about it, and when the responses were read, he spoke out strong and sure.

At the door the reverend shook hands with him. "It is a pleasure to have you with us, Brother Brennen."

"It's a pleasure to be here, Reverend," Brennen said. "I may not always agree with you, Parson, but you're a good man, a very good man. You can expect me next Sunday, sir."

Walking up the street, Brennen said, "My ideas haven't changed, but Sanderson is a decent man, entitled to a decent attendance at his church, and his congregation should be ashamed. Ashamed, I say!"

Brennen was alone in his saloon next day. Brother Elisha had given an impassioned sermon on the sinfulness of man and the coming of the Great Day, and he scared them all hollow.

You never saw such a changed town. Ralston, who spoke only two languages, American and profane, was suddenly talking like a Baptist minister at a Bible conference and looking so sanctimonious it would fair turn a man's stomach.

Since Brother Elisha started preaching, the two emptiest places in town were the church and the saloon. Nor would I have you thinking wrong of the saloon. In my day in the West, a saloon was a club, a meeting place, a forum, and a source of news all put together. It was the only place men could gather to exchange ideas, do business, or hear the latest news from the outside.

And every day Brother Elisha went up the mountain.

One day when I stopped by the saloon, Brennen was outside watching Brother Elisha through his field glasses.

"Is he prayin'?" I asked.

"You might say. He lifts his arms to the sky, rants around some, then he disappears over the hill. Then he comes back and rants around some more and comes down the hill."

"I suppose he has to rest," I said. "Prayin' like that can use up a sight of energy."

"I suppose so," he said doubtfully. After a moment or two, he asked, "By the way, Marshal, were you ever in Mobeetie?"

By that time most of that great blank space on the mountainside had grown up to grass, and it grew greenest and thickest right where Brother Elisha walked, and that caused more talk.

Not in all this time had Brother Elisha been seen to take on any nourishment, not a bite of anything, nor to drink, except water from the well.

When Sunday came around again the only two in church were Brennen and me, but Brennen was there, all slicked up mighty like a winning gambler, and when the reverend's wife passed the plate, Brennen dropped in a twenty-dollar gold piece. Also, I'd heard he'd had a big package of groceries delivered around to the one-room log parsonage.

The town was talking of nothing but Brother Elisha, and it was getting so a man couldn't breathe the air around there, it was so filled with sanctified hypocrisy. You never saw such a bunch of overnight gospel-shouters.

Now I can't claim to be what you'd call a religious man, yet I've a respect for religion, and when a man lives out his life under the sun and the stars, half the time riding alone over mountains and desert, then he usually has a religion although it may not be the usual variety. Moreover, I had a respect for the reverend.

Brennen had his say about Brother Elisha, but I never did, although there was something about him that didn't quite tally.

Then the miracle happened.

It was a Saturday morning and Ed Colvin was shingling the new livery barn, and in a town the size of Red Horse nobody could get away from the sound of that hammer, not that we cared, or minded the sound. Only it was always with us.

And then suddenly we didn't hear it anymore.

Now it wasn't noontime, and Ed was a working sort of man, as we'd discovered in the two months he'd been in town. It was not likely he'd be quitting so early.

"Gone after lumber," I suggested.

"He told me this morning," Brace said, "that he had enough laid by to last him two days. He was way behind and didn't figure on quitting until lunchtime."

"Wait," I said, "we'll hear it again."

Only when some time passed and we heard nothing we started for the barn. Ed had been working mighty close to the peak of what was an unusually steep roof.

We found him lying on the ground and there was blood on his head and we sent for the doc.

Now Doc McDonald ain't the greatest doctor, but he was all we had aside from the midwife and a squaw up in the hills who knew herbs. The doc was drunk most of the time these days and showing up with plenty of money, so's it had been weeks since he'd been sober.

Doc came over, just weaving a mite, and almost as steady as he usually is when sober. He knelt by Ed Colvin and looked him over. He listened for a heartbeat and he held a mirror over his mouth, and he got up and brushed off his knees. "What's all the rush for? This man is dead!"

We carried him to Doc's place, Doc being the undertaker, too, and we laid him out on the table in his back room. Ed's face was dead white except for the blood, and he stared unblinking until the doc closed his eyes.

We walked back to the saloon feeling low. We'd not known Ed too well, but he was a quiet man and a good worker, and we needed such men around our town. Seemed a shame for him to go when there were others, mentioning no names, who meant less to the town.

That was the way it was until Brother Elisha came down off the mountain. He came with long strides, staring straight before him, his face flushed with happiness that seemed always with him these days. He was abreast of the saloon when he suddenly stopped.

It was the first time he had ever stopped to speak to anyone, aside from his preaching.

"What has happened?" he asked. "I miss the sound of the hammer. The sounds of labor are blessed in the ears of the Lord."

"Colvin fell," Brace said. "He fell from the roof and was killed."

Brother Elisha looked at him out of his great dark eyes and he said, "There is no death. None pass on but for the Glory of the Lord, and I feel this one passed before his time."

"You may think there's no death," Brace said, "but Ed Colvin looks mighty dead to me."

He turned his eyes on Brace. "O, ye of little faith: Take me to him."

When we came into Doc McDonald's the air was foul with liquor, and Brace glared at Doc like he'd committed a blasphemy. Brother Elisha paused briefly, his nose twitching, and then he walked through to the back room where Ed Colvin lay.

We paused at the door, clustered there, not knowing what to expect, but Brother Elisha walked up and bowed his head, placing the palm of his right hand on Colvin's brow, and then he prayed. Never did I know a man who could make a prayer fill a room with sound like Brother Elisha, but there at the last he took Ed by the shoulders and he pulled him into a sitting position and he said, "Edward Colvin, your work upon this earth remains unfinished. For the Glory of the Lord . . . *Rise!*"

And I'll be forever damned if Ed Colvin didn't take a long gasping breath and sit right up on that table. He looked mighty confused and Brother Elisha whispered in his ear for a moment and then with a murmur of thanks Ed Colvin got up and walked right out of the place.

We stood there like we'd been petrified, and I don't know what we'd been expecting, but it wasn't this. Brother Elisha said, "The Lord moves in mysterious ways His wonders to perform." And then he left us.

Brace looked at me and I looked at Ralston and when I started to speak my mouth was dry. And just then we heard the sound of a hammer.

When I went outside people were filing into the street and they were looking up at that barn, staring at Ed Colvin, working away as if nothing had happened. When I passed Damon, standing in the bank door, his eyes were wide open and his face white. I spoke to him but he never even heard me or saw me. He was just standing there staring at Colvin.

By nightfall everybody in town was whispering about it, and when Sunday morning came they flocked to hear him preach, their faces shining, their eyes bright as though with fever.

When the reverend stepped into the pulpit, Brennen was the only one there besides me.

Reverend Sanderson looked stricken, and that morning he talked in a low voice, speaking quietly and sincerely but lacking his usual force. "Perhaps," he said as we left, "perhaps it is we who are wrong. The Lord gives the power of miracles to but few."

"There are many kinds of miracles," Brennen replied, "and one miracle is to find a sane, solid man in a town that's running after a red wagon."

As the three of us walked up the street together we heard the great rolling voice of Brother Elisha: "And I say unto you that the gift of life to Brother Colvin was but a sign, for on the morning of the coming Sabbath we shall go hence to the last resting place of your loved ones, and there I shall cause them all to be raised, and they shall live again, and take their places among you as of old!"

You could have dropped a feather. We stood on the street in back of his congregation and we heard what he said, but we didn't believe it, we couldn't believe it.

He was going to bring back the dead.

Brother Elisha, who had brought Ed Colvin back to life, was now going to empty the cemetery, returning to life all those who had passed on . . . and some who had been helped.

"The Great Day has come!" He lifted his long arms and spread them wide, and his sonorous voice rolled against the mountains. "And men shall live again for the Glory of All Highest! Your wives, your mothers, your brothers and fathers, they shall walk beside you again!"

And then he led them into the singing of a hymn and the three of us walked away.

That was the quietest Sunday Red Horse ever knew. Not a whisper, all day long. Folks were scared, they were happy, they were inspired. The townsfolk walked as if under a spell.

Strangely, it was Ed Colvin who said it. Colvin, the man who had gone to the great beyond and returned . . . although he claimed he had no memory of anything after his fall.

Brace was talking about the joy of seeing his wife again, and Ed said quietly, "You'll also be seeing your mother-in-law."

Brace's mouth opened and closed twice before he could say anything at all, and then he didn't want to talk. He stood there like somebody had exploded a charge of powder under his nose, and then he turned sharply around and walked off.

"I've got more reason than any of you to be thankful,"

Ed said, his eyes downcast. "But I'm just not sure this is all for the best."

We all glanced at each other. "Think about it." Ed got up, looking kind of embarrassed. "What about you, Ralston? You'll have to go back to work. Do you think your uncle will stand for you loafing and spending the money he worked so hard to get?"

"That's right," I agreed, "you'll have to give it all back."

Ralston got mad. He started to shout that he wouldn't do any such thing, and anyway, if his uncle came back now he would be a changed man, he wouldn't care for money any longer, he—

"You don't believe that," Brennen said. "You know darned well that uncle of yours was the meanest skinflint in this part of the country. Nothing would change him."

Ralston went away from there. Seemed to me he wanted to do some thinking.

When I turned to leave, Brennen said, "Where are you going?"

"Well," I said, "seems to me I'd better oil up my six-shooters. There's three men in that Boot Hill that I put there. Looks like I'll have it to do over."

He laughed. "You aren't falling for this, are you?"

"Colvin sounds mighty lively to me," I said, "and come Sunday morning Brother Elisha has got to put up or shut up."

"You don't believe that their time in the hereafter will have changed those men you killed."

"Brennen," I said, "if I know the Hame brothers, they'll come out of their graves like they went into them. They'll come a-shootin'."

There had been no stage for several days as the trail had been washed out by a flash flood, and the town was quiet and it was scared. Completely cut off from the outside, all folks could do was wait and get more and more frightened as the Great Day approached. At first everybody had been filled with happiness at the thought of the dead coming back, and then suddenly, like Brace and Ralston, everybody was taking another thought.

There was the Widow McCann who had buried three husbands out there, all of them fighters and all of them mean. There were a dozen others with reason to give the matter some thought, and I knew at least two who were packed and waiting for the first stage out of town.

Brace dropped in at the saloon for his first drink since Brother Elisha started to preach. He hadn't shaved and he looked mighty mean. "Why'd he pick on this town?" he burst out. "When folks are dead they should be left alone. Nobody has a right to interfere with nature thataway."

Brennen mopped his bar, saying nothing at all.

Ed Colvin dropped around. "Wish that stage would start running. I want to leave town. Folks treat me like I was some kind of freak."

"Stick around," Brennen said. "Come Sunday the town will be filled with folks like you. A good carpenter will be able to stay busy, so busy he won't care what folks say about him. Take Streeter there. He'll need a new house now that his brother will be wanting his house back."

Streeter slammed his glass on the bar. "All right, damn it!" he shouted angrily, "I'll build my own house!"

Ralston motioned to me and we walked outside. Brace was there, and Streeter joined us. "Look," Ralston whispered, "Brace and me, we've talked it over. Maybe if we were to talk to Brother Elisha . . . maybe he'd call the whole thing off."

"Are you crazy?" I asked.

His eyes grew mean. "You want to try those Hame boys again? Seems to me you came out mighty lucky the last time. How do you know you'll be so lucky again? Those boys were pure-dee poison."

That was gospel truth, but I stood there chewing my cigar a minute and then said, "No chance. He wouldn't listen to us."

Ed Colvin had come up. "A man doing good works," he said, "might be able to use a bit of money. Although I suppose it would take quite a lot."

Brace stood a little straighter but when he turned to Colvin, the carpenter was hurrying off down the street. When I turned around there was Brennen leaning on the doorjamb, and he was smiling.

Friday night when I was making my rounds I saw somebody slipping up the back stairs of the hotel, and for a moment his face was in the light from a window. It was Brace.

Later, I saw Ralston hurrying home from the direction of the hotel, and you'd be surprised at some of the folks I spotted slipping up those back stairs to commune with Brother Elisha. Even Streeter, and even Damon.

Watching Damon come down those back stairs I heard a sound behind me and turned to see Brennen standing there in the dark. "Seems a lot of folks are starting to think this resurrection of the dead isn't an unmixed blessing."

"You know something?" I said thoughtfully. "Nobody has been atop that hill since Brother Elisha started his walks. I think I'll just meander up there and have a look around."

"You've surprised me," Brennen said. "I wouldn't have expected you to be a churchgoing man. You're accustomed to sinful ways."

"Why, now," I said, "when I come into a town to live,

I go to church. If the preacher is a man who shouts against things, I never go back. I like a man who's for something.

"Like you know, I've been marshal here and there, but never had much trouble with folks. I leave their politics and religion be. Folks can think the way they want, act the way they please, even to acting the fool. All I ask is they don't make too much noise and don't interfere with other people.

"They call me a peace officer, and I try to keep the peace. If a growed-up man gets himself into a game with a crooked gambler, I don't bother them . . . if he hasn't learned up to then, he may learn, and if he doesn't learn, nothing I tell him will do him any good."

"You think Colvin was really dead?"

"Doc said so."

"Suppose he was hypnotized? Suppose he wasn't really dead at all?"

After Brennen went to bed I saddled up and rode out of town. Circling around the mountain I rode up to where Brother Elisha used to go to pray. Brennen had left me with a thought, and Doc had been drinking a better brand of whiskey lately.

Brace had drawn money from the bank, and so had Ralston, and old Mrs. Greene had been digging out in her hen coop, and knowing about those tin cans she buried there after her husband died kind of sudden, I had an idea what she was digging up.

I made tracks. I had some communicatin' to do and not many hours to do it in.

I spent most of those hours in the saddle. Returning to Red Horse the way I did brought me to a place where the trail forked, and one way led over behind that mountain with the burnt-off slope. When I had my horse out of sight I drew up and waited.

It was just growing gray when a rider came down the mountain trail and stopped at the forks. It was Ed Colvin.

We hadn't anything to talk about right at the moment so I just kept out of sight in the brush and then followed. He seemed like he was going to meet somebody and I had a suspicion it was Brother Elisha. And it was.

"You got it?" Ed Colvin asked.

"Of course. I told you we could fool these yokels. Now let's—"

When I stepped out of the brush I was holding a shotgun. I said, "The way of the transgressor is hard. Give me those saddlebags, Delbert."

Brother Elisha stared at me. "I fear there is some mistake," he said with dignity. "I am Brother Elisha."

"I found those cans and sacks up top of the hill. The ones where you kept your grub and the grass seed you scattered." I stepped in closer.

"You are Delbert Johnson," I added, "and the wires over at Russian Junction say you used to deal a crooked game of faro in Mobeetie. Now give me the saddlebags."

The reverend has a new church now, and a five-room frame parsonage to replace his tiny cabin. The dead of Red Horse sleep peacefully and there is a new iron fence around the cemetery to keep them securely inside. Brennen still keeps his saloon, but he also passes the collection plate of a Sunday, and the results are far better than they used to be.

There was a lot of curiosity as to where the reverend came by the money to do the building, and the good works that followed. Privately, the reverend told Brennen and me about a pair of saddlebags he found inside the parsonage door that Sunday morning. But when anyone else asked him he had an answer ready.

"The ravens have provided," he would say, smiling gently, "as they did for Elijah."

Nobody asked any more questions.

DESPERATE MEN

They were four desperate men, made hard by life, cruel by nature, and driven to desperation by imprisonment. Yet the walls of Yuma Prison were strong and the rifle skill of the guards unquestioned, so the prison held many desperate men besides these four. And when prison walls and rifles failed, there was the desert, and the desert never failed.

Fate, however, delivered these four a chance to test the desert. In the early dawn the land had rolled and tumbled like an ocean storm. The rocky promontory over the river had shifted and cracked in an earthquake that drove fear into the hearts of the toughest and most wicked men in Arizona. For a minute or two the ground had groaned and roared, dust rained down from cracks in the roofs of the cells, and in one place the perimeter wall had broken and slid off, down the hillside. It was as if God or the Devil had shown them a way.

Two nights later, Otteson leaned his shaven head closer to the bars. "If you're yellow, say so! I say we can make it! If Isager says we can make it through the desert, I say we go!"

"We'll need money for the boatmen." Rodelo's voice was low. "Without money we will die down there on the shores of the gulf."

All were silent, three awaiting a word from the fourth. Rydberg knew where the army payroll was buried. The government did not know, the guards did not know, only Rydberg. And Otteson, Isager, and Rodelo knew he knew.

He was a thin, scrawny man with a buzzard's neck and a buzzard's beak for a nose. His bright, predatory eyes indicated his hesitation now. "How . . . how much would it take?" he asked.

"A hundred," Otteson suggested, "not more than two. If we had that much we could be free."

Free . . . no walls, no guards, no stinking food. No sweating one's life out with backbreaking labor under the blazing sun. Free . . . women, whiskey, money to spend . . . the click of poker chips, the whir of the wheel, a gun's weight on the hip again. No beatings, no solitary, no lukewarm, brackish drinking water. Free to come and go . . . a horse between the knees . . . women . . .

He said it finally, words they had waited to hear. "There's the army payroll. We could get that."

The taut minds of Otteson, Rodelo, and Isager relaxed slowly, easing the tension, and within the mind of each was a thought unshared.

Gold . . . fifteen thousand in gold coins for the taking! A little money split four ways, but a lot of money for one!

Otteson leaned his bullet head nearer. "Tomorrow night," his thick lips barely moved as he whispered, "tomorrow night we'll go out. If we wait longer they'll have the wall repaired."

"There's been guards posted ever since the quake," Rodelo protested.

Otteson laughed. "We'll take care of them!" From under the straw mattress he drew a crude, prison-made knife. "Rydberg can take care of the other with his belt."

Cunningly fashioned of braided leather thongs, it concealed a length of piano wire. When the belt was removed and held in the hands it could be bent so the loop of the steel wire projected itself, a loop large enough to encircle a man's head . . . then it could be jerked tight and the man would die.

Rodelo leaned closer. "How far to the gold?"

"Twenty miles east. We'll need horses."

"Good!" Otteson smashed a fist into a palm. "East is good! They'll expect us to go west into California. East after the gold, then south into the desert. They'd never dream we'd try that! It's hot as sin and dry as Hades, but I know where the water holes are!"

Their heads together, glistening with sweat in the hot, sticky confines of their cells, they plotted every move, and within the mind of three of the men was another plot: to kill the others and have the gold for himself.

"We'll need guns." Rydberg expressed their greatest worry. "They'll send Indians after us."

The Indians were paid fifty dollars for each convict returned alive—but it had been paid for dead convicts, too. The Yaquis knew the water holes, and fifty dollars was twice what most of them could make in a month if they could find work at all.

"We'll have the guns of the two guards. When we get to Rocky Bay, we'll hire a fisherman to carry us south to Guaymas."

• • •

The following day their work seemed easy. The sun was broiling and the guards unusually brutal. Rydberg was knocked down by a hulking giant named Johnson. Rydberg just brushed himself off and smiled. It worried Johnson more than a threat. "What's got into him?" he demanded of the other guards. "Has he gone crazy?"

Perryman shrugged. "Why worry about it? He's poison mean, an' those others are a bad lot, too. Otteson's worst of all."

"He's the one I aim to get," Johnson said grimly, "but did you ever watch the way he lifts those rocks? Rocks two of us couldn't budge he lifts like they were so many sacks of spuds!"

It was sullen dark that night; no stars. There was thunder in the north and they could hear the river. The heat lingered and the guards were restless from the impending storm. At the gap where the quake had wrecked the wall were Perryman and Johnson. They would be relieved in two hours by other guards.

They had been an hour on the job and only now had seated themselves. Perryman lit a cigarette and leaned back. As he straightened to say something to Johnson he was startled to see kicking feet and clawing hands, but before he could rise, a powerful arm came over his shoulder, closing off his breath. Then four men armed with rifles and pistols went down the side of Prison Hill and walked eastward toward the town.

One hour before discovery. That was the most they could expect, yet in half that time they had stolen horses and headed east. Otteson had been shrewd. He had grabbed Perryman's hat from the ground. Both Isager and Rodelo had hats of a sort. Rydberg was without any covering for his shaven head.

Two hours after their escape they reached the adobe. Rydberg led the way inside the ruin, and they dug up the gold from a far corner. Each man took a sack, and then they turned their horses to the south and the desert.

"Each year," Otteson said, "the fishermen come to Rocky Bay. They live there while they fish, and then return to their homes down the gulf. Pablo told me, and he said to keep Pinacate on my left and head for the coast at Flat Hill. The bay is on a direct line between the hill and the coast."

Pablo had been killed by a blow on the head from a guard's gun, but he had been planning escape with Otteson. Dawn came at last and the clouds slid away leaving the sun behind . . . and the sun was hot.

From the Gila River to the Mexican border there was nothing. Only desert, cacti, rocks, and the sun, always the sun. There was not even water until one almost reached the border. Water was found only in *tinajas*, basins that captured rain and retained it until finally evaporated by the sun. Some of the *tinajas* were shaded and held the water for a long time, and in others there was just sand. Sometimes water impregnated the sand at the bottom. These things a man must know to survive on that devil's trail.

Their route from the Gila to the border was approximately fifty miles as the buzzard flies, but a man does not ride as the buzzard flies, not even in a lonely and empty land. There are clusters of rock, broken lava, upthrust ledges, and clumps of cacti. And there are always, inevitably, arroyos. Seventy miles would be closer to the truth, seventy miles of desert in midsummer.

The border was a vague line which in theory left them free of pursuit, but in 1878 officers of the law often ignored lines of demarcation—and the Indians did not notice them at all. Actually, the border was their halfway point, for they had a rough distance of one hundred and forty miles to traverse.

Behind them two guards lay dead, and the hostler only lived because Rodelo was not, by nature, a killer. Rodelo had the sleeping man's hands and feet tied before he got his eyes open. Then he gagged and left him. They stole four horses and three canteens and filled the canteens at the pump. Otteson, Rydberg, and Isager took it for granted the hostler had been killed.

They rode hard for twenty miles, and then they had the added weight of the gold. Otteson knew the way from Pablo and he pointed it out occasionally as they rode. But he did not offer his back to his companions.

Four battered and desperate men headed south under the glaring sun. Dust lifted, they sweated, and their lips grew dry. They pushed their horses, for distance was important. Otteson called a halt, finally. He was a heavy man and the hard riding sapped the strength of his horse.

"Where is it we're gonna find water?" Isager noted the hesitation before Otteson replied. Isager knew the desert, but not this area. Otteson only had the knowledge Pablo had given him and he didn't want to tell too much.

"Near Coyote Peak there's water. Maybe ten miles yet."

Isager tested the weight of his canteen. Rodelo drank several good gulps and returned his canteen to its place behind his saddle. Rydberg, who had brought the guard's water bottle, drank also. Otteson made a motion of drinking, but Isager watched his Adam's apple. It did not move.

Isager was a lean man, not tall, and narrow of jaw and cheekbone. He weighed one hundred and fifty pounds and carried no ounce of fat. He had been sent to Yuma after killing a marshal, which would have been his sixth notch if he had been a man for carving notches. It was noteworthy that in selecting a weapon he had taken a pistol. Isager was nothing if not practical. The pistol was his favorite weapon, and the four would be close together. By the time they had spread out to where a rifle might be useful, he would have a rifle. Of that he was positive.

Rodelo knew nothing of the desert but much of men. When younger he had sailed to the West Coast of Africa and had seen men die of the sun. He had replaced the bandanna that covered his head when working in the prison yard with a hat stolen from the livery, knowing the sun would be vicious on their shaven skulls. They depended upon Otteson, and he was not to be trusted. Isager alone he respected: he liked none of them. Rydberg did not guess what the others knew—that they would soon be minus a man.

They walked their horses now. Behind them was no dust, but pursuit was certain. It was the Indians who worried them, for fifty dollars was a lot of money to an Indian. Two hundred dollars for them all.

The air wavered and changed before them, seeming to flow and billow with heat waves. On their right was the Gila Range, and the desert grew more rugged. Otteson watched when Rydberg drank, when he passed his hand over his bare skull, saw him put water on his head. Otteson was complacent, confident.

Isager's mouth was dry, but he did not touch the canteen. A mere swallow at dusk could do more good than a bucket now. He watched the others with cat eyes. Rydberg took another pull. The heat baked the desert and reflected in their faces like heat from a hot stove. Twice they stopped for rest, and each time it was Otteson and Isager who stopped in what little shade there was. Rydberg swayed as he dismounted.

"Hot!" he gasped. "How much further to water?"

"Not far." Otteson looked at Rydberg's horse. It was the best.

Isager took water from his canteen and wiped out his horse's mouth and nostrils. Rodelo thought this was a good idea and did likewise.

"Let's wait until dark," Rydberg suggested. "I'm hot. My head aches. That sun is killing me."

"You want to get caught by them Injuns? Or them laws from Yuma?"

They moved on, and Rydberg's skull was pocked with sun blisters. The dust grew thicker, the air was dead, the desert a pink and red reflector for the sun. Rydberg swayed drunkenly, and Rodelo swore mentally and reflected that it must be 120 degrees or more.

Rydberg began to mutter. He pulled at his dry canteen. He tried again, shook it, and there was no sound. Otteson looked straight before him. Isager said nothing, and only Rodelo looked around as the man swayed drunkenly in his saddle.

"I'm out of water," Rydberg said. "How about a drink?"

"On the desert," Otteson said, "each man drinks his own water. You'll have to wait."

The dust and sun and thirst turned their world into a red hell of heat waves and blurred blue mountains. The hooves of their horses dragged. Rydberg muttered, and once he croaked a snatch of song. He mumbled through thin, cracked lips, and the weird face above the scraggly neck became even more buzzardlike. His skull was fiery red now, and it bobbed strangely as he weakened. Suddenly he shouted hoarsely and pointed off across the desert.

"Water!" he gabbled. "Water, over there!"

"Mirage," Rodelo said, and the others were silent, riding.

"Gimme a drink." Rydberg rode at Otteson and grabbed at his canteen.

The big man moved his horse away, striking at the skinny hand. "Go to hell," he said coldly.

Rydberg grabbed at him, lost balance, and fell heavily into the sand. He struggled to get up, then fell again.

Rodelo looked at him. His own canteen was empty. "The damn fool," Isager said, "why didn't he get him a hat?"

Nobody else spoke. Then Otteson reached for the canteen on Rydberg's horse, but Isager was closer and unhurriedly appropriated it. He also took the rifle. "Take the horse if you like," he said, "you're a heavy man."

Otteson glared at Isager, and Rodelo moved in and took the gold. "Are you going to leave him here like that?" he demanded.

Otteson shrugged. "He asked for it."

"He wouldn't live until night," Isager said. "Stay if you want."

Rodelo drew Rydberg into the shade of an ironwood tree. Then he mounted and followed. Why had they grabbed the empty canteen and the rifle when they could have gotten their hands on Rydberg's share of the gold?

A thin shadow of doubt touched him. Then the answer was plain and he cursed himself for a fool. Nearly two hundred gold coins he now carried, and it was considerable weight. They preferred that he carry the extra gold until . . . his jaw set hard, but within him there was a cold shock of fear.

They thought he was going to die! They thought— He'd show them. From deep within him came a hard burning defiance. He'd show them.

It had been midafternoon when they left Rydberg. It

was two hours later when they came up to Coyote Peak. Otteson was studying the rocks around and suddenly he turned sharply left and rode into an arroyo. Twenty minutes later they stood beside the *tinaja*.

Despair mounted within Rodelo. It was only a hollow of rock with a few gallons of water in the bottom. They filled their canteens, then watered the horses. When the horses had finished the water was gone.

"We'll rest a few hours," Isager suggested, "then go on after dark."

Isager ignored the shade and lay down on his side with his face toward the two men and his weapons and water close behind him.

Rodelo found a spot in soft sand, well back in the shadow of the rocks. He stared at the others and thought exhaustion had made them stupid. Both had relaxed upon hard, rocky ground. The least move would awaken them. They would get no rest that way. While this was soft sand. . . . He relaxed luxuriously.

He awakened with a start. It was cold, dark, and silent. With sudden panic, he sprang to his feet. "Isager!" he shouted. "Ott!" And the desert gave back only echoes. He felt for his canteen, and it was gone. He ran to where his horse had been picketed, and it, too, was gone.

He had slept and they had left him. They had taken the gold, the horse, the canteen . . . only his pistol remained. He had that only because they had feared to awaken him.

He rushed to a rise of ground, scrambled, slipped on the rocks, and skinned his knees. Then he got to the top and stared off to the southeast. All he could see was the soft, velvety darkness, the cool of the desert night, and the unspeaking stars.

He was alone.

For the first time he was frightened. He was horribly,

unspeakably frightened. Rodelo hated being alone, he feared loneliness, and he knew the power of the desert to kill.

Then his fear left him, his thoughts smoothed out and the panic ended. They could not move fast without knowing the country better than they did. They would travel at a walk, and if they did, he might overtake them. He was younger than either, and he was strong. He had never found a trial that could test his endurance.

A glance at the stars told him they could have no more than an hour's start. How much would that mean at night in unfamiliar desert? Three miles? Five miles?

Doubt came. Could he make up the distance? They would never suspect pursuit. Suppose the day came and he was still without water? But what would waiting gain? This was not a spring, and the *tinaja* was empty.

He could wait for death, or for capture on the verge of death, or he could fight. He returned to the *tinaja* and found perhaps a cup of water in the bottom. He thrust his head into the basin and sucked it up. Then he straightened, glanced at the stars for direction, and struck out for the southeast, walking steadily.

Otteson and Isager rode side by side. Each man led a horse, and on those horses were the gold sacks. The issue between them was clear now. Isager knew he was faster with a gun, and Otteson knew it also. Therefore, the big man would wait for a moment when the killing was a sure thing.

Neither man mentioned Rydberg nor Rodelo. It was like Otteson to ignore what was past. Isager thought of Rodelo with regret—he had liked the younger man, but this was a matter of survival. They walked their horses, careful not to tire them. Once, encountering a nest of boulders, they circled some distance to get past them. Over the next two hours this allowed Rodelo to gain considerable ground.

The first day netted them sixty miles of distance but twenty of it had been up the Gila for the gold, and the next forty angling toward the border. Daylight found them near the border and Otteson looked back. Nothing but heat waves. "They'll be coming," Isager said. "They'll find Rydberg by the buzzards. Then they'll find Rodelo. That gives them a line on us even if they don't find our trail."

Ahead of them on their right was a cluster of mesas, on their left ahead high and blue on the horizon, the bulk of Pinacate, a fifteen-mile-long ridge that towered nearly five thousand feet into the brassy sky.

The coolness left the desert as the sun lifted. Both men knew the folly of haste. Moreover they had each other to watch. Neither wanted to go ahead, and this slowed their pace. Isager wished it had been Otteson back there rather than Rodelo. He had seen the big man get to his feet and had done likewise. Both had chosen stony ground, as a sound sleep might be their last sleep. Otteson had saddled up, glanced at the sleeping man, and then with a shrug had gathered up Rodelo's gear and horse. To stop him would mean a shoot-out, and neither knew which side Rodelo would join if awakened by gunfire. He had mounted up and taken Rydberg's horse. Neither had planned on abandoning the young man when they stopped, but this was a case of survival of the fittest and Rodelo had given them an opportunity to decrease their number by one more.

"You sure the fishermen come there at this time of the year?"

"Pablo said so. He planned to go this way himself. Rocky Bay, they call it. From Flat Hill we go right down to the water. How could a man mistake a bay? And if the fishermen aren't there, we'll wait."

Not long after that they came up to Tinajas Altas where they watered the horses and refilled their canteens. Isager looked over the back trail from beside the tanks. He saw no dust, no movement. Once he believed he saw something stir down there, but it could have been nothing more than a coyote or a mountain sheep. A horse would make dust.

They rested, drank water again, and ate a little of the hardtack and jerky they had smuggled from the prison, food hoarded against this effort. An hour passed, then a second hour. The rest meant much to them and to their horses. Otteson got up carefully, facing Isager. "Reckon we'd better move on. I won't feel safe until we're on that fishin' boat headed south."

Up on the mesa's side among the talus, something moved. Isager's quick eye saw it and recognized it in the same instant with a start of inward surprise. Otteson's back was to the talus, but he saw a flicker of something in Isager's eyes. "What's the matter?" he exclaimed, starting to turn.

He caught himself, his eyes turning ugly. "Figured I'd turn an' you'd shoot me? Don't try nothin' like that."

Rodelo was on the slope behind and slightly above Otteson and about thirty yards back from him. His face was ghastly and red, his prison jeans were torn from cacti and rocks, but he clutched a businesslike .44 in his fist. He lifted it and took careful sight, shifting his feet as he did so. A rock rolled under his foot.

Otteson whipped around, quick as a cat. His rifle blasted from the hip and he missed. He never fired again.

He went down, clawing at the rocks and gravel on which he had fallen, blood staining their pink to deep crimson. Isager held his smoking Colt and looked up the slope at Rodelo.

The younger man had recovered his balance and they stared at each other over their guns.

"You might miss," Isager said. "I never do."

"Why don't you shoot, then?"

"I want company. Two can make it easier than one. Much easier than three."

"Then why didn't you let him kill me?"

"Because he wanted to kill me himself. You need me. I know the desert and you don't."

Rodelo came over the rocks, stepping carefully. "All right," he said. "Gimme water."

Isager holstered his gun. "There's the *tinaja*. Drink an' we'll push on." He looked at Rodelo with curious respect. "How'd you catch up so fast?"

"You rode around things. I walked straight to your dust. You rested. I couldn't afford to."

"Good man." Isager mounted up. Nothing was said about what happened. "If we play it smart now, we'll leave each other alone. Together we can make it through."

One thing they had not forgotten. The knowledge of the *tinajas* lay dead in the skull of Otteson.

"We'll have to make our water last. It won't be far now. That's Pinacate."

The mountain bulked before them now, and by the time the stars were out it loomed huge on the horizon. They slept that night and when they awakened, Rodelo looked around at Isager. His cheekbones were slashes of red from the sun, his eyes deep sunken. Stubble of beard covered his cheeks and his shirt was stiff with sweat and dust. "I smell the sea," he said, low-voiced. "I can smell the sea."

When they started on once more, they kept the mountain between them and the sun, saving themselves from the heat. Once they found a water hole but the mud was cracked and dry in the bottom. Isager's brown face was shadowed with red, Otteson's hat pulled low over his cold eyes.

The horses were gaunt and beaten. Several times the men dismounted and led the horses to spare them. Their hunger was a gnawing, living thing within them, and their spare canteens were dry, their own very low. The eyes of the men were never still, searching for water. Yet it was not enough to look. One had to know. In the desert water may be within a few feet and give no indication of its presence. And then, from the top of a rise, they saw the gulf!

"There it is." Rodelo stared, hollow-eyed. "Now for that bay."

A squarish flat hill was before them. They circled and saw the gulf due west of it. "S'pose that's it?" Isager asked doubtfully.

"You can see for yourself that it's a big bay." The tension between them was back: they were watching each other out of the corners of their eyes again.

Isager stood in his stirrups and looked south. Land stretched away until it ended in a point. There was a hint of sea in that direction but he was not sure. "All right," he said, "but I don't see any boats."

The plain sloping down to the bay was white with soda and salt. Long sand spits extended into the milky blue water. Here and there patches showed above the surface. "Looks mighty shallow," Rodelo said doubtfully. "Don't seem likely a boat would come in here."

Isager hefted his canteen, feeling its lightness with fear. "We'd better hunt for water."

South of them, the rocky bluff shouldered against the sky, dark and rugged. North the beach lay flat and empty . . . frightening in its emptiness. The horses stood, heads down and unmoving. The rocky bluff looked promising, but the salt on his lips frightened Isager. Behind them they heard a deep, gasping sigh and they turned. The paint packhorse was down.

It had sunk to the sand and now it lay stretched out, the hide on its flanks hanging like loose cloth in the hollows of its ribs.

Isager removed the gold from the horse, and with the gold off, it struggled to rise. Isager glanced at Rodelo, hesitant to use both hands to help the horse. "Go ahead," Rodelo said, "help him."

Together they got the horse up, and then they turned south. The salty crust crunched and broke beneath their feet. Sometimes they sank to their ankles; the horses broke through at every step. They often stopped to rest and Isager glanced at Rodelo. "We better have a truce," he said, his eyes shifting away, then back. "You couldn't make it without me."

Rodelo's lips thinned over his white teeth. "Don't need you. You knew the desert. I know the sea."

"The desert's still with us," Isager said. Suddenly the water in Rodelo's canteen was more precious than gold. He was waiting for a chance to go for his gun.

The white glare around them forced their eyes to thin slits, while soda dust settled over them in a thin cloak. They stared at each other, as wild and thin as the gaunt, skeletonlike horses, white and shadowy things that seemed to waver with unreality in the heat. The milky water, undrinkable, and taunting them, whispered secret obscenities along the blue-white beach. "There'll be a fishing boat," Isager said. "No reason to kill each other. Maybe there's water beyond that bluff."

"There'll be no boat." Rodelo stated it flatly. "This is the wrong bay."

Isager stared, blinking slowly. "Wrong bay?" he said stupidly.

"Look!" Rodelo shouted harshly. "It's too shallow! We've come to the wrong place!"

Isager's dry tongue fought for his lips. There was no hope then.

"Give me your gun," Rodelo said, "and I'll take you there."

"So you can kill me?" Isager drew back, his eyes cold and calculating.

"I know where the bay is," Rodelo said. "Give me your gun."

Isager stared. Was it a trick? How could he actually know?

Suddenly, Rodelo shrugged. "Come on, then! I'll take my chances on you!" He pointed toward the dark bluff. "Look! That's a water sky. There's water beyond that point. Another bay!"

He took a step and a bullet kicked dust at his feet. He grabbed for his gun and whirled on Isager, but the gunfighter had already faced the hillside. Four Indians were coming down the hill, riding hard. As Rodelo turned, Isager stepped his feet apart and fired. An Indian's horse stumbled and went down, throwing the rider head over heels.

Rodelo dropped to one knee and shot under the belly of his horse. He saw an Indian drop and he fired again and missed. A bullet hit Isager and turned him half around. He staggered, and the half-dead horse lunged clumsily away. A hoof went through the crust and the horse fell heavily and lay panting, one white sliver of bone showing through the hide of the broken leg.

Isager fell, pulled off balance by the fall of the horse, and Rodelo fired again and again. His gun muzzle wavered and the shots kicked up dust. Isager rolled over behind the downed horse. He knew from harsh experience that accuracy was more essential than speed. He steadied his gun barrel. The Indian who had been thrown was rushing him. The brown body loomed large and he could see sweat streaks on the man's chest. He squeezed off his shot and saw the Indian stumble in midstride and then pitch over on his face.

Isager pushed himself to his knees, then got up. The beach weaved slowly, sickeningly beneath him. He turned his head stiffly and looked toward Rodelo. The fallen man looked like a bundle of old clothes, but as Isager looked, the bundle moved. Rodelo uncoiled himself and got up. Blood covered his face from a cut on his cheek. He stared at his empty gun, then clumsily began feeding shells into the chambers.

Across the wavering sand the two men stared at each other, then Rodelo laughed hoarsely. "You look like hell!" he said, grinning from his heat-blasted face.

Isager's brain seemed to spin queerly and he blinked. What was the matter with him? A pain bit suddenly at his side, and he clasped the pain with his hand. His fingers felt damp and he drew them away, staring stupidly at the blood dripping from his fingers.

"You copped one," Rodelo said. "You're hit."

Isager swayed. Suddenly he knew this was it, right here on this dead-white beach washed by an ugly weedy sea. It was no way for a cowhand to cash in his chips. "Beat it," he said hoarsely. "There's more coming."

"How do you know that?"

"That's why they rushed. To get us an' claim the reward. If they'd been alone they would have taken their time." His knees felt buttery and queer. "There's one good horse. Take the gold an' beat it. I'm done in, so I'll hold them off."

He went to his knees. "Only . . ." His voice trailed off and he waited, his eyes begging Rodelo to wait a minute longer, then he managed the words, "get some of that money to Tom Hopkins's wife. He . . . he was that marshal. Funny thing, funny . . . Never meant to kill him. He came at me an' it was just reflex . . . jus' . . . just drew an' shot."

"All right," Rodelo said, and he meant it. He turned and disappeared into the blinding light.

Isager lay down behind the fallen horse. He slid the rifle from its scabbard and waited.

Sheriff Bill Garden and two Apache trackers found Isager a few hours later. Gunfire from the advance party of six Yaquis had led them to this desolate beach. The convict was curled up behind a dying horse, surrounded by bright brass shells ejected from his rifle. Two of the Apache horses were gone and only one of the horses ridden by the convicts was alive. He was standing head down on the hillside not far away.

Horse tracks trailed away from the body of Isager, a faint trail toward the bluff to the south. Bill Garden glanced after them. The remaining scouts were still after the last man. He turned and looked down at Isager. "Lord a-mighty," he said. "What a place to die!"

Far off across the water there was a flash of white, a jib shaken out to catch the wind . . . a boat had left the fishing beds at Rocky Bay and was beating its way southward toward Guaymas.

THE COURTING
OF GRISELDA

When it came to Griselda Popley, I was down to bedrock and showing no color.

What I mean is, I wasn't getting anyplace. The only thing I'd learned since leaving the Cumberland in Tennessee was how to work a gold placer claim, but I was doing no better with that than I was with Griselda.

Her pa, Frank Popley, had a claim just a whoop and a holler down canyon from me. He had put down a shaft on a flat bench at the bend of the creek and he was down a ways and making a fair clean-up.

He was scraping rock down there and panning out sixty to seventy dollars a day, and one time he found a crack where the gold had seeped through and filled in a space under a layer of rock, and he cleaned out six hundred dollars in four or five minutes.

It sure does beat all how prosperity makes a man critical of all who are less prosperous. Seems like some folks no sooner get two dollars they can rattle together than they start looking down their noses at folks who only have two bits.

We were right friendly while Popley was sinking his

shaft, but as soon as he began bringing up gold he started giving me advice and talking me down to Griselda. From the way he cut up, you'd have thought it was some ability or knowledge of his that put that gold there. I never saw a man get superior so fast.

He was running me down and talking up that Arvie Wilt who had a claim nearby the Popley place, and Arvie was a man I didn't cotton to.

He was two inches taller than my six feet and three, and where I pack one hundred and eighty pounds on that lean a frame, most of it in my chest, shoulders, and arms, Arvie weighed a good fifty pounds more and he swaggered it around as if almighty impressed with himself.

He was a big, easy-smiling man that folks took to right off, and it took them a while to learn he was a man with a streak of meanness in him that was nigh onto downright viciousness. Trouble was, a body never saw that mean streak unless he was in a bind, but when trouble came to him, the meanness came out.

But Arvie was panning out gold, and you'd be surprised how that increased his social standing there on Horse Collar Creek.

Night after night he was over to the Popleys', putting his big feet under their table and being waited on by Griselda. Time to time I was there, too, but they talked gold and how much they weighed out each day while all I was weighing out was gravel.

He was panning a fine show of color and all I had was a .44 pistol gun, a Henry rifle, and my mining tools. And as we all know it's the high card in a man's hand to be holding money when he goes a-courting.

None of us Sacketts ever had much cash money. We were hardworking mountain folk who harvested a lean corn crop off a side-hill farm, and we boys earned what clothes weren't made at home by trapping muskrats or coon. Sometimes we'd get us a bear, and otherwise we'd live on razorback hog meat or venison.

Never will forget the time a black bear treed old Orrin, that brother of mine, and us caught nine miles from home and none of us carrying iron.

You ever tackle a grown bear with a club? Me and Tyrel, we done it. We chunked at him with rocks and sticks, but he paid them no mind. He was bound and determined to have Orrin, and there was Orrin up high in the small branches of that tree like a 'possum huntin' persimmons.

Chunking did no good, so Tyrel and me cut us each a club and we had at that bear. He was big and he was mean, but while one of us closed in on him before, the other lambasted him from behind. Time to time we'd stop lambasting that bear to advise Orrin.

Finally that old bear got disgusted and walked off and Orrin came down out of that tree and we went on to the dance at Skunk Hollow School. Orrin did his fiddling that night from a sitting stool because the bear had most of his pants.

Right now I felt like he must have felt then. Every day that Griselda girl went a-walking past my claim paying me no mind but switching her skirts until I was fair sweating on my neck.

Her pa was a hard man. One time I went over there for supper like I had when I'd been welcome, back when neither of us had anything. He would stand up there in his new boots, consulting a new gold watch every minute or two, and talking high and mighty about the virtues of hard work and the application of brains. And all the time that Arvie Wilt was a-setting over there making big eyes at Griselda.

If anything, Arvie had more gold than Popley did and

he was mighty welcome at table, but for me the atmosphere was frosting over a mite, and the only reason I dug in and held on was that I'd scraped my pot empty of beans and for two days I'd eaten nothing but those skimpy little wild onions.

Now when it came right down to it, Popley knew I'd worked hard as either of them, but I was showing no color and he wanted a son-in-law who was prosperous, so needing to find fault, he taken issue with me on fighting.

We boys from the high-up hills aren't much on bowing and scraping, but along about fighting time, you'll find us around. Back in the Cumberland I grew up to knuckle-and-skull fighting, and what I hadn't learned there I picked up working west on a keelboat.

Pa, he taught us boys to be honest, to give respect to womenfolk, to avoid trouble when we could, but to stand our ground when it came to a matter of principle, and a time or two I'd stood my ground.

That old six-shooter of mine was a caution. It looked old enough to have worn out three men, but it shot true and worked smooth. My hands are almighty big but I could fetch that pistol faster than you could blink. Not that I made an issue of it because Pa taught us to live peaceable.

Only there was that time down to Elk Creek when a stranger slicked an ace off the bottom, and I taken issue with him.

He had at me with a fourteen-inch blade and my toothpick was home stuck in a tree where I'd left it after skinning out a deer, so I fetched him a clout alongside the skull and took the blade from him. A friend of his hit me from behind with a chair, which I took as unfriendly, and then he fetched out his pistol, so I came up a-shooting.

Seemed like I'd won myself a name as a bad man to trouble, and it saved me some hardship. Folks spoke polite and men seeking disagreement took the other side of the road, only it gave Popley something he could lay a hand to, and he began making slighting remarks about men who got into brawls and cutting scrapes.

Words didn't come easy to me and by the time I'd thought of the right answer I was home in bed, but when Popley talked I felt like I was disgracing Griselda by coming a-courting.

So I went back to my claim shanty and looked into the bean pot again, but it was still empty, and I went a-hunting wild onions.

Nobody could ever say any of us Sacketts fought shy of work, so I dug away at my claim until I was satisfied there was nothing there but barren gravel. Climbing out of that shaft I sat down and looked at my hole card.

There was nothing left but to load up my gear on that spavined mule I had and leave the country. I was out of grub, out of cash money, and out of luck. Only leaving the country meant leaving Griselda, and worst of all, it meant leaving her to Arvie Wilt.

Time or two I've heard folks say there's always better fish in the sea, but not many girls showed me attention. Many a time I sat lonely along the wall, feared to ask a girl to dance because I knew she'd turn me down, and no girl had paid me mind for a long time until Griselda showed up.

She was little, she was pert, and she had quick blue eyes and an uptilted nose and freckles where you didn't mind them. She'd grown into a woman and was feeling it, and there I was, edged out by the likes of Arvie Wilt.

Popley, he stopped by. There I was, a-setting hungry and discouraged, and he came down creek riding that big brown mule and he said, "Tell, I'd take it kindly if you stayed away from the house." He cleared his throat because I had a bleak look to my eye. "Griselda is coming up to marrying time and I don't want her confused. You've got nothing, and Arvie Wilt is a prosperous mining man. Meaning no offense, but you see how it is."

He rode on down to the settlement and there was nothing for me to do but go to picking wild onions. The trouble was, if a man picked all day with both hands he couldn't pick enough wild onions to keep him alive.

It was rough country, above the canyons, but there were scattered trees and high grass plains, with most of the ridges topped with crests of pine. Long about sundown I found some deer feeding in a parklike clearing.

They were feeding, and I was downwind of them, so I straightened up and started walking toward them, taking my time. When I saw their tails start to switch, I stopped.

A deer usually feeds into the wind so he can smell danger, and when his tail starts to wiggle he's going to look up and around, so I stood right still. Deer don't see all too good, so unless a body is moving they see nothing to be afraid of. They looked around and went back to feeding and I moved closer until their tails started again, and then I stopped.

Upshot of it was, I got a good big buck, butchered him, and broiled a steak right on the spot, I was that hungry. Then I loaded the best cuts of meat into the hide and started back, still munching on wild onions.

Down on the creek again the first person I saw was Griselda, and right off she began switching her skirts as she walked to meet me.

"I passed your claim," she said, "but you were not there."

She had little flecks of brown in her blue eyes and she stood uncomfortably close to a man. "No, ma'am, I've give . . . given . . . it up. Your pa is right. That claim isn't up to much."

"Are you coming by tonight?"

"Seems to me I wore out my welcome. No, ma'am, I'm not coming by. However, if you're walking that way, I'll drop off one of these here venison steaks."

Fresh meat was scarce along that creek, and the thought occurred that I might sell what I didn't need, so after leaving a steak with the Popleys, I peddled the rest of it, selling out for twelve dollars cash money, two quarts of beans, a pint of rice, and six pounds of flour.

Setting in my shack that night I wrassled with my problem and an idea that had come to me. Astride that spavined mule I rode down to the settlement and spent my twelve dollars on flour, a mite of sugar, and some other fixings, and back at the cabin I washed out some flour sacks for aprons, and made me one of those chef hats like I'd seen in a newspaper picture. Then I set to making bear-sign.

Least, that's what we called them in the mountains. Most folks on the flatland called them doughnuts, and some mountain folk did, but not around our house. I made up a batch of bear-sign and that good baking smell drifted down along the creek, and it wasn't more than a few minutes later until a wild-eyed miner came running and falling up from the creek, and a dozen more after him.

"Hey! Is that bear-sign we smell? Is them doughnuts?"

"Cost you," I said. "I'm set up for business. Three doughnuts for two bits."

That man set right down and ate two dollars' worth and by the time he was finished there was a crowd around reaching for them fast as they came out of the Dutch oven.

Folks along that creek lived on skimpy bacon and beans, sometimes some soda biscuits, and real baking was unheard-of. Back to home no woman could make doughnuts fast enough for we Sackett boys who were all good eaters, so we took to making them ourselves. Ma often said nobody could make bear-sign like her son, William Tell Sackett.

By noon I was off to the settlement for more makings, and by nightfall everybody on the creek knew I was in business. Next day I sold a barrel of doughnuts, and by nightfall I had the barrel full again and a washtub also. That washtub was the only one along the creek, and it looked like nobody would get a bath until I'd run out of bear-sign.

You have to understand how tired a man can get of grease and beans to understand how glad they were to taste some honest-to-gosh, down-to-earth doughnuts.

Sun-up and here came Arvie Wilt. Arvie was a big man with a big appetite and he set right down and ran up a bill of four dollars. I was making money.

Arvie sat there eating doughnuts and forgetting all about his claim.

Come noon, Griselda showed up. She came a-prancing and a-preening it up the road and she stayed around, eating a few doughnuts and talking with me. The more she talked the meaner Arvie got.

"Griselda," he said, "you'd best get along home. You know how your pa feels about you trailing around with just any drifter."

Well, sir, I put down my bowl and wiped the flour off my hands. "Are you aiming that at me?" I asked. "If you are, you just pay me my four dollars and get off down the pike."

He was mean, like I've said, and he did what I hoped

he'd do. He balled up a fist and threw it at me. Trouble was, he took so much time getting his fist ready and his feet in position that I knew what he was going to do, so when he flung that punch, I just stepped inside and hit him where he'd been putting those doughnuts.

He gulped and turned green around the jowls and white around the eyes, so I knocked down a hand he stuck at me and belted him again in the same place. Then I caught him by the shirt front before he could fall and backhanded him twice across the mouth for good measure.

Griselda was a-hauling at my arms. "Stop it, you awful man! You hurt him!"

"That ain't surprising, Griselda," I said. "It was what I had in mind."

So I went back to making bear-sign, and after a bit Arvie got up, with Griselda helping, and he wiped the blood off his lips and he said, "I'll get even! I'll get even with you if it's the last thing I do!"

"And it just might be," I said, and watched them walk off together.

There went Griselda. Right out of my life, and with Arvie Wilt, too.

Two days later I was out of business and broke. Two days later I had a barrel of doughnuts I couldn't give away and my private gold rush was over. Worst of all, I'd put all I'd made back into the business and there I was, stuck with it. And it was Arvie Wilt who did it to me.

As soon as he washed the blood off his face he went down to the settlement. He had heard of a woman down there who was a baker, and he fetched her back up the creek. She was a big, round, jolly woman with pink cheeks, and she was a first-rate cook. She settled down to making apple pies three inches thick and fourteen inches across and she sold a cut of a pie for two bits and each pie made just four pieces.

She also baked cakes with high-grade all over them. In mining country rich ore is called high-grade, so miners got to calling the icing on cake high-grade, and there I sat with a barrel full of bear-sign and everybody over to the baker woman's buying cake and pie and such-like.

Then Popley came by with Griselda riding behind him on that brown mule, headed for the baker woman's. "See what a head for business Arvie's got? He'll make a fine husband for Griselda."

Griselda? She didn't even look at me. She passed me up like a pay-car passing a tramp, and I felt so low I could have walked under a snake with a high hat on.

Three days later I was back to wild onions. My grub gave out, I couldn't peddle my flour, and the red ants got into my sugar. All one day I tried sifting red ants out of sugar; as fast as I got them out they got back in until there was more ants than sugar.

So I gave up and went hunting. I hunted for two days and couldn't find a deer, nor anything else but wild onions.

Down to the settlement they had a fandango, a real old-time square dance, and I had seen nothing of the kind since my brother Orrin used to fiddle for them back to home. So I brushed up my clothes and rubbed some deer grease on my boots, and I went to that dance.

Sure enough, Griselda was there, and she was with Arvie Wilt.

Arvie was all slicked out in a black broadcloth suit that fit him a little too soon, and black boots so tight he winced when he put a foot down.

Arvie spotted me and they fetched to a halt right beside me. "Sackett," Arvie said, "I hear you're scraping bottom again. Now my baker woman needs a helper to rev up her pots and pans, and if you want the job—"

"I don't."

"Just thought I'd ask,"—he grinned maliciously— "seein' you so good at woman's work."

He saw it in my eyes so he grabbed Griselda and they waltzed away, grinning. Thing that hurt, she was grinning, too.

"That Arvie Wilt," somebody said, "there's a man will amount to something. Popley says he has a fine head for business."

"For the amount of work he does," somebody else said, "he sure has a lot of gold. He ain't spent a day in that shaft in a week."

"What do you mean by that?"

"Ask them down to the settlement. He does more gambling than mining, according to some."

That baker woman was there, waltzing around like she was light as a feather, and seeing her made me think of a Welshman I knew. Now you take a genuine Welshman, he can talk a bird right out of a tree . . . I started wondering . . . how would he do with a widow woman who was a fine baker?

That Welshman wasn't far away, and we'd talked often, the year before. He liked a big woman, he said, the jolly kind and who could enjoy making good food. I sat down and wrote him a letter.

Next morning early I met up with Griselda. "You actually marrying that Arvie?"

Her pert little chin came up and her eyes were defiant. "A girl has to think of her future, Tell Sackett! She can't be tying herself to a—a—ne'er-do-well! Mr. Wilt is a serious man. His mine is very successful," her nose tilted, "and so is the bakery!"

She turned away, then looked back, "And if you expect any girl to like you, you'd better stop eating those onions! They're simply awful!"

And if I stopped eating wild onions, I'd starve to death.

Not that I wasn't half-starved, anyway.

That day I went further up the creek than ever, and the canyon narrowed to high walls and the creek filled the bottom, wall to wall, and I walked ankle deep in water going through the narrows. And there on a sandy beach were deer tracks, old tracks and fresh tracks, and I decided this was where they came to drink.

So I found a grassy ledge above the pool and alongside an outcropping of rock, and there I settled down to wait for a deer. It was early afternoon and a good bit of time remained to me.

There were pines on the ridge behind me, and the wind sounded fine, humming through their needles. I sat there for a bit, enjoying the shade, and then I reached around and pulled a wild onion from the grass, lifting it up to brush away the sand and gravel clinging to the roots. . . .

It was sundown when I reached my shanty, but I didn't stop, I rode on into the settlement. The first person I saw was the Welshman. He was smiling from ear to ear, and beside him was the baker woman.

"Married!" he said cheerfully. "Just the woman I've been looking for!"

And off down the street they went, arm in arm.

Only now it didn't matter anymore.

For two days then I was busy as all get-out. I was down to the settlement and back up above the narrows of the canyon, and then I was down again.

Putting my few things into a pack, and putting the saddle on that old mule of mine, I was fixing to leave the claim and shanty for the last time when who should show up but Frank Popley.

He was riding his brown mule with Griselda riding behind him, and they rode up in front of the shack. Griselda slid down off that mule and ran up and threw her arms around me and kissed me right on the lips.

"Oh, Tell! We heard the news! Oh, we're so happy for you! Pa was just saying that he always knew you had the stuff, that you had what it takes!"

Frank Popley looked over at me and beamed. "Can't keep a good man down, boy! You sure can't! Griselda, she always said, 'Pa, Tell is the best of the lot,' an' she was sure enough right!"

Suddenly a boot crunched on gravel, and there was Arvie, looking mighty mean and tough, and he was holding a Walker Colt in his fist, aimed right at me.

Did you ever see a Walker Colt? Only thing it lacks to be a cannon is a set of wheels.

"You ain't a-gonna do it!" Arvie said. "You can't have Griselda!"

"You can have Griselda," I heard myself say, and was astonished to realize that I meant it.

"You're not fooling me! You can't get away with it." And his thumb came forward to cock that pistol.

Like I said, Arvie wasn't too smart or he'd have cocked his gun as he drew it, so I just fetched out my six-shooter and let the hammer slip from under my thumb as it came level.

Deliberately, I held it a little high, and the .44 slug smashed him in the shoulder. It knocked him sidewise and he let go of that big pistol and staggered back two steps and sat down hard.

"You're a mighty disagreeable man, Arvie," I said,

"and not much account. When the boys down at the set-tlement start finding the marks you put on those cards you'll have to leave the country, but I reckon you an' Griselda deserve each other."

She was looking at me with big eyes and pouty lips because she'd heard the news, but I wasn't having any.

"You-all been washing gold along the creek," I said, "but you never stopped to think where those grains of gold started from. Well, I found and staked the mother lode, staked her from Hell to breakfast, and one day's take will be more than you've taken out since you started work. I figure now I'll dig me out a goodly amount of money, then I'll sell my claims and find me some friends that aren't looking at me just to see what I got."

They left there walking down that hill with Arvie astride the mule making pained sounds every time it took a step.

When I had pulled that wild onion up there on that ledge overlooking the deer run, there were bits of gold in the sand that clung to the roots, and when I scraped the dirt away from the base of that outcrop, she was all there . . . wire gold lying in the rock like a jewelry store window.

Folks sometimes ask me why I called it the Wild Onion Mining Company.

END OF THE DRIVE

We came up the trail from Texas in the spring of '74, and bedded our herd on the short grass beyond the railroad. We cleaned our guns and washed our necks and dusted our hats for town; we rode fifteen strong to the hitching rail, and fifteen strong to the bar.

We were the Rocking K from the rough country back of the Nueces, up the trail with three thousand head of longhorn steers, the first that spring, although the rivers ran bank full and Comanches rode the war trail.

We buried two hands south of the Red, and two on the plains of the Nation, and a fifth died on Kansas grass, his flesh churned under a thousand hoofs. Four men gone before Indian rifles, but the death-songs of the Comanches were sung in the light of a hollow moon, and the Kiowa mourned in their lodges for warriors lost to the men of the Rocking K.

We were the riders who drove the beef, fighting dust, hail, and lightning, meeting stampedes and Kiowa. And we who drove the herd and fought our nameless, unrecorded battles often rode to our deaths without glory, nor with any memory to leave behind us.

The town was ten buildings long on the north side of the street, and seven long on the south, with stock corrals to the east of town and Boot Hill on the west, and an edging of Hell between.

Back of the street on the south of town were the shacks of the girls who waited for the trail herds, and north of the street were the homes of the businessmen and merchants, where no trail driver was permitted to go.

We were lean and hard young riders, only a few of us nearing thirty, most of us nearer to twenty. We were money to the girls of the line, and whiskey to the tenders of bars, but to the merchants we were lean, brown young savages whose brief assaults on their towns were tolerated for the money we brought.

That was the year I was twenty-four, and only the cook was an older man, yet it was my fifth trip up the trail and I'd seen this town once before, and others before that. And there were a couple I'd seen die, leaving their brief scars on the prairie that new grass would soon erase.

I'd left no love in Texas, but a man at twenty-four is as much a man as he will be, and a girl was what I wanted. A girl to rear strong sons on the high plains of Texas, a girl to ride beside me in the summer twilight, to share the moon with me, and the high stars over the caprock country.

For I had found a ranch, filed my claims, and put my brand on steers, and this drive was my last for another man, the last at a foreman's wages. When I rode my horse up to the rail that day, I saw the girl I dreamed about . . . the girl I wanted.

She stood on the walk outside the store and she lifted a hand to shade her eyes, her hair blowing light in the wind, and her figure was long and slim and the sun caught red lights in her hair. Her eyes caught mine as I rode tall in the leather, the first man to come up the street.

She looked grave and straight and honestly at me, and it seemed no other girl had ever looked so far into my heart. At twenty-four the smile of a woman is a glory to the blood and a spark to the spirit, and carries a richer wine than any sold over a bar in any frontier saloon.

I'd had no shave for days, and the dust of the trail lay on my clothes, and sour I was with the need of bathing and washing. When I swung from my saddle, a tall, lonely man in a dusty black hat with spurs to my heels, she stood where I had seen her and turned slowly away and walked into the store.

We went to the bar and I had a drink, but the thing was turning over within me and thinking of the girl left no rest for me. She was all I could think about and all I could talk about that afternoon.

So when I turned from the bar Red Mike put a hand to my sleeve. "It's trouble you're headed for, Tom Gavagan," he said. "It's been months since you've seen a girl. She's a bonny lass, but you know the rule here. No trail hand can walk north of the street, nor bother any of the citizens."

"I'm not one to be breakin' the law, Mike, but it is a poor man who will stop shy of his destiny."

"This is John Blake's town," he said.

The name had a sound of its own, for John Blake was known wherever the trails ran; wherever they came from and where they ended. He was a hard man accustomed to dealing with hard men, and when he spoke his voice was law. He was a square, powerful man, with a name for fair dealing, but a man who backed his words with a gun.

"It is a time for courting," I said, "although I want trouble with no man. And least of all John Blake."

When I turned to the door I heard Red Mike behind me. "No more drinking this day," he said. "We've a man to stand behind."

When the door creaked on its spring a man looked around from his buying, and the keeper of the store looked up, but the girl stood straight and tall where she was, and did not turn. For she knew the sound of my heels on the board floor, and the jingle of my Spanish spurs.

"I am selling the herd this night," I said, when I came to stand beside her, "and I shall be riding south with the morning sun. I hope not to ride alone."

She looked at me with straight, measuring eyes. "You are a forward man, Tom Gavagan. You do not know me."

"I know you," I said, "and know what my heart tells me, and I know that if you do not ride with me when I return to Texas, I shall ride with sorrow."

"I saw you when you rode into town last year," she said, "but you did not see me."

"Had I seen you I could not have ridden away. I am a poor hand for courting, knowing little but horses, cattle, and grass, and I have learned nothing that I can say to a girl. I only know that when I saw you there upon the walk it seemed my life would begin and end with you, and there would be no happiness until you rode beside me."

"You are doing well enough with your talk, Tom Gavagan, and it is a fine thing that you do it no better or you'd be turning some poor girl's head."

She put her money on the counter and met the glance of the storekeeper without embarrassment, and then she turned and looked at me in that straight way she had and said, "My uncle is Aaron McDonald, and he looks with no favor upon Texas men."

"It is my wish to call on you this night," I said, "and the choice of whether I come or not belongs to you and no one else."

"The house stands among the cottonwoods at the street's far end." Then she added, "Come if you will . . . but it is north of the street."

"You can expect me," I replied.

And turning upon my heel I walked from the store and heard the storekeeper say, "He is a Texas man, Miss June, and you know about the ordinance as well as anyone!"

Once more in the sunshine I felt a strength within me that was beyond any I had ever known, and an exhilaration. Lined along the street were fourteen riders. They loitered at the street corners and relaxed on the benches on the walk in front of the barber shop. A group of them waited for me before the saloon. They were my army, battle tested and true. With them I could take on this town or any other.

Then I saw John Blake.

He wore a black frock coat and a wide-brimmed black planter's hat. His guns were out of sight, but they were there, I had no doubt.

"Your men aren't drinking?" he commented.

"No."

"Red Mike," Blake said. "I remember him well from Abilene, and Tod Mulloy, Rule Carson, and Delgado. You came ready for trouble, Gavagan."

"The Comanches were riding, and the Kiowa."

"And now?"

"I will be going north of the street tonight, John, but not for trouble. I was invited."

"You know the rule here." He looked at me carefully from his hooded eyes. "It cannot be."

"There are other ways to look, John, and I am not a trouble-hunting man."

"The people who live here have passed an ordinance. This is their town and I am charged with enforcing their laws." He stated this flatly, and then he walked away, and I stood there with a lightness inside me and an awareness of trouble to come.

The cattle were checked and sold to Bob Wells. We rode together to the bank and when we went in John Blake stood square on his two feet, watching.

McDonald was a narrow man, high-shouldered and thin, dry as dust and fleshless. He looked at me and gave a brief nod and counted over the money for the cattle, which was my employer's money, and none of it mine but wages.

He watched me put the gold and greenbacks in a sack and he said, "Your business here is finished?"

"I've some calls to make."

"You are welcome," he said, "south of the street."

"Tonight I shall come to call on your niece. She has invited me."

"You must be mistaken." He was a cold man with his heart in his ledgers and his dollars. "You are welcome here to do whatever business you have, and beyond that you are not welcome."

"I am not a drunk, wandering the streets and looking for trouble. I am one who has been entrusted with these two thousand cattle and now, like you, with this money. But, unlike you, I will carry this payment across many dangerous miles back to Texas. My honesty and character are not in question there."

"Mr. McDonald," Wells protested, "this is a good man. I know this man."

"We put up with your kind," McDonald said, "south of the street."

I could see my attempt had been wasted on him. The issue was not character but class. McDonald had decided to put himself above me and there was no chance he'd be seeing it differently.

"Five times I have come over the trail," I told him, "and I have seen towns die. Markets and conditions change, and neither of us has been in this country long enough to be putting on airs."

"Young man, let me repeat. South of the street you and your kind are welcome, north of it you become a subject for John Blake. As for this town . . . I am the mayor and it will not die."

"I have spoken with Mr. Blake. He is aware of my plans." I glanced over at the marshal and deep in his eyes something glinted, but whether it was a challenge or amusement I couldn't be sure. "I know him, Mr. McDonald," I said, "and he knows me."

Rocking K men were in the saloons that night, and Rocking K men were south of the street, but I sat at the campfire near the chuck wagon and Red Mike joined me there.

"If you'll be riding, I'll saddle your horse."

"Saddle two, then."

"Ah? It's like that, is it?"

"A man must find out, Mike, one never knows. If she's the girl I want, she will ride with me tonight."

We were young then, and the West was young, with

the land broad and bright before us. We knew, whatever the truth was, that every horse could be ridden, every man whipped, every girl loved. We rode with the wind then, and sang in the rain, and when we fought it was with the same savage joy as that of the Comanches who opposed us, these fierce, proud warriors who would ride half a thousand miles to fight a battle or raid a wagon train. And no Bruce ever rode from the Highlands with a finer lot of fighting men than rode this day with the Rocking K.

"And John Blake?"

"Stay out of it, Mike, and keep others out. John Blake is a stubborn man, and if we go against him there will be killing in the town. This is a personal matter and does not concern the brand."

With a mirror nailed to the chuck wagon's side I shaved and combed my hair and made myself ready for courting. It was much to expect of any girl, to ride to Texas with a man she did not know, and yet in those days when men constantly moved such things happened. There were few men from whom to choose in those wild small towns, and the best were often moving and had to be taken on the fly. And to me this was the girl and now was the time.

There was John Blake to consider, a man seasoned in the wars of men and cattle, who knew all the dodges and all the tricks, and whatever a man might invent he had known before. Each herd had a man who wished to prove himself against a trail town marshal, never grasping the difference between the skilled amateur and the hardened professional. John Blake looked upon men with vast patience, vast understanding, and used a gun only when necessary, but when he used it he used it coldly, efficiently, and deliberately.

In a black broadcloth suit with my hat brim down, I

rode up the middle of the street with the reins in my left hand, my right resting on my thigh near my gun.

Tonight I was more than a Texas man a-courting, I was a challenge to the rule of John Blake, and it was something I had no liking for. No man from the Texas trails had been north of the street since he had been marshal, and it was assumed that no man would.

Outside the town a Rocking K rider dozed on the ground near his horse, and grazing close by was another horse, saddled and bridled for travel.

John Blake was not in sight, but when I passed the livery stable Tod Mulloy was seated under the light, minding his own business, and on the edge of the walk near the eating house Rule Carson smoked a cigar. Inside, over coffee, were Delgado and Enright. They would not interfere, but would be on hand if needed. Nor did I doubt that the rest of them were scattered about town, just waiting for my call.

At the end of the street when I turned north John Blake was awaiting me. And I drew up.

"I'd hoped it would not come to this, John, but a man must go a-courting. He must go where his heart would take him, and I think in my place, you would go, no matter what."

He considered that, a square black block of a man looking as solid as rock and as immovable. "It might be," he agreed, after a moment, "but is it courting you are about, or is this a Texas challenge to me?"

"I wouldn't go risking the lady's reputation by asking her to sneak away and meet me after dark. This is no challenge."

He nodded. "If it was," he replied, "I'd stop you, for kill or be killed is my job when it comes to an issue, but I'd stop no decent man from courting . . . although if I were giving advice about the woman in question—"

"Don't," I said. "A man with his heart set isn't one to listen."

"You're not out of the woods," Blake added. "Believe me, I've nothing against you or any decent man making a decent call. It's the drunks and the fighting I want to keep south of the street. However, that is a thing of yesterday for me. I have quit my job."

"Quit!"

"Aye. McDonald told me to keep you south of the street tonight, or lose my job. He has grown arrogant since he took office, and I work for the town, not just the mayor. I was hired to keep the peace, and that only. So I've quit."

The stubborn foolishness of McDonald angered me, yet in a sense I could not blame the man, for generally we were a wild crowd and if a man did not understand us he might easily believe us capable of any evil. At the same time I had pride in my promises, and I had said I would call.

"If you've actually quit, I'd like to take advantage of the fact you're no longer marshal here."

He shot me a quick look. "I want nobody hurt, Gavagan. I've quit, but I've still a feeling for the town."

"It would be like this . . ." and he listened while I explained the idea that had come to me.

"It must be carefully done, no fighting, do you hear?"

Turning my horse I rode back to talk with Carson, Mulloy, Enright, and Delgado. Immediately after I had finished they scattered out to talk to the others and take their positions.

"I saw them going up to the house with their rifles," Carson said. "Carpenter who owns the store is there, with Wilson, Talcott, and some I do not know by name, but all have businesses along the street, so I think it will work."

Circling through the darkness I rode up to the house among the poplars, but stopped across the street. It had been quiet for the boys from the Rocking K and they ached to blow off steam and dearly loved a joke. So this might work.

Leaving my horse I crossed the alley where the shadows were deep and drew near the house. I heard subdued voices beneath the trees.

"I don't like it," Carpenter was saying. "Once that Texas crowd know Blake has quit they will blow the lid off."

"It was a fool idea. John Blake has kept the peace."

"Tell that to McDonald. He would have Blake on some other excuse if not this. The man will have nobody who won't kowtow to him."

Suddenly there was a crashing and splintering of wood from the street, followed by a gunshot and a chorus of Texas yells that split the night wide open, and then there was another outburst of firing and a shattering of glass.

"There they go!" Carpenter stepped out of the shadows into the moonlight. "What did I tell you?"

Down the street charged four Rocking K riders, yelling and shooting. It reminded me of the old days when I was a youngster on my first trip up the trail.

The front door slammed open and McDonald came rushing out, an angry man by the sound of him. "What's that? What's going on?"

The night was stabbed and slashed by the blaze of gunshots, and intermingled with them was the smashing of glass and raucous yells. The boys were having themselves a time.

"You fired Blake," Carpenter said, "and the lid's off."

"We'll see about that!" McDonald said. "Come on!"

They rushed for the street in a mass, and when they

did I moved closer, stepped over the fence, and crossed the lawn to the house.

Suddenly as it had started, and just as we had planned, a blanket dropped upon the town. Not a shout, a shot, or a whisper. By the time McDonald got there the hands would be seated around, playing cards and talking, looking upon the world with the wide-eyed innocence of a bunch of two-year-olds.

The door opened under my rap and June stood there in a pale blue dress, even more lovely than I had expected.

"Why, it's you! But—!" She looked beyond me into the night. "Where is Uncle Aaron?"

"May I come in?"

Startled, she looked up at me again, then stepped back and I went in and closed the door behind me. Hat in hand I bowed to Mrs. McDonald, who was behind her.

The room was stiff, cluttered and lacking in comfort, with plush furniture and a false, unused elegance. There was too much bric-a-brac, and not a place where a man could really sit. Suddenly I remembered the spaciousness of the old Spanish-style houses I had known in Texas.

"We heard shooting," June said.

"Oh, that? Some confusion in town. I believe your uncle went down to put a stop to it."

She looked at me carefully, and I seemed to sense a withdrawing, a change that I could not quite grasp.

"You're not dressed for riding," I said.

She flushed. "You surely didn't believe . . . you weren't *serious*?" She looked at me in amazement. "I thought . . . I mean, it was rather fun, but . . . could you imagine, *me* going with *you* . . ."

Something went out of me then and I stood there feeling the fool I undoubtedly was. Some fine, sharp flame flickered within me as though caught in a gust of wind, then snuffed out and left me empty and lost . . . it might have been the last spark of my boyhood. A man must grow up in so many ways.

On the street she had seemed beautiful and strong and possessed of a fine courage, and in the romantic heart of me I had believed she was the one, that she was my dream, that she was the girl who rode in my thoughts in the dust of the drag or the heat of the flank.

She stared at me, half astonished, and within me there was nothing at all, not sorrow, not bitterness, certainly not anger.

"Good night," I said. "I am sorry that I intruded."

She had cost me a dream, but suddenly I was aware that she would have cost me the dream anyway, for that was what I had been in love with . . . a dream.

Opening the door, I was about to leave when Aaron McDonald pushed past me. Anger flashed in his eyes, and his face paled with fury that was in him. "Look here!" he shouted. "You—!"

"Shut up, you arrogant windbag," I said, and walked on out the door leaving him spluttering. And to the others who were outside, I said, "Get out of my way," and they stepped back and the gate creaked on rusty hinges when I stepped out.

A hand on the pommel of my saddle, I stood for a moment under the stars, cursing myself for seven kinds of an idiot. Like any child I had been carried away . . . who did I think I was, anyway?

Yet although the fire was out the smoke lifted, and I hesitated to step into the saddle, knowing the finality of it. The things a man will wish for are harder to leave behind than all his wants, and who, at some time in his life, does not dream of gathering into his arms and carrying away the girl he loves?

The men of the Rocking K came from the saloons and

stood around me, and when they looked at my face, something seemed to shadow theirs, for I think my dream was one lived by them all, and had it come true with me then all their lonely dreaming might be true also.

"We'll be going," I said.

Yet there was a thing that remained to be done, for as I had lost something this day, I had gained something, too.

"I'll join you at the wagon," I told them, and turning at right angles I rode between the buildings toward the south of town.

It was a simple room of rough boards with one window, a small stove, and a bed. John Blake had his coat off and he was packing, but he turned to face whoever was at the door.

"John," I said, "she would not come and I was a fool to expect it. I have grown a little tonight, I think."

"You have grown a little," he agreed, "but don't expect too much of it, for there will be other times. Each time one grows, one loses a little, too."

"John," I said, "there are cattle on the plains of Texas and I've land there. When I come north again I'll be driving my own herd. It is a big job for one man."

"So?"

"There will be rivers to cross and the Comanches will be out, but there's a future in it for the men who make the drives.

"I like the way you straddle a town, and I like a man with judgment and principle. It is a rare thing to find a man who will stand square on what he believes, whether it is making a rule or an exception to it. So if you'll ride with me it's a partnership, share and share alike."

A square, solid, blocky man in a striped white shirt and black sleeve garters, he looked at me carefully from those cool gray eyes, and then he said, quite seriously, "I've little to pack," he said, "for a man who has never had anything but a gun travels light."

THE LONESOME GODS

Who can say that the desert does not live? Or that the dark, serrated ridges conceal no spirit? Who can love the lost places, yet believe himself truly alone in the silent hills? How can we be sure the ancient ones were wrong when they believed each rock, each tree, each stream or mountain possessed an active spirit? Are the gods of those vanished peoples truly dead, or do they wait among the shadows for some touch of respect, the ritual or sacrifice that can again give them life?

It is written in the memories of the ancient peoples that one who chooses the desert for his enemy has chosen a bitter foe, but he who accepts it as friend, who will seek to understand its moods and whims, shall feel also its mercy, shall drink deep of its hidden waters, and the treasures of its rocks shall be opened before him. Where one may walk in freedom and find water in the arid places, another may gasp out his last breath under the desert sun and mark the sands with the bones of his ending.

Into the western wastelands, in 1807, a man walked dying. Behind him lay the bodies of his companions and the wreck of their boat on the Colorado River. Before him lay the desert, and somewhere beyond the desert the shores of the Pacific.

Jacob Almayer was a man of Brittany, and the Bretons are an ancient folk with roots among the Druids and those unknown people who vanished long ago, but who lifted the stones of Karnak to their places. He was a man who had walked much alone, a man sensitive to the wilderness and the mores of other peoples and other times, and now he walked into the desert with only the miles before him.

The distance was immeasurable. He was without water, without food, and the vast waste of the desert was the sickly color of dead flesh deepening in places to rusty red or to the hazy purple of distance. Within the limits of his knowledge lay no habitation of men except the drowsy Spanish colonies along the coast. Yet, colonies or not, the sea was there, and the men of Brittany are born to the sea. So he turned his face westward and let the distance unroll behind him.

Now he had not long to live. From the crest of the ridge he stared out across the unbelievable expanse of the desert. The gourd that hung from his shoulder was empty for many hours. His boots were tatters of leather, his cheeks and eyes sunken, his lips gray and cracked.

Morning had come at last, and Jacob Almayer licked the dew from the barrel of his rifle and looked westward. Although due west was the way he had traveled and due west he should continue, off to his right there lay the shadow of an ancient trail, lying like the memory of a dream across the lower slope of the mesa.

The trail was old. So old the rocks had taken the patina of desert time, so old that it skirted the curve of an ancient beach where once lapped the waters of a vanished sea. The old trail led away in a long, graceful sweep, toward the west-northwest, following the high ground toward some destination he could not guess.

West was his logical route. Somewhere out there the road from Mexico to the California missions cut diagonally across the desert. By heading directly west he might last long enough to find that road, yet the water gourd was dry and the vast sun-baked basin before him offered no promise. The ancient folk who made this path must have known where water could be found, yet if the sea had vanished from this basin might not the springs have vanished also?

Jacob Almayer was a big man, powerful in the chest and broad in the shoulders, a fighter by instinct and a man who would, by the nature of him, die hard. He was also a man of ironic, self-deriding humor, and it was like him to have no illusions now. And it was like him to look down the ancient trail with curious eyes. For how many centuries had this trail been used? Walked by how many feet, dust now these hundreds of years? And for how long had it been abandoned?

Such a path is not born in a month, nor are the stones marked in a year. Yet the ages had not erased the marks of their passing, although without this view from the crest it was doubtful if the trail could be seen. But once seen and recognized for what it was, following it should not be hard. Moreover, at intervals the passing men had dropped stones into neat piles.

To mark the miles? The intervals were irregular. To break the monotony? A ritual, perhaps? Like a Tibetan spinning a prayer wheel? Was each stone a prayer? An invocation to the gods of travelers? Gods abandoned for how long?

"I could use their help," Jacob Almayer said aloud, "I could use them now." Either path might lead to death, and either might lead to water and life, but which way?

Curiosity triumphed, or rather, his way of life triumphed. Had it not always been so with him? And those others who preceded him? Was it not curiosity more than desire for gain that led them on? And now, in what might be the waning hours of life, it was no time to change.

Jacob Almayer looked down the shimmering basin and he looked along the faint but easy sweep of the trail. He could, of course, rationalize his choice. The trail led over high ground, along an easier route; trust an Indian to keep his feet out of the heavy sand. Jacob Almayer turned down the trail, and as he did so he stooped and picked up a stone from the ground.

The sun lifted into the wide and brassy sky and the basin swam with heat. The free-swinging stride that had carried him from the Colorado was gone now, but the trail was good and he walked steadily. He began to sweat again, and smelled the odors of his unwashed clothes, his unbathed body; the stale smell of old sweat. Yet the air he breathed, however hot, was like wine—like water, one could almost swallow it. Soon he came to a pile of stones and he dropped the stone he carried and picked up another, then walked on.

Upon his shoulder the gourd flopped loosely, and his dry tongue fumbled at the broken flesh of his lips. After several hours he stopped sweating, and when he inadvertently touched the flesh of his face it felt hot and dry. When he paused at intervals he found it becoming harder and harder to start again but he kept on, unable to rest for long, knowing that safety if it came would be somewhere ahead.

Sometimes his boots rolled on rocks and twisted his feet painfully, and he could feel that his socks were stuck to his blistered feet with dried blood. Once he stumbled and fell, catching himself on his hands, but clumsily so that the skin was torn and lacerated. For a long minute he held himself on his hands and knees, staring drunkenly at the path beneath him, caught in some trancelike state when he was neither quite conscious nor quite unconscious, but for the moment was just flesh devoid of animation. Finally he got to his feet and, surprised to find himself there, he started on, walking with sudden rapidity as if starting anew. Cicadas hummed in the cacti and greasewood, and once he saw a rattler coil and buzz angrily, but he walked on.

Before him the thread of the trail writhed among the rocks, emerged, and then fell away before him to a lower level, so faint yet beckoning, always promising, drawing him into the distance as a magnet draws filings of iron. He no longer thought, but only walked, hypnotized by his own movement. His mind seemed to fill with the heat haze and he remembered nothing but the rocks, dropping and carrying stones with the deadly persistence of a drunken man.

Now the trail skirted the white line of an ancient beach, where the sand was silver with broken shell and where at times he came upon the remains of ancient fires, blackened stones, charred remains of prehistoric shells and fish bones.

His eyes were bloodshot now, slow to move and hard to focus. Dust devils danced in the desert heat waves. He clung to the thread of the path as to the one thing in this shimmering land of mirages that was real, that was familiar.

Then he tripped.

He fell flat on his face, and he lay still, face against the gravel of the partial slope, the only sound that of his hoarse breathing. Slowly he pushed himself up, got into a sitting position. Drunkenly he stared at his palms, scraped and gouged by the fall. With infinite and childish concentration he began to pick the sand from the wounds, and then he licked at the blood. He got up then, because it was his nature to get up. He got up and he recovered his gun, making an issue of bending without losing balance, and triumphant when he was successful.

He fell twice more in the next half hour, and each time it took him longer to rise. Yet he knew the sun was past its noontime high, and somehow he must last out the day. He started on but his mouth was dry, his tongue musty, and the heat waves seemed all around him. He seemed to have, at last, caught up with the mirage, for it shimmered around him and washed over him like the sea but without freshness, only heat.

A man stood in the trail before him.

An Indian. Jacob Almayer tried to cry out but he could not. He started forward, but the figure of the man seemed to recede as he advanced . . . and then the Indian's arm lifted and pointed.

Almayer turned his head slowly, looking toward the ridge of upthrust rock not far off the trail. Almayer tried to speak, but the Indian merely pointed.

Jacob Almayer leaned back and tried to make out the looks of the Indian, but all he could see was the brown skin, breechclout, and some sort of a band around his head. Around his shoulders was some sort of a fur jacket. A *fur* jacket? In this heat? Almayer looked again at the rocks; when he looked back, the Indian was gone.

The rocks were not far away and Almayer turned toward them, but first he stopped, for where the Indian had been standing there was a pile of stones. He walked toward it and added his stone to the pile. Then he picked up another and turned toward the ridge. There was a trail here, too. Not quite so plain as the other, but nevertheless, a trail.

He walked on, hesitating at times, reluctant to get

away from the one possibility of safety, but finally he reached the ridge where the trail rounded it, and he did likewise, and there in a corner of the rocks was white sand overgrown with thin grass, a clump of mesquite, a slim cottonwood tree, and beneath it, a pool of water.

Jacob Almayer tasted the water and it was sweet; he put a little on his lips, and it had the coolness of a bene-diction. He put some in his mouth and held it there, let-ting the starved tissues of his mouth absorb the water, and then he let a little trickle down his throat, and felt it, all the way to his stomach. After a while he drank, and over his head the green leaves of the cottonwood brushed their green and silver palms in whispering ap-plause. Jacob Almayer crept into the shade and slept. He awoke to drink, then slept again, and in the paleness of the last hours of night he awakened and heard a faint stir upon the hillside opposite the ridge beside which he lay. He squinted his eyes, then widened them, trying to see, and then he did see.

There were men there, men and women, and even he in his half-delirium and his half-awareness knew these were like no Indians he had seen. Each carried a basket and they were gathering something from among the squat green trees on the hill. He started up and called out, but they neither turned nor spoke, but finally com-pleted their work and walked slowly away.

Daylight came . . . one instant the sky was gray, and then the shadows retreated into the canyons and the dark places among the hills, and the sun crowned the distant ridges with gold, then bathed them in light, and the last faltering battalions of the shadows withered and died among the rocks and morning was there. In the early light Jacob Almayer drank again, drank deep now, and long.

His thirst gone, hunger remained, but he stood up and

looked over at the hill. Had he seen anything? Or had it been his imagination? Had it been some fantasy of his half-delirium? Leaving the spring he crossed the small valley toward the hillside and climbed it. As he walked, he searched the ground. No footsteps had left their mark, no stones unturned, no signs of a large body of people moving or working.

The trees . . . he looked at them again, and then he recalled a traveler who had told him once of how the Indians gathered the nuts from these pines . . . from the piñon. He searched for the cones and extracted some of the nuts. And then he gathered more, and more. And that evening he killed a mountain sheep near the spring.

At daylight he resumed his walk, but this time his gourd was filled with water, and he carried fresh meat with him, and several pounds of the nuts. As Jacob Almayer started to walk, he picked up a stone, and then an idea came to him.

How far would an Indian walk in a day? Those who followed this trail would probably have no reason for hurry. Would they walk fifteen miles? Twenty? Or even thirty? Or would distance depend on the water supply? For that was the question that intrigued him. Where they stopped there would be water. The solution was to watch for any dim trail leading away from the main route toward the end of the day.

Soon he found another pile of the stones, and he dropped the one he carried, and picked up another. And at nightfall he found a dim trail that led to a flowing spring, and he camped there, making a fire and roasting some of his meat. As he ate and drank, as he watched his fire burn down, as he thought of the trail behind and the trail ahead, he looked out into the darkness.

Jacob Almayer was a Breton, and the folk of Brittany are sensitive to the spirits of the mountains and forest. He looked out into the darkness beyond the firelight and he said aloud, "To the spirits of this place, my respects, humble as they are, and in my heart there will always be thanks for you, as long as I shall live."

The fire fluttered then, the flames whipping down, then blazing up, brighter than ever. From far off there came the distant sound of voices. Were they chanting, singing? He couldn't tell . . . it might have been the wind.

RUSTLER ROUNDUP

CHAPTER 1

Judge Gardner Collins sat in his usual chair on the porch. The morning sunshine was warm and lazy, and it felt good just to be sitting, half awake and half asleep. Yet it was time Doc Finerty came up the street so they could cross over to Mother Boyle's for coffee.

Powis came out of his barbershop and sat down on the step. "Nice morning," he said. Then, glancing up the street and across, he nodded toward the black horse tied at the hitching rail in front of the stage station. "I see Finn Mahone's in town."

The judge nodded. "Rode in about an hour after daybreak. Reckon he's got another package at the stage station."

"What's he getting in those packages?" Powis wondered. "He gets more than anybody around here."

"Books, I reckon. He reads a lot."

Powis nodded. "I guess so." He looked around at the

judge and scratched the back of his neck thoughtfully. "Seen anything more of Miss Kastelle?"

"Remy?" The judge let the front legs of his chair down.

"Uh-huh. She was in yesterday asking me if I'd heard if Brewster or McInnis were in town."

"I've lost some myself," Collins said. "Too many. But Pete Miller says he can't find any sign of them, and nobody else seems to."

"You know, Judge," Powis said thoughtfully, "one time two or three years back I cut hair for a trapper. He was passing through on the stage, an' stopped overnight. He told me he trapped in this country twenty years ago. Said there was some of the most beautiful valleys back behind the Highbinders anybody ever saw."

"Back in the Highbinders, was it?" Judge Collins stared thoughtfully at the distant, purple mountains. "That's Finn Mahone's country."

"That's right," Powis said.

Judge Collins looked down the street for Doc Finerty. He scowled to himself, only too aware of what Powis was hinting. The vanishing cattle had to go somewhere. If there were pastures back in the Highbinders, it would be a good place for them to be hidden, and where they could stay hidden for years.

That could only mean Finn Mahone.

When he looked around again, he was pleased to see Doc Finerty had rounded the corner by the Longhorn Saloon and was cutting across the street toward him. The judge got up and strolled out to meet him and they both turned toward Mother Boyle's.

Doc Finerty was five inches shorter than Judge Gardner Collins's lean six feet one inch. He was square built, but like many short, broad men he was quick moving and was never seen walking slow when by himself. He and the judge had been friends ever since they first met, some fifteen years before.

Finerty was an excellent surgeon and a better doctor than would have been expected in a western town like Laird. In the hit-and-miss manner of the frontier country, he practiced dentistry as well.

Judge Collins had studied law after leaving college, reading in the office of a frontier lawyer in Missouri. Twice, back in Kansas, he had been elected justice of the peace. In Laird his duties were diverse and interesting. He was the local magistrate. He married those interested, registered land titles and brands, and acted as a notary and general legal advisor.

There were five men in Laird who had considerable academic education. Aside from Judge Collins and Doc Finerty there were Pierce Logan, the town's mayor and one of the biggest ranchers; Dean Armstrong, editor and publisher of *The Branding Iron;* and Garfield Otis, who was, to put it less than mildly, a bum.

"I'm worried, Doc," the judge said, over their coffee. "Powis was hinting again that Finn Mahone might be rustling."

"You think he is?"

"No. Do you?"

"I doubt it. Still, you know how it is out here. Anything could be possible. He does have a good deal of money. More than he would be expected to have, taking it easy like he does."

"If it was me," Doc said, "I'd look the other way. I'd look around that bunch up around Sonntag's place."

"They are pretty bad, all right." Judge Collins looked down at his coffee. "Dean was telling me that Byrn Sonntag killed a man over to Rico last week."

"Another?" Doc Finerty asked. "That's three he's killed this year. What was it you heard?"

"Dean didn't get much. He met the stage and Calkins told him. Said the man drew, but Sonntag killed him. Two shots, right through the heart."

"He's bad. Montana Kerr and Banty Hull are little better. Miller says he can't go after them unless they do something he knows about. If you ask me, he doesn't want to."

Finerty finished his cup. "I don't know as I blame him. If he did we'd need another marshal."

The door opened and they both looked up. The man who stepped in was so big he filled the door. His hair was long and hung around his ears, and he wore rugged outdoor clothing that, while used, was reasonably clean and of the best manufacture.

He took off his hat as he entered, and they noted the bullet hole in the flat brim of the gray Stetson. His two guns were worn with their butts reversed for a cross draw, for easier access while riding and to accommodate their long barrels.

"Hi, Doc! How are you, Judge?" He sat down beside them.

"Hello, Finn! That mountain life seems to agree with you!" Doc said. "I'm afraid you'll never give me any business."

Finn Mahone looked around and smiled quizzically. His lean brown face was strong, handsome in a rugged way. His eyes were green. "I came very near cashing in for good." He gestured at the bullet hole. "That happened a few days ago over in the Highbinders."

"I didn't think anybody ever went into that country but you. Who was it?" the judge asked.

"No idea. It wasn't quite my country. I was away over east, north of the Brewster place on the other side of Rawhide."

"Accident?" Finerty asked.

Mahone grinned. "Does it look like it? No, I think I came on someone who didn't want to be seen. I took out. Me, I'm not mad at anybody."

The door slammed open and hard little heels tapped on the floor. "Who owns that black stallion out here?"

"I do," Finn replied. He looked up, and felt the skin tighten around his eyes. He had never seen Remy Kastelle before. He had not even heard of her.

She was tall, and her hair was like dark gold. Her eyes were brown, her skin lightly tanned. Finn Mahone put his coffee cup down slowly and half turned toward her.

He had rarely seen so beautiful a woman, nor one so obviously on a mission.

"I'd like to buy him!" she said. "What's your price?"

Finn Mahone was conscious of some irritation at her impulsiveness. "I have no price," he said, "and the horse is not for sale." A trace of a smile showed at the corners of his mouth.

"Well," she said, "I'll give you five hundred dollars."

"Not for five thousand," he said quietly. "I wouldn't sell that horse any more . . . any more than your father would sell you."

She smiled at that. "He might . . . if the price was right," she said. "It might be a relief to him!"

She brushed on by him and sat down beside Judge Collins.

"Judge," she said, "what do you know about a man named Finn Mahone? Is he a rustler?"

There was a momentary silence, but before the judge could reply, Finn spoke up. "I doubt it, ma'am. He's too lazy. Rustlin' cows is awfully hot work."

"They've been rustling cows at night," Remy declared. "If you were from around here you would know that."

"Yes, ma'am," he said mildly, "I guess I would. Only sometimes they do it with a runnin' iron or a cinch ring.

Then they do it by day. They just alter the brands a little with a burn here, an' more there."

Finn Mahone got up. He said, "Ma'am, I reckon if I was going to start hunting rustlers in this country, I'd do it with a pen and ink."

He strolled outside, turning at the door as he put his hat on to look her up and down, very coolly, very impudently. Then he let the door slam after him. Across the room the back door of the restaurant opened as another man entered.

Remy felt her face grow hot. She was suddenly angry. "Well! Who was that?" she demanded.

"That was Finn Mahone," Doc Finerty said gently.

"Oh!" Remy Kastelle's ears reddened.

"Who?" The new voice cut across the room like a pistol shot. Texas Dowd was a tall man, as tall as Mahone or Judge Collins, but lean and wiry. His gray eyes were keen and level, his handlebar mustache dark and neatly twisted. He might have been thirty-five, but was nearer forty-five. He stood just inside the back door.

Stories had it that Texas Dowd was a bad man with a gun. He had been in the Laird River country but two years, and so far as anyone knew his gun had never been out of its holster. The Laird River country was beginning to know what Remy Kastelle and her father had found out, that Texas Dowd knew cattle. He also knew range, and he knew men.

"Finn Mahone," Judge Collins replied, aware that the name had found acute interest. "Know him?"

"Probably not," Dowd said. "He live around here?"

"No, back in the Highbinders. I've never seen his place, myself. They call it Crystal Valley. It's a rough sixty miles from here, out beyond your place." He nodded to Remy.

"Know where the Notch is? That rift in the wall?" Collins continued. "Well, the route to his place lies up that Notch. I've heard it said that no man should travel that trail at night, and no man by day who doesn't know it. It's said to be one of the most beautiful places in the world. Once in a while Mahone gets started talking about it, and he can tell you things . . . but that trail would make your hair stand on end."

"He come down here often?" Dowd asked carefully.

"No. Not often. I've known three months to go by without us seeing him. His place is closer to Rico."

"Name sounded familiar," Dowd said. He looked around at Remy. "Are you ready to go, ma'am?"

"Mr. Dowd," Remy said, her eyes flashing, "I want that black stallion Mahone rides. That's the finest horse I ever saw!"

"Miss Kastelle," Finerty said, "don't get an idea Mahone's any ordinary cowhand or rancher. He's not. If he said he wouldn't sell that horse, he meant it. Money means nothing to him."

Judge Collins glanced at Finerty as the two went out. "Doc, I've got an idea Dowd knows something about Finn Mahone. You notice that look in his eye?"

"Uh-huh." Doc lit a cigar. "Could be, at that. None of us know much about him. He's been here more than a year, too. Gettin' on for two years. And he has a sight of money."

"Now don't you be getting like Powis!" Judge Collins exclaimed. "I like the man. He's quiet, and he minds his own business. He also knows a good thing when he sees it. I don't blame Remy for wanting that horse. There isn't a better one in the country!"

Finn Mahone strode up the street to the Emporium. "Four boxes of forty-four rimfire," he said.

He watched while Harran got down the shells, but his mind was far away. He was remembering the girl. It had been a long time since he had seen a woman like that. Women of any kind were scarce in this country. For a moment, he stood staring at the shells, then he ordered a few other things, and gathering them up, went out to the black horse. Making a neat pack of them, he lashed them on behind the saddle. Then he turned and started across the street.

He worried there was going to be trouble. He could feel it building up all around him. He knew there were stories being told about him, and there was that hole in his hat. There was little animosity yet, but it would come. If they ever got back into the Highbinders and saw how many cattle he had, all hell would break loose.

Stopping for a moment in the sunlight in front of the Longhorn, he finished his cigarette. "Mahone?"

He turned.

Garfield Otis was a thin man, not tall, with a scholar's face. He had been a teacher once, a graduate of a world-famous university, a writer of intelligent but unread papers on the Battles of Belarius and the struggle for power in France during the Middle Ages. Now he was a hanger-on around barrooms, drunk much of the time, kept alive by a few odd jobs and the charity of friends.

He had no intimates, yet he talked sometimes with Collins or Finerty, and more often with young Dean Armstrong, the editor of *The Branding Iron*. Armstrong had read Poe, and he had read Lowell, and had read Goethe and Heine in the original German. He quickly sensed much of the story behind Otis. He occasionally bought him drinks, often food.

Otis, lonely and tired, also found friendship in the person of Lettie Mason, whose gambling hall was opposite the Town Hall, and Finn Mahone, the strange rider from the Highbinder Hills.

"How are you, Otis?" Finn said, smiling. "Nice morning, isn't it?"

"It is," Otis responded. He passed a trembling hand over his unshaven chin. "Finn, be careful. They are going to make trouble for you."

"Who?" Finn's eyes were intent.

"I was down at Lettie's. Alcorn was there. He's one of those ranchers from out beyond Rawhide. One of the bunch that runs with Sonntag. He said you were a rustler."

"Thanks, Otis." Finn frowned thoughtfully. "I reckoned something like that was comin'. Who was with him?"

"Big man named Leibman. Used to be a sort of a bruiser on the docks in New York. Lettie doesn't take to him."

"She's a good judge of men." Finn hitched up his gun belts. "Reckon I'll trail out of town, Otis. Thanks again."

At Lettie's he might have a run-in with some of the bunch from Rawhide, and he was not a trouble hunter. He knew what he was when aroused, and knew what could happen in this country. Scouting the hills as he always did, he had a very good idea of just what was going on. There was time for one drink, then he was heading out. He turned and walked into the Longhorn.

Red Eason was behind the bar himself this morning. He looked up as Mahone entered, and Finn noticed the change in his eyes.

"Rye," Finn said. He waited, his hands on the bar while the drink was poured. He was conscious of low voices in the back of the saloon and glanced up. Two men were sitting there at one of the card tables. One was a slender man of middle age with a lean, high-boned face. He was unshaven, and his eyes were watchful. The other was a big man, even bigger than Mahone was himself. The man's face was wide and flat, and his nose had been broken.

The big man got up from the table and walked toward him. At that moment the outer door opened and Dean Armstrong came in with Doc Finerty and Judge Collins. They halted as they saw the big man walking toward Mahone.

Armstrong's quick eyes shifted to Banty Hull. The small man was seated in a chair half behind the corner of the bar. If Mahone turned to face the big man who Armstrong knew to be named Leibman, his back would be toward Hull. Dean Armstrong rarely carried a gun, but he was glad he was packing one this morning.

Leibman stopped a few feet away from Mahone. "You Finn Mahone?" he demanded. "From back in the Highbinders?"

Mahone looked up. "That's my name. That's where I live." He saw that the other man had shifted until he was against the wall and Leibman was no longer between them.

"Hear you got a lot of cattle back in them hills," Leibman said. "Hear you been selling stock over to Rico."

"That's right."

"Funny thing, you havin' so many cows an' nobody knowin' about it."

"Not very funny. I don't recall that anybody from Laird has ever been back to see me. It's a pretty rough trail. You haven't been back there, either."

"No, but I been to Rico. I seen some of them cows you sold."

"Nice stock," Mahone said calmly. He knew what was coming, but Leibman wasn't wearing a gun.

"Some funny brands," Leibman said. "Looked like some of them had been altered."

"Leibman," Finn said quietly, "you came over here huntin' trouble. You'd know if you saw any of those cattle that none of them had but one brand. You know nobody else has seen them, so you think you can get away with an accusation and cover it up by trouble with me.

"You want trouble? All right, you've got it. If you say there was an altered brand on any of those cattle, *you're a liar!*"

Leibman sneered. "I ain't wearin' a gun!" he said. "Talk's cheap."

"Not with me, it isn't," Mahone said. "With me talk is right expensive. But I don't aim to mess up Brother Eason's bar, here. Nor do I aim to let your pal Alcorn slug me from behind or take a shot at me.

"So what we're going to do, you and me, is go outside in the street. You don't have a gun, so you can use your hands."

Without further hesitation he turned and walked into the street. "Judge," he said to Collins, "I'd admire if you'd sort of keep an eye on my back. Here's my guns." He unbuckled his belts and passed them to the judge.

Alcorn and Banty Hull, watched by Doc Finerty and Armstrong, looked uneasily at each other as they moved into the street. Mahone noticed the glance. This wasn't going the way they had planned.

Leibman backed off and pulled off his shirt, displaying a hairy and powerfully muscled chest and shoulders.

Remy Kastelle came out of the Emporium and, noticing the crowd, was starting across the street when Pierce Logan walked up to her.

He was a tall man, perfectly dressed, suave and intelligent. "How do you do, Miss Kastelle!" he said, smiling.

She nodded up the street. "What's going on up there?"

Logan turned quickly, and his face tightened. "Looks like a fight starting," he said. "That's Leibman, but who can be fighting him?"

Then he saw Mahone. "It's that fellow from the Highbinders, Mahone."

"The one they're calling a rustler?" Remy turned quickly. She failed to note the momentary, pleased response to her reference to Mahone as a rustler. Her eyes quickened with interest. "He tricked me. I hope he takes a good beating!"

"He will!" Logan said dryly. "Leibman is a powerful brute. A rough-and-tumble fighter from the East."

"I'm not so sure." Texas Dowd had walked up behind them. He was looking past them gravely. "I think your man Leibman is in for a whipping."

Logan laughed, but glanced sharply at Dowd. He had never liked the Lazy K foreman. He had always had an unpleasant feeling that the tall, cold cattleman saw too much, and saw it too clearly. There was also a sound to Dowd's voice, something in his way of talking that caught in Logan's mind. Stirred memories of . . . someone.

"Wouldn't want to bet, would you?" Logan asked.

"Yes, I'll bet."

Remy glanced around, surprised and puzzled. "Why, Mr. Dowd! I would never have imagined you to be a gambling man."

"I'm not," Dowd said.

"You think it's a sure thing, then?" Logan asked, incredulously.

"Yes," Dowd replied.

"Well, I think you're wrong for a hundred dollars," Logan said.

"All right." Dowd looked at Remy. "I'll be inside, buying what we need, Miss Remy."

"Aren't you even going to watch it?" Logan demanded.

"No," Dowd said. "I've seen it before." He turned and walked into the store.

"Well!" Logan looked at Remy, astonished. "That foreman of yours is a peculiar man."

"Yes." She looked after Dowd, disturbed. "He sounded like he had known something of Mahone before. Now let's go!"

"You aren't going to watch it?" Pierce Logan was shocked in spite of himself.

"Of course! I wouldn't miss it for the world!"

Finn Mahone knew fighters of Leibman's type. The man had won many fights. He had expected Mahone to avoid the issue, but Mahone's calm acceptance and his complete lack of excitement were disturbing the bigger man. Mahone pulled off his shirt.

Leibman's face hardened suddenly. If ever he had looked at a trained athlete's body, he was looking at it now. With a faint stir of doubt he realized he was facing no common puncher, no backwoods brawler. Then his confidence came back. He had never been whipped, never . . .

He went in with a rush, half expecting Mahone to be the boxer type who might try to evade him. Finn Mahone had no intention of evading anything. As Leibman rushed, he took one step in and smashed Leibman's lips into pulp with a straight left. Then he ducked and threw a right to the body.

Stopped in his tracks, Leibman's eyes narrowed. He feinted and clubbed Mahone with a ponderous right. Mahone took it and never even wavered, then he leaped in, punching with both hands!

Slugging madly, neither man giving ground, they stood spraddle-legged in the dust punching with all their power. Leibman gave ground first, but it was to draw Finn on, and when Mahone rushed, Leibman caught him with a flying mare and threw him over his back!

Finn hit the ground in a cloud of dust, and as a roar went up from the crowd, he leaped to his feet and smashed Leibman back on his heels with a wicked right to the jaw. Leibman ducked under another punch and tried to throw Mahone with a rolling hip-lock. It failed when Mahone grabbed him and they both tumbled into the dust. Finn was up first, and stepped back, wiping the dust from his lips. Leibman charged, and Finn side-stepped, hooking a left to the bigger man's ear.

Leibman pulled his head down behind his shoulder. Then he rushed, feinted, and hit Mahone with a wicked left that knocked him into the dust. He went in, trying to kick, but Finn caught his foot and twisted, throwing Leibman off balance.

Finn was on his feet then, and the two men came together and began to slug. The big German was tough; he had served his apprenticeship in a hard school. He took a punch to the gut, gasped a long breath, and lunged. Then Finn stepped back and brought up a right uppercut that broke Leibman's nose.

Finn walked in, his left a flashing streak now. It stabbed and cut, ripping Leibman's face to ribbons. Suddenly, Judge Collins realized something that few in the crowd understood. Until now, Mahone had been playing with the big man. What happened after that moment was sheer murder.

The left was a lancet in the shape of a fist. The wicked right smashed again and again into Leibman's body, or clubbed his head. Once Finn caught Leibman by the arm and twisted him sharply, at the same time bringing up a smashing right uppercut. Punch-drunk and swaying, Leibman was a gory, beaten mass of flesh and blood.

Finn looked at him coolly, then measured him with a left and drove a right to the chin that sounded when it hit like an ax hitting a log. Leibman fell, all in one piece.

Without a word or a glance around, Finn walked to his saddle and picked up his shirt. Then he dug into his saddlebags and took out a worn towel. Judge Collins came over to him. "Better put these on first," he said.

Finn glanced at him sharply, then smiled. "I reckon I had," he said. He mopped himself with the towel, then slid into his shirt. With the guns strapped on his lean hips, he felt better.

His knuckles were skinned despite the hardness of his hands. He looked up at Collins. "Looks like they were figurin' on trouble."

"That's right. There's rumors around, son. You better watch yourself."

"Thanks." Mahone swung into the saddle. As he turned the horse he glanced to the boardwalk and saw the girl watching him. Beside her was a tall, handsome man with powerful shoulders. He smiled grimly, and turned the horse away down the street, walking him slowly.

Texas Dowd appeared at Logan's elbow. Pierce turned and handed him a hundred dollars. "You'd seen him fight before?" he asked.

Dowd shrugged. "Could be. He's fought before."

"Yes," Logan said thoughtfully, "he has." He glanced at Dowd again. "What do you know about him?"

Texas Dowd's face was inscrutable. "That he's a good man to leave alone," he said flatly.

Dowd turned stiffly and strode away. Nettled, Logan stared after him. "Where did you find him?" he asked.

Remy smiled faintly. "He came up over the border when I was away at school. Dad liked the way he played poker. He started working for us, and Dad made him foreman. There was a gunman around who was making trouble. I never really got it straight, but the gunman died. I heard Dad telling one of the hands about it."

Behind them Texas Dowd headed down the street. He made one brief stop at Lettie Mason's gambling hall and emerged tucking a single playing card into his breast pocket. Then he mounted his horse and rode hard down the trail toward the Highbinders. . . .

Finn Mahone walked the black only to the edge of town, then broke the stallion into a canter and rapidly put some miles behind him. Yet no matter how far or fast he rode, he could not leave the girl behind him. He had seen Remy Kastelle, and something about her gave him a lift, sent fire into his veins. Several times he was on the verge of wheeling the horse and heading back.

She was his nearest neighbor, her range running right up to the Rimrock. But beyond the Rimrock nobody ever tried to come. Finn slowed the black to a walk again, scowling as he rode. His holdings were eighty miles from Rawhide where Alcorn and Leibman lived. There was no reason for them jumping him, unless they needed a scapegoat. The talk about rustling was building up, and if they could pin it on him, there were plenty of people who would accept it as gospel.

People were always suspicious of anyone who kept to himself. Nobody knew the Highbinder country like he did. If they had guessed he had nearly five thousand acres of top grassland, there might have been others trying to horn in.

Crystal Valley, watered by Crystal Creek, which flowed into the Laird, was not just one valley, it was three. In the first, where his home was, there were scarcely three hundred acres. In the second there were more than a thousand acres, and in the third, over three thousand. There was always water here, even in the driest weather, and the grass always grew tall. Three times the number of cattle he now had could never have kept it down.

High, rocky walls with very few passes made it impossible for cattle to stray. The passes were okay for a man on foot, or in one or two cases, a man on a mountain horse, but nothing more.

After a while he reined in and looked off across the rolling country toward the Kastelle spread. It was a good ranch, and Remy was making it a better one. She knew cattle, or she had someone with her who did. He smiled bitterly because he knew just who that someone was.

Finn Mahone got down from his horse and rolled and lighted a cigarette. As he faced north, he looked toward the Kastelle ranch with its Lazy K brand. Southwest of him was McInnis and his Spur outfit. The McInnis ranch was small, but well handled, and until lately, prosperous.

East of him was the town of Laird, and south and just a short distance west of Laird, the P Slash L ranch of Pierce Logan.

Northeast of town was Van Brewster's Lazy S, and north of that, the hamlet of Rawhide. Rawhide was a settlement of ranchers, small ranchers such as Banty Hull, Alcorn, Leibman, Ringer Cobb, Ike Hibby, Frank Salter, and Montana Kerr. It was also the hangout of Byrn Sonntag.

He had not been joking when he suggested the best

way to look for rustlers was with a pen and ink. There are few brands that cannot be altered, and it was a curious thing that the brands of the small group of cattlemen who centered in Rawhide could be changed very easily into Brewster's Lazy S or McInnis's Spur.

Finn Mahone was a restless man. There was little to do on his range much of the time, so when not reading or working around the place, he rode. And his riding had taken him far eastward along the ridge of the Highbinders, eastward almost as far as Rawhide.

Mounting, Finn turned the stallion toward the dim trail that led toward the Notch. It was a trail not traveled but by himself. A trail no one showed any desire to follow.

Ahead of him a Joshua tree thrust itself up from the plain. It was a lone sentinel, the only one of its kind in many miles. He glanced at it and was about to ride by when something caught his eye. He reined the horse around and rode closer. Thrust into the fiber of the tree was a playing card. A hole had been shot through each corner.

"Well, I'll be damned!" he said. "Texas Dowd. He finally figured out I was here—" His comment to the stallion stopped abruptly, and he replaced the card, looking at it thoughtfully. Then, on a sudden inspiration, he wheeled the stallion and rode off fifty feet or so, then turned the horse again. His hand flashed and a gun was in it. He fired four times as rapidly as he could trigger the gun. Then he turned the horse and rode away.

There were four more holes in the card, just inside the others. A message had been sent, and now the reply given.

·   ·   ·

The great wall of the Rimrock loomed up on his left. It was a sheer, impossible precipice from two to six hundred feet high and running for all of twelve miles. For twenty miles further there was no way over except on foot. It was wild country across the Rim, and not even Finn Mahone had ever explored it thoroughly.

Straight ahead was the great rift in the wall. Sheer rock on one side, a steep slope on the other. Down the bottom ran the roaring, brawling Laird River, a tumbling rapids with many falls. The trail to Crystal Valley skirted the stream and the sheer cliff. Eight feet wide, it narrowed to four, and ran on for three miles, never wider than that.

After that it crossed the Laird three times, then disappeared at a long shale bank that offered no sign of a trail. The shale had a tendency to shift and slide at the slightest wrong move. It was that shale bank that defeated ingress to the valley. There was a way across. An outlaw had shown it to Finn, and he'd heard it from an Indian.

By sighting on the white blaze of a tree, and a certain thumblike projection of rock, one could make it across. Beneath the shale at this point there was a shelf of solid rock. A misstep and one was off into loose shale that would start to slide. It slid, steeper and steeper, for three hundred yards, then plunged off, a hundred feet below, into a snarl of lava pits.

Once across the slides, the trail was good for several miles, then wound through a confusion of canyons and washes. At the end one rode through a narrow stone bottleneck into the paradise that was Crystal Valley.

Finn Mahone dismounted at the Rimrock, and led his horse to the edge of the river. While the black was drinking, he let his eyes roam through the trees toward the Notch, then back over the broad miles of the Lazy K.

Remy Kastelle. The name made music in his mind. He

remembered the flash of her eyes, her quick, capable walk.

The sun was warm, and he sat down on the bank of the stream and watched the water. Until now he had known peace, and peace was the one thing most to be desired. His cattle grew fat on the grassy valley lands, there were beaver and mink to be trapped, deer to be hunted. Occasionally, a little gold to be panned from corners and bends of the old creek bank. It had been an easy, happy, but lonely life.

It would be that no longer. For months now he had seen the trouble building in Laird Valley. He had listened to the gossip of ranch hands in Rico, the cattle buyers and the bartenders. He had heard stories of Byrn Sonntag, of Montana Kerr, of Ringer Cobb.

Simple ranchers? He had smiled at the idea. No man who knew the Big Bend country would ever suggest that, nor any man who had gone up the trail to Dodge and Hays. They were men whose names had legends built around them, men known for ruthless killing.

Frank Salter was just as bad. Lean and embittered, Salter had ridden with Quantrill's guerrillas, then he had trailed west and south. He had killed a man in Dimmit, another in Eagle Pass. He was nearly fifty now, but a sour, unhappy man with a rankling hatred for everything successful, everything peaceful.

Of them all, Sonntag was the worst. He was smooth, cold-blooded, with nerves like chilled steel. He had, the legends said, killed twenty-seven men.

Looking on from a distance Mahone had the perspective to see the truth. Until lately, there had been no suspicion of rustling. No tracks had been found; there had reportedly been no mysterious disappearances of cattle. The herds had been weeded patiently and with intelligence.

Abraham McInnis suddenly awakened to the realization that the thousand or more cattle he had believed to be in the brakes were not there. The rustlers had carefully worked cattle down on the range so there would always be cattle in sight. They had taken only a few at a time, and they had never taken a cow without its calf, and vice versa.

McInnis had gone to town and met with Brewster, and Van had returned to his own ranch. For three days he covered it as he had not covered it since the last roundup. At the very least, he was missing several hundred head of cattle. The same was true of Collins, the Kastelles, and Pierce Logan.

All of this was known to Finn Mahone. Stories got around in cattle country, and he was a man who listened much and remembered what he heard. Moreover, he could read trail sign like most men could read a newspaper.

He mounted the stallion and started over the trail for Crystal Valley.

Pierce Logan was disturbed. He was a cool, careful man who rarely made mistakes. He had moved the outlaws into Rawhide, had made sure they all had small holdings, had given them their brands. Then he had engineered, from his office in town and his ranch headquarters, the careful job of cattle theft that had been done. Byrn Sonntag was a man who would listen, and Byrn was a man who could give orders. The stealing had been so carefully done that it had been going on for a year before the first rumbles of suspicion were heard.

Even then, none of that suspicion was directed toward Rawhide. When Rawhide ranchers came to Laird they were quiet and well behaved. In Rawhide they had their own town, their own saloon, and when they felt like a bust, they went, under orders, to Rico.

Logan had understood that sooner or later there would be trouble. He had carefully planned what to do beforehand. He had dropped hints here and there about Finn Mahone, choosing him simply because he lived alone and consequently was a figure of mystery and some suspicion. He had never mentioned Finn's name in connection with rustling. Only a couple of times he had wondered aloud what he found to do all the time, and elsewhere he had commented that whatever he did, it seemed to pay well.

Pierce Logan had seen Mahone but once before, and that time from a distance. He had no animosity toward him, choosing the man cold-bloodedly because he was the best possible suspect.

His plan was simple. When Mahone was either shot, hung for rustling, or run out of the country, the pressure would be off, the ranchers would relax, and his plans could continue for some time before suspicion built up again. If in the process of placing the blame on Mahone he could remove some of the competition from the picture, so much the better. He had a few plans along those lines.

His was not a new idea. It was one he had pondered upon a good deal before he came west to Laird. He had scouted the country with care, and then had trusted the gathering of the men to Sonntag.

Everything had gone exactly as planned. His seeds of suspicion had fallen on fertile soil, and his rustlers had milked the range of over five thousand head of cattle before questions began to be asked. No big bunches had been taken, and he had been careful to leave no bawling cows or calves on the range. The cattle had been shoved down on the open country on the theory that as long as plenty of cattle were in sight, few questions would be asked.

Two things disturbed him now. One of them was the fact that Finn Mahone had proved to be a different type of man than he had believed. He had defeated Leibman easily and thoroughly, and in so doing had become something of a local hero. Moreover, the way he had done it had proved to Logan that he was not any ordinary small-time rancher, to be tricked and deluded. Also, despite himself, he was worried by what Dowd had said.

The unknown is always disturbing. Although he and Dowd had little to do with one another, Texas Dowd had the reputation of being a tough and capable man. The fact that he knew Mahone and had referred to him as dangerous worried Logan. In his foolproof scheme, he might have bagged some game he didn't want.

The second disturbing factor was Texas Dowd himself. Pierce Logan's easy affability, his personality, his money, and his carefully planned influence made no impression on Dowd. Logan knew this, and also knew that Dowd was suspicious of him. He doubted that Dowd had any reason for his suspicion. Yet, any suspicion was a dangerous thing.

Pierce Logan had been careful to see that some of his own cattle were rustled. He had deliberately planned that. It made no difference to him how they were sold; he got a big share of the money in any event, and it paid to avoid suspicion. Also, he had gone easy on the Lazy K, because Texas Dowd was a restless rider, a man forever watching his grazing land, forever noticing cattle. Also, Pierce Logan was pretty sure he would someday own the Lazy K.

Along with his plans for the Laird Valley, two other things were known only to Pierce Logan. One was that he was himself a fast man with a gun, with nine killings behind him. The second was that he could handle his fists.

He had seen Leibman fight before, and had always been quite sure he could whip him, if need be. Until today he had never seen a man he was not positive he could beat. Finn Mahone was a puzzle. Especially as he noted that Finn had never let himself go with Leibman. He had toyed with him, making a fight of it and obviously enjoying himself. Then suddenly, dramatically, he had cut him down.

Pierce Logan made his second decision that night. Earlier, he had decided that Dowd must be killed. That night he decided that his plans for Finn Mahone must be implemented quickly. Mahone must be used and then removed from the scene, thoroughly.

He got up and put on his wide white hat, then strolled out on the boardwalk, pausing to light a cigarette. It was a few minutes after sundown, and almost time to go to supper at Ma Boyle's. His gray eyes shifted, and saw the man dismounting behind the livery stable.

Logan finished his smoke, then stepped down off the porch and walked across to the stable. His own gray nickered when it saw him, and he walked in, putting a hand on the horse's flank. Byrn Sonntag was in the next stall.

Speaking softly, under his breath, Logan said, "Watch when Mahone makes his next shipment. Then get some altered brands into them and let me know as soon as it's done."

"Sure," Sonntag said. He passed over a sheaf of bills to Logan. "I already taken my cut," Sonntag said.

Logan felt a sharp annoyance, but stilled it. "Dowd," he said, "looks like trouble. Better have one of the boys take care of it."

Sonntag was quiet for a minute, then he replied,

"Yeah, an' it won't be easy. Dowd's hell on wheels with a gun."

Pierce Logan left the barn and walked slowly down the street. He scowled. It was the first time he had ever heard Sonntag hesitate over anything.

Byrn Sonntag was pleased beyond measure when he encountered Mexie Roberts in the Longhorn. He passed him the word, then went on and sat in on a poker game. When the game broke up several hours later he was a winner by some two hundred dollars.

Mexie Roberts joined him on the trail. He was a slight, brown man with a sly face. "You know Texas Dowd?" Sonntag demanded.

"*Sí.*" Roberts studied Sonntag.

"Kill him."

"How much?"

Sonntag hesitated. Then he drew out his winnings. "Two hundred," he said, "for a clean job . . . one hundred now."

CHAPTER 2

The Rimrock that divided the open range of Laird Valley from Mahone's holdings was almost as steep and difficult to scale from the inside. Finn Mahone had often studied the mountains, and knew there was an old, long-unused path that seemed to lead toward the crest. His black stallion was a mountain-bred horse, and he took the trail without hesitation.

The steep mountainside was heavily timbered with pine, mingled with cedar and manzanita. The earth under the trees was buried deep under years and years of pine needles, except where here and there rock cropped out of the earth: the rough granite fingers of the mountain.

Several times he reined in to let the stallion breathe easier, and while resting the horse, he turned in the saddle to study the land around him. Below him, stretched out like something seen in a dream, were the three links in the Crystal Valley chain, and along the bottom the tumbling silver of Crystal Creek.

His stone cabin, built in a cleft of the mountain, was invisible from here, but he could just see the top of the dead pine that towered above the forest to mark the opening into the trail to Rico. It was a trail rarely used except when he drove his cattle to the railroad siding in the desert town.

Rico was as turbulent as Laird was peaceful, and it was a meeting ground of the cattlemen from Laird, the sheep men from the distant Ruby Hills, and the miners who worked a few claims in the Furbelows. Rico had no charms for Finn Mahone, and he avoided the town and the consequences of trouble there.

His occasional visits to Laird had built friendships. He had come to enjoy his contacts with Judge Collins, Doc Finerty, Dean Armstrong, and Otis.

Big, quiet, and slow to make friends, he had bought drinks for and accepted drinks from these men, and had, at the insistence of Otis, gone around to see Lettie Mason. Her house of entertainment was frowned upon by the respectable, but offered all Laird possessed in the way of theater and gambling. Lettie had heard Mahone was in town and sent Otis to bring him to call.

She was a woman of thirty-four who looked several years younger. She had lived in Richmond, New York, San Francisco, and New Orleans, and had for eight years of her life been married to a man of old but impoverished family who had turned to gambling as a business.

Lettie Mason had met three of the men in Laird before she came west. Two of these were Finn Mahone and Texas Dowd, and the third was Pierce Logan.

Since her arrival she had been in the company of Logan many times, and he had never acknowledged their previous meeting. After some time Lettie became convinced that he had forgotten the one night they met. It was not surprising, since he had been focused on the cards that her husband had been holding and she was introduced by her married name. Dowd was a frequent visitor at the rambling frame house across from the combination city hall and jail, but Mahone had been there only twice.

One other man in Laird knew a little about Lettie Mason. That man was Garfield Otis, who probably knew her better than all the rest. Otis, lonely, usually broke, and always restless, found in her the understanding and warmth he needed. She fed him at times, gave him drinks more rarely, and confided in him upon all subjects. She was an intelligent, astute woman who knew a good deal about men and even more about business.

Finn Mahone, riding the mountainside above Crystal Valley, could look upon Laird with detachment. Consequently, his perspective was better. In a town where he had no allegiances and few friendships, he could see with clarity the shaping and aligning of forces. He was a man whom life had left keenly sensitive to impending trouble, and as he had seen it develop before, he knew the indications.

Until the fight with Leibman, he had believed he was merely a not-too-innocent bystander. Now he knew he was, whether he liked it or not, a participant. Behind the rising tide of trouble in the Laird basin there appeared to be a shrewd intelligence, the brain of a man or woman who knew what he or she wanted and how to get it.

Understanding nothing of that plan, Mahone could still detect the tightening of strings. Some purpose of the mind behind the trouble demanded that he, Finn Mahone, be marked as a rustler and eliminated.

He was nearing the crest and the trail had leveled off and emerged from the pine forest.

He must have another talk with Lettie. He knew her of old, and knew she was aware of all that happened around her, that men talked in her presence and she listened well. They had met in New Orleans in one of those sudden contacts deriving from the war. He had found her taking shelter in a doorway during a riot, and escorted her home. She was, he learned, making a success of gambling where her husband had failed. He had died, leaving her with little, but that little was a small amount of cash and a knowledge of gambling houses.

Her husband, who had drawn too slow in an altercation with another gambler, had tried to beat the game on his own. Lettie won a little, and then bought into a gambling house, preferring the house percentage to the risk of a single game. Kindhearted, yet capable and shrewd, she made money swiftly.

Finn reined in suddenly and spoke softly to the stallion. Before him was a little glade among the trees, a hollow where the water from a small stream gathered before trickling off into a rippling brook that eventually reached Crystal Creek. A man was coming out of the trees and walking down to the stream. The man lay down beside the stream and drank. Dismounting, Finn held the big horse motionless and stood behind a tree, watching.

When the man arose, Finn saw that he was an Indian,

no longer young. Two braids fell over his shoulders from under the battered felt hat, and there was a knife and a pistol on his belt.

The Indian looked around slowly, then turned and started back toward the woods. Yet some sense must have warned him he was being watched, for he stopped suddenly and turned to stare back in Finn's direction.

Moving carefully, Finn stepped from behind the tree and mounted his horse. Then he walked the horse down into the glade and toward the Indian.

The fellow stood there quietly, his black eyes steady, watching Finn approach. *"How Kola?"* Finn gave the Sioux greeting because he knew no other. He reined in. "Is your camp close by?"

The Indian gestured toward the trees, then turned and led the way. Sticks had been gathered for a fire, and some blankets were dropped on the ground. Obviously, the Indian had just arrived. Two paint ponies stood under the trees, and the Indian's new rifle, a Winchester, leaned against a tree.

Finn took out his tobacco and tossed it to the Indian. "Traveling far?"

"Much far." The Indian dug an old pipe from his pocket and stoked it with tobacco, then he gestured toward the valley. "Your house?"

"Yes, my house, my cows."

The Indian lit his pipe and smoked without speaking for several minutes. Finn rolled a cigarette and lighted it, waiting. The Indian nodded toward the valley. "My home . . . once. Long time no home."

"You've come back, huh?" Finn took his cigarette from his lips and looked at the glowing end. "Plenty of beaver here. Why not stay?"

The Indian turned his head to look at him. "Your home now," he suggested.

"Sure," Mahone said. "But there's room enough for both of us. You don't run cattle, I don't trap beaver. You and me, friends, huh?"

The Indian studied the proposition. "Sure," he said, after a while. "Friends." Then he added, "Me Shoshone Charlie."

"My name's Finn Mahone." He grinned at the Indian. "You been to Rawhide . . . the little town?"

"Rawhide no good. Rico no good. Plenty bad white man. Too much shootin'." Charlie nodded. "Already see two white man, ride much along big river. One white man tall, not much meat, bad cut like so," he indicated a point over the eye. "Other white man short, plenty thick. Bay pony."

Frank Salter and Banty Hull. They had been scouting the upper Laird River Canyon. That was on this side of Rico, and beyond the Rimrock from the Laird Valley. It was far off their own range. If they were scouting along there, the chances were they were looking for the route he took to Rico on his cattle drives. He forded the river in the bottom of that canyon.

"Thanks. Those men are plenty bad." Mahone watched the light changing on the mountainside across the Crystal Valley. The Indian knew plenty, and given time, might talk. He had a feeling he had won a friend in the old man.

"I'm headin' back," he said, "after a bit. Suppose you need sugar, tobacco? You come to see me. Plenty of coffee, too. I always have some in the pot, and if I'm not home, you get a cup and have some. Better not go into Rawhide, unless you have to." The Indian watched him as he rode away.

He was restless, knowing things were coming to a head. It disturbed him that Remy thought of him as a rustler. The girl had stirred him more deeply than he liked to admit. Yet, even as he thought of that, he knew it went further. She was so much the sort of person he had always wanted.

If he had read the bullet-marked playing card right, Texas Dowd finally knew he was on the range. The fact that he was riding for her would account for the excellent cattle she had, and the condition of her grass. In his months of riding the Highbinders, he had watched with interest the shifting of the Lazy K cattle. The ground was never grazed too long, and the cattle were moved from place to place with skill instead of allowing them to range freely. They had been shifted to the lowlands during the spring months and then, as hotter weather drew near, moved back where there was shade and greener grass from subirrigated land near the hills.

Dowd would know that Finn Mahone was no rustler, whatever else he might think of him.

Once home, he stabled his horse, gave it a brisk rubdown, and went into the house. After a leisurely supper he brewed an extra pot of coffee, hot and black, and sat down by the lamp. He picked up a book, but found himself thinking instead of the girl with golden hair who had watched his fight from the boardwalk. He recalled the flash of her eyes as he had told her he refused to sell the stallion. He sighed, and settled in to a few hours of reading.

In the rambling adobe house on the Lazy K, Remy walked into the spacious, high-ceilinged living room, and sat down. "Dad," she asked suddenly, "have you ever heard of a man named Mahone?"

Frenchy Kastelle sat up in his chair and put his book

down. He was a lean, aristocratic man with white hair at his temples and dark, intelligent eyes. He was French mixed with California Spanish, and he had lived on the San Francisco waterfront in exciting and dangerous times. Finally, he had gone into the cattle business in Texas.

His knowledge of cattle was sketchy, but he got into a country where there was free range, and made the most of it. Yet he was just puttering along and breaking even when Texas Dowd rode over the border on a spent horse. The two became friends, and he hired the taciturn Texan as foreman. Few better cattlemen lived, and the ranch prospered, but newcomers began crowding in, and at Dowd's suggestion, they abandoned the ranch and moved westward to the distant Laird River Valley.

The route had been rough, and not unmarked with incident. Texas Dowd had proved himself a fighting man as well as a cattleman.

Frenchy knew how to appreciate a fighting man. Casual and easygoing in bearing, he was a wizard with cards and deadly with a gun. He was, he confessed, a man who loved his leisure. He was willing enough to leave his ranch management to the superior abilities and energies of Remy and Dowd.

He looked at his daughter with interest. For the past two years he had been aware that she was no longer a child, that she was a young lady with a mind of her own. He had looked at first with some disquiet, being entirely foreign to the problem of what to do about a young lady who was blossoming into such extravagant womanhood.

This was the first time she had ever manifested anything more than casual interest in any man, although Frenchy was well aware that Pierce Logan had been taking her to dances in Laird.

"Mahone?" He closed his book and placed it on the

table. "Isn't he that chap who lives back in the mountains? Buys a lot of books, I hear."

He studied his daughter shrewdly. "Why this sudden interest?"

"Oh, nothing. Only there was a fight today, and this Mahone fellow whipped that brute Leibman from over at Rawhide. Gave him an awful beating."

"Whipped Leibman?" Kastelle was incredulous. "I'd like to have seen that. Leibman used to fight on the coast, rough-and-tumble fights for a prize. He was a bruiser."

"Dowd won money on Mahone, and from the way he acts I think he knows something about him. He seemed so sure that he would beat Leibman."

"Then why not ask him?" Kastelle suggested.

"I know, Dad," she protested, "but he won't tell me anything. As far as that goes, I don't even know anything about Dowd!"

"Well, it is sometimes best not to ask too much about a man; judge him by his actions . . . that's a courtesy that I have taken advantage of as much as anyone. Texas Dowd is the best damned cattleman that ever came west of the Mississippi, and that includes Jesse Chisholm, Shanghai Pierce, or any of them! What more do you want?"

"What do you know about him?" Remy demanded. "What did he do before he came to us? He had been shot, but who had done it? Who, in all this world, could make Texas Dowd run?"

Kastelle shrugged and lifted his eyebrows. "A man may run from many things, Remy. He may run from fear of killing as much as fear of death. Fewer run for that reason, but a good man might.

"I've never asked him any questions and he hasn't volunteered anything. However, there are a few things one may deduce. He's been in the army at some time, as one can see by the way he sits a horse and carries his shoulders. He's been in more than one fight, as he is too cool in the face of trouble not to have had experience.

"Moreover, he's been around a lot. He knows New Orleans and Natchez, for instance. He also knows something about St. Louis and Kansas City, and he's hunted buffalo. Also, he knows a good deal about Mexico and speaks Spanish fluently. We know all these things, but what is important is that he is not only our foreman but our friend. He has shown us that, and that is the only thing that has any real meaning."

Remy walked out on the wide flagstone terrace in front of the ranch house. The stars were very bright, and the breeze was cool. Looking off in the distance she could see the dark loom of the Highbinders, jagged along the skyline. She tried to tell herself she was only interested in Mahone because of that magnificent horse, but she knew it was untrue.

She detected a movement near the corrals, and saw Dowd's white shirt. She left the terrace and walked toward him across the hard-packed earth of the yard. "Texas!" she called.

He turned, a lean, broad-shouldered figure, the moonlight silver on his hat. "Howdy, Remy," he said. "Out late, ain't you?"

"Texas," she demanded abruptly, "what do you know about Finn Mahone?" Then hastily, to cover up—"I mean, is he a rustler?"

Texas Dowd drew on his cigarette, and it glowed brightly. "No, ma'am, I don't guess he is. Howsoever, men change. He wouldn't have been once, but he might be now. But offhand, I'd say no. I'd have to be shown proof before I'd believe it."

"Where did you know him?"

"Don't rightly recall saying I did," Dowd said. "Maybe it was just a name that sounded familiar. Maybe he just looked like somebody I used to know."

"Where?" she persisted.

"Remy," Dowd said slowly, "I want to tell you something. You stay clear of Finn Mahone! He's a dangerous man, as dangerous to women in some respects as he is to men! I don't believe there's a man on this range could face him with a gun unless it was Byrn Sonntag."

"Not even you?"

He dropped his cigarette and toed it into the dust. "I don't know, Remy," he said quietly. He drew a long breath. "The hell of it is," he said, sighing bitterly, "I may have to find out."

He turned abruptly and walked away from her toward the bunkhouse. She started to speak, then hesitated, staring after him.

Remy Kastelle practically lived in the saddle. Her white mare, Roxie, loved exploring as much as she did, but in the next few days Remy studiously avoided the wide ranges toward the Highbinders in the west. But, time and again she would find her eyes straying toward the high pinnacle that marked the entrance to the Notch.

Then one day she mounted and turned her horse toward the Rimrock. As she drew closer, her eyes lifted toward the great red wall of the mountain. It was like nothing she had ever seen. In all her riding she had never come this far to the west, although she was aware that Lazy K cattle fed as far as the wall itself.

When she drew near, she turned the mare and rode along toward the Notch. She was riding in that direction when she saw the bullet-marked card on the Joshua tree.

Curiously, she stared at it. This was not the first time she had seen a card with the corners drilled by bullets. Many times she had seen Texas Dowd shoot in just that way. It was the first time she had ever seen the other four bullet holes. She studied the card for a while, then shrugged and rode on. It meant nothing to her.

She rode on, and the sun was warm in her face. She knew she should be turning back, but was determined to see the Notch at close hand. A shoulder of the rock jutted out before her and she rounded it, and the air was suddenly filled with the rushing roar of the Laird River. To her left was a dim trail up through the pines. Scarcely thinking what she was doing she turned the white mare up the trail into the Notch.

Remy told herself she was riding this way because she wanted to see the Notch, and because she was curious about Crystal Valley. Carefully, she kept her mind away from Finn Mahone. The tall rider could mean nothing to her. He was just another small rancher, and a brawler in the bargain.

Yet Dowd's warning, and his obvious respect for Mahone, stuck in her mind. Who was Finn Mahone? What was he?

The trail dipped suddenly and she hesitated. Only eight feet wide here, and a sheer drop off to her right. The tracks of Mahone's stallion showed plainly. "If he did it, I can!" she told herself, and spoke to the horse. They moved on, and the trail narrowed, almost imperceptibly. Roxie shied nervously at the depth to her right, and Remy bit her lip thoughtfully as she studied the trail. It would be impossible to turn around now. For better or worse, she must keep going.

When the narrow trail finally ended she was nearing the bank of the Laird. She had heard that three crossings must be made, and she hesitated again, looking at the sky. There was going to be little time. The thought of going back over the trail in the dark frightened her.

She forded the Laird and rode up the opposite bank. The side from which she had just come was sheer cliff, towering upward to a height of nearly four hundred feet. The trail was narrow but solid, some fifteen feet above the tumbling Laird.

The country was wild and picturesque. In all her life she had never seen such magnificent heights of sheer rock, nor such roaring beauty as the rushing rapids below her. Tall trees towered against the sky, and when there was a glade or open hillside on her right the grass was green and thick. Entranced by the sheer beauty, she rode on, passing a waterfall that let the Laird go rolling over its brink in a smooth, glassy stream of power, thundering to the stones thirty feet below.

This was the country of which she had heard, the country that was almost unknown to the outside world. She pressed on, forgetful of the dwindling afternoon, and thinking only of the beauty of the landscape. She forded the Laird again, a swift, silent stream this time, and her road came out under great trees, turning the afternoon into a dim twilight as though she rode through a magnificent cathedral of towering columns.

Roxie was as interested as she herself, the mare's ears forward, twitching and curious. They continued, came out in a steep-walled canyon, and forded the stream for the third time. Again it was white water, but slower than below. The trail took her out of the canyon then, and across a valley of some fifty acres, the river, wider and deeper, was backed up behind a natural dam until there was a small lake among the trees. A bird flew up from the water, but she caught only a glimpse and could not identify it.

Then suddenly the trail channeled again and she was

in another narrow-mouthed canyon. Great crags leaned over the trail here, and the river was no longer near, but had taken a turn away to the right. Then, riding out of the canyon, she stopped, staring across the first of the dreaded shale banks.

Evening had come, although it was still light, and there was no sound but the soft whisper of the wind in the trees. This was a lonely land, a land where nothing seemed to move, nothing seemed to stir, not even a leaf.

Looking up, she saw the long, steep slide of shale, and looking down, she saw that the shale disappeared in growing darkness below. But when she looked off to the right now, there was no canyon wall, no river. There was only a vast and empty silence, and the somber shadows of twilight lying over a gloomy desert. These were the lava pits, a trackless, lifeless region of blowholes and jagged rock. It lay below her, something like a hundred feet below.

Roxie shied at the bank, and backed away nervously. There was a route across. That much Remy knew. Yet how it went, or how one knew where to enter, she could not guess. Hopelessness overwhelmed her, and anger, too. Anger at herself for failing now, and for persisting so long.

Fortunately, they would not be worried at home. She often rode to the McInnis ranch, or to Brewster's. Occasionally, she stayed all night. But the thought of staying in this lonely place at night frightened her. She did not want to turn around, yet the slate bank was appalling in its silent uncertainty.

Dismounting, she walked up to it, and stepped in with a tentative foot. Her boot sank, and almost at once the shale began to slide under her feet. She drew back, pale and disturbed.

Roxie pulled back nervously; the mare was obviously afraid and wanted none of it. Standing there, trying to make up her mind, Remy was suddenly startled.

A horseman was riding out of the darkness on the far side, and he rode now up to the edge of the awful drop-off into the lava pits. From across the distance she could hear he was singing, some low, melancholy song.

Remy stood still, her heart caught suddenly by the loneliness of the man, and the low, dreaming voice made the night seem suddenly alive with sadness. Stirred, she stood still, her lips parted as though to call, watching, and listening. It was only when he turned his horse to ride on that she became aware of herself.

She called out, and the man reined in his horse suddenly, and turned, listening. Then she called again. "Hey, over there! How do I get across?"

"What the devil?" It was Mahone. The realization made her eyes widen a little. "Who is it?" he demanded. "What are you doing here?"

"It's Remy Kastelle!" she said. "I started for a look at Crystal Valley! Can you help me over?"

He sat his horse, staring across the way, his face no more than a light spot in the darkness. She could almost imagine him swearing, and then he moved his horse to a new position. "All right," he called, "start toward me. Come straight along until I tell you to stop. How's that mare of yours? Is she skittish?"

"A little," Remy admitted, "but I think she'll be all right."

"Then come on."

Roxie hesitated, put a hoof into the shale, and snorted. Remy spoke soothingly, and the mare quieted. Mahone called again, and the sight of the stallion on the other side of the bank seemed to encourage the white mare. Gingerly, she moved into the slate. It sank sickeningly, then seemed to reach solid footing. Stepping with infinite care, the mare moved on.

When they had gone something over twenty yards, Mahone called to her, and she reined in.

"Now be very careful!" he shouted. "See that tall pine up there? Turn her head and ride that way. Count her steps, and when she has gone thirty steps, stop her again."

Her heart pounding, Remy spoke to the mare, and Roxie moved out, very slowly. This was a climb, and the shale slid around her hooves. Once the mare slipped and seemed about to fall, but scrambled and got her feet under her once more.

When they had gone thirty steps, Mahone called again. When she looked, she saw he had shifted position. "Now ride right to me!" he said.

It was so dark now she could make him out only by his face and the brightness of some of the studs on the stallion's bridle. She turned again, and after stumbling and sliding for another fifty yards, the mare scrambled onto solid earth and stopped, trembling in every limb.

Remy slid to the ground and her knees melted under her. "I wouldn't do that again," she protested, "for all the money in the world! How do you ever live in such a place?"

Mahone laughed. "I like it!" he said. "Wait until you see Crystal Valley!"

She started to get up and he helped her. The touch of his hand made her start, and she looked up at him in the darkness, just distinguishing the outline of his face. She sensed his nearness and moved back, strangely disturbed. Something about this man did things to her, and she was angered by it.

"But what will we do?" she protested. "Isn't there another slide? Longer than this?"

He grinned and nodded. She saw his white teeth in the darkness. "Yes, there is, but I'll put a rope on your saddle horn for luck and lead the mare by the bridle reins."

"Are you trying to frighten me?" she flared.

"No, not a bit. If you were riding ahead of me, and my horse didn't know the trail, I'd want your rope on my saddle horn. This next slide is a dilly!"

They started on, and he rode rapidly, eager to get the last of the dim light. The sky was still a little gray. When they reached the edge of the slide it was abysmally dark. He reined in abruptly. "Too dark," he told her. "We'll get off and wait until the moon comes up. It should be over the rim in about an hour. By moonlight we can make it."

He walked over to some trees and tied the two horses loosely. Gathering some sticks, he built a fire. When the dry sticks blazed up, he looked across at her and grinned. "Seems sort of strange. This is the first time a woman's ever crossed that slate bank, unless it was some Indian."

Remy looked at him gravely, then stretched her hands toward the fire. Surprisingly, the evening was quite cool, and the air was damp. Mahone knelt beside the fire and fed dry sticks into it, then looked up at her. "Your name is Kastelle?" he said. "It's an odd name. It has a ring to it, somehow."

"Perhaps you knew my father?" she suggested. "Before we came here we lived in Texas, and before that he was a gambler in San Francisco, what used to be called the Barbary Coast. They called him Frenchy."

He was looking at the fire. "Frenchy Kastelle?" He shook his head thoughtfully. "Seems like I would remember."

"I gathered from what my foreman said today that you know *him*." Remy leaned back, looking at the fire. "His name is Texas Dowd."

"Did this Dowd say he knew me?"

"No, he didn't, but he won money on your fight. He won a bet from Pierce Logan. Logan was sure Leibman would win."

"This Pierce Logan must know Leibman," Mahone commented. "No man risks his money on a stranger."

It was something she had not considered. Still, Logan got around a good deal, and he might have met the big German. But she was not to be turned from her main interest. "That's why I thought Dowd knew you. He seemed so sure."

"He might know me. In cattle country men get to know others by name lots of times, or maybe you meet in a bar, or in passing."

"Were you ever in Mexico?" It was a shot in the dark, but she noticed that Finn picked up a stick and began poking the fire. Why, she could not have guessed, but suddenly she felt she had touched the nerve of the whole story.

"Mexico? I reckon most every man who lives along the border gets into Mexico. Right pretty country . . . some of it. Fine folks, too."

They were silent for a moment.

"What's it like in there?" Remy indicated the trail toward Crystal Valley.

"Like a little bit of heaven," he said. "Quiet, peaceful, green . . . the most beautiful spot I ever saw. There's something about living back in these hills that gives a man time to think, to consider. Then, I like to read. Back there I can sit on my porch for hours, or over a fire in the cabin, and read all I like."

"How about your cattle? Don't you ever work them?"

He shrugged, and poked thoughtfully at the fire. "They aren't much trouble," he said. "No other cattle can get to them. I brand the calves while out riding around.

Carry a running iron with me all the time. That way the work never gets much behind."

He stood up. "The moon's higher. We'd better go."

Remy knew one thing. She would never forget that night ride across that mile of treacherous shale. It was a ride she would never want to make alone, even by day. Yet she was dozing in her saddle and half asleep when they pulled up at the cabin.

"Go on in," he said. "I'll put up the horses."

She went up the steps and opened the door. It was dark but warm inside. She was struck at once by that warmth. An empty house, empty for hours on a chill night, shouldn't have been warm. She struck a light, and saw the candle on the table. When she lighted it, she turned slowly, half expecting to see someone in the room, but it was empty.

Puzzled, she walked to the fireplace and, with the poker, stirred the coals. They glowed red. Then she saw the coffeepot and, stooping, touched it with her hand. It was warm, almost hot.

She straightened then, and looked around. The room was small, but comfortable, having none of the usual marks of bachelor quarters. Surprisingly, it was neat. The few clothes she saw were hung on pegs, the pots and pans were polished and shining, the dishes on the shelves were neatly stacked, and all was clean. Only one cup stood on the table. In it were a few coffee grounds.

Remy was standing there looking at that cup when Finn came in. He tossed his hat to a peg across the room and it caught. He glanced at the cup, then at her eyes. "We'll warm the coffee up," he said, "and then have something to eat."

She turned and looked at him thoughtfully. "The coffee," she said, and there was a question in her voice, "is warm. Almost hot!"

"Good," he said. She stared at him while he stirred the fire. "We'll eat right away, then."

"Can I help?"

"If you like." He got some plates down and put them on the table.

Why she should be disturbed, she didn't know. Obviously, there was someone else around. She had understood that Finn Mahone lived alone in the valley. Who was here with him? Where was she now?

Why must it be a woman? Remy didn't know why, but she wondered if it was. There was nothing effeminate about the room, yet it was almost too neat, too perfect. From her experience with cattlemen and cowhands, they usually lived in something that resembled a boar's nest. This was anything but that.

She looked up suddenly to see him watching her with a covert smile. "Would you like to see the rest of the house?" he suggested. She had the feeling that she amused him, and her spine stiffened.

"No, I don't think I'd care to! It isn't at all necessary!"

He grinned and picked up the candle. "Come on," he said.

She hesitated, then followed. She was curious.

The next room was a bedroom with a wide, spacious bed, much resembling an old four-poster. She thought it was, but when she drew nearer she could see it was homemade. On the floor was an Indian rug, and here, too, there were pegs on the walls. There were three pictures.

She started toward them, but he turned away and went into a third room. She followed him, then stopped. Here was a wide, homemade writing desk, and around her the walls were lined with books. The candlelight gleamed on the gold lettering, and she looked at them curiously. How her father would love this room! She could imagine his eyes lighting up at the sight of so many books.

They returned to the other room and he got the coffee and filled two new cups. They ate, almost in silence, but Remy found her eyes straying again and again to that empty cup. If Finn Mahone noticed, he gave no sign.

When they had finished eating, she helped him stack the few dishes. Somewhere not far off a wolf howled, a weird, yapping chorus that sounded like more than a dozen.

She stopped in the act of putting away the last of the food. "It's nice here," she said, "but so quiet. How do you ever stand it . . . alone?"

"I manage." His smile was exasperating. "It is quiet, but I like the stillness."

The problem of the night was before them, but Remy avoided the thought, trying to appear quiet, assured. She should have been frightened or worried. She told herself that would be the maidenly thing. Yet she wasn't. She was curious, and a little disturbed.

Sometimes she saw his eyes on her, calm and amused, and she wondered what he was thinking. No other man had ever upset her so much, nor had she met any other who was so difficult to read. Dowd was older, a simple, quiet man, and if he did not talk about some things, it was something she could understand. Somewhere he had been hurt, deeply hurt.

There was none of that in Finn Mahone. He was simply unreadable.

"You're going to have trouble, you know," she said suddenly.

"Trouble?" He accepted the word, seemed to revolve it in his mind. "I think so. It's been coming for some time.

But don't be sure it will only be for me. Before this is over, there will be trouble for all of us."

She looked at him, surprised. "How do you mean?"

He tossed a stick on the fire. "How long has this rustling been going on? They say some five thousand cattle have disappeared. I would say that is about ten percent of what there is on the range around here, yet who has actually *seen* any rustlers?

"Who has seen any cattle being moved? Who has heard of any being shipped? Why were there always cattle on the lower ranges, and none up in the canyons?"

"Why?" Remy watched him, curious and alert.

He looked up at her, and his eyes, she noted, were a strange darkish green. He ran his fingers through his hair. "Why? Because the rustlers have taken cattle slowly, carefully, a few at a time, and when they have taken them they have moved other cattle down from the canyons where they could be seen, so no suspicion would be aroused."

He looked at her with a wry smile. "Five thousand cattle are a lot of cattle! And they are gone. Gone like shadows or a bunch of ghosts. You think that doesn't take planning?"

"You know who is behind it?"

"No. But now that people are accusing me, I aim to find out!"

"We haven't lost many, Dowd says."

Finn nodded. "Want to know why? Because that foreman of yours is a right restless hombre. He keeps moving around. He's up in every canyon and draw on your range. He knows it like the back of his hand. They don't dare take any chances with him. Whoever is behind this rustling doesn't aim to get caught. He means to go on, handling as many cows as he can without suspicion."

"You're a strange man," Remy said suddenly.

He turned his head and looked at her, the firelight dancing and flickering on his cheek. "Why?"

"Oh, living here all alone. Having all those books, and yet fighting like you did down there in the street."

He shrugged. "It's not so strange. Many men who fight also read. As for living alone, it's better that way." His face darkened, and he got to his feet. "It saves trouble. I don't like killing."

"Have you killed so many?" Somehow she didn't believe so. Somehow it didn't seem possible.

"No, but there's one I don't want to kill," he said. "That's one reason I'm back here. That's one reason I'll stay here unless I have to come out."

Remy arose and stood facing him. How tall he was! He stood over her, and looked down, and for an instant their eyes met. She felt hot color rising over her face, and his hands lifted as if to take her by the arms. She stood very still, and her knees were trembling. Suddenly the room seemed to tilt, and she swayed, her eyes wide and dark.

He dropped his hands abruptly and went around the chairs toward the porch. "You sleep in there." He jerked a thumb toward the wide bed. "I'll stay out there with the horses for a while, then sleep in here by the fire."

He was gone. Remy stared after him, her lips parted, her heart beating fast. She knew with an awful lost and empty feeling that if he had taken hold of her at that moment he could have done as he pleased with her. She passed a hand over her brow, and hurried into the other room, closing the door.

CHAPTER 3

Pierce Logan had made his decision. A long conference with Sonntag and Frank Salter had convinced him that the time had come to make a definite move.

He disliked definite moves, yet had planned for them if it became necessary. His way had always been the careful way, to weed the range of cattle by taking a few here and a few there, until his own wealth grew, and the others were weakened. Then, bit by bit, to take what he wanted.

All in all the Rawhide outfit were making more money than they had ever made, but none of them were content. They wanted a lot of money quick, and they wanted action.

"If they don't git what they want, Pierce," Sonntag said, "they'll begin to drift. I know every man jack of 'em! They don't like none o' this piecin' along."

"Dowd's gettin' suspicious," Salter said. His eyes were cold gray. Pierce Logan had an idea that the old guerrilla didn't like him. "We got t' git rid of Dowd!"

"That's been seen to," Sonntag said. "Any day now."

Pierce Logan had returned to Laird filled with disquiet and anger at his plans deliberately being altered, but it was an anger that slowly seeped away as a plan began to evolve in his mind. A plan whereby he could come out with most of the profits himself. If those fools insisted on starting an out-and-out war, he would appear to be an innocent bystander. His cowhands were men known on the range. None of them were rustlers. Logan had been careful to see to that, and to keep the rustlers off his ranch except when they were getting some of his own cattle. When that happened, he managed to see that his hands were busy elsewhere.

Several of the men who worked for him, like Nick

James and Bob Hunter, had ridden for McInnis or Judge Collins. They were known to be capable, trustworthy men. Carefully, Pierce Logan examined his own position. His meetings with Sonntag had always been secret, and there was no way anyone could connect him with the rustling.

Sonntag had done something about Texas Dowd. From what he had said, the foreman of the Lazy K would die very soon. When Dowd was out of the picture, his most formidable enemy would be removed. And in the meanwhile, he had the problem of pinning decisive evidence on Mahone.

So far as anyone knew he had avoided Rawhide. His connection with those ranchers was unknown. In any plans to move against the rustlers, as ranchers the Rawhide group would be included, and so know all the plans made against them. While considered a rough, tough crowd, no suspicion had been directed at them so far.

If anyone suspected them it would be Texas Dowd.

The only other possible joker in the deck would be Finn Mahone. Now, once suspicion was pinned on him, the Rawhide gang could hit the ranches hard, and it could be attributed to Mahone's "gang." Logan meant to sow that thought in the minds of the Laird ranchers: that Mahone had acquired a gang.

He was perfectly aware that Judge Collins, Doc Finerty, and Dean Armstrong did not believe Mahone a rustler. His evidence would have to convince even them.

Once the blame was saddled on the man from the Highbinders, he would turn the Rawhide bunch loose on some wholesale raids that would break McInnis and Brewster, Collins and Kastelle. The raids would still be carefully planned, but no longer would the rustlers take cattle in dribbles, and they would kill anyone who saw them.

The new plan was to clean up while they had Mahone to blame it on. When the big steal was over, when Mahone was shown to be guilty, then killed, and Logan was left in power, he would marry Remy Kastelle and own Laird Valley.

From there, a man might go far. He might, by conniving, be appointed governor of the Territory. He might do a lot of things. A man with money and no scruples could do much, and he meant to see that none remained behind to mark the trail he had taken to wealth.

But in all his speculations and planning he overlooked one man. He did not think of Garfield Otis.

Otis was a drunkard. A man who practically lived on whiskey. He neither intended nor wanted to swear off. He drank because he liked whiskey and because he wanted to forget what he would like to have done, and live in the present. He was always around, and a man who is always around and taken for granted by everyone hears a great deal. If he is a man of intelligence, he learns much more than people give him credit for.

Had Pierce Logan realized it, only one man in the Laird Valley suspected him. That man was Otis.

Texas Dowd smelled something odorous in the vicinity of Rawhide. He knew men, and if Banty Hull, Montana Kerr, and the rest were peaceful ranchers, then he was the next Emperor of China. He knew all about Sonntag. He did not like Logan, but did not suspect he was the brain behind the rustling.

Neither did Otis. But stumbling along the street one evening, Otis had seen Logan ostentatiously lighting a cigarette in front of his office. Later, he had seen him cross the street and enter the livery stable. Seated on the edge of the walk, he had seen Logan leave the stable, and a moment later a rider headed off across the country. The rider was a big man.

Otis was only mildly curious at the moment. Yet he wondered who the man was. The man had seemed very big, and in the Laird Valley country only five men were of that size. Logan himself, Judge Collins, Finn Mahone, Leibman, and Byrn Sonntag.

Dean Armstrong was bent over the desk when Otis opened the door. He looked up. "Hi, Otis!" he called cheerfully. "Come on back and sit down!"

"Mahone been in town?"

Dean shook his head. "Not that I know of. No, I'm sure he hasn't been back since the fight. He said he would bring me a book he was telling me about, and he never forgets, so I guess he hasn't been in."

Then the man wasn't Finn Mahone.

The idea had never been a practical one, anyway. What would Mahone want with Logan? And meeting him in secret? It wouldn't make sense. It had certainly not been Judge Collins. That left only Leibman and Byrn Sonntag. Otis shoved his hands down in his pockets and watched Armstrong's pen scratching over the paper. "Dean," he asked, "what do you know about Pierce Logan?"

"Logan?" Armstrong put his pen down and leaned his forearms on the desk. Then he shook his head. "Just what everyone knows. He's got one of the best ranches in the valley. Been here about two or three years. He owns the livery stable, and has a partnership in the hotel. I think he has a piece of the Longhorn, too."

Dean picked up his pen again, frowning at the paper. "Why?"

"Oh, just wondering. No reason. Nice-looking man. Do you suppose he'll marry that Kastelle girl?"

"Looks like it." Dean scowled again. Somehow the idea didn't appeal to him. "If he does he'll control over half the range in Laird Valley."

Otis was restless. He got up. "Yes, you're right about that. And if McInnis and Brewster decided to sell out, he would own it all." He turned to go.

"Wait a minute and I'll walk over to the Longhorn with you."

Then Armstrong glanced at Otis. "Have you eaten?"

Garfield Otis hesitated, then he turned and smiled. "Why, no. Come to think of it, I haven't."

"Then let's stop by Ma Boyle's and eat before we have a drink."

They walked out together, and Armstrong locked the door after him. Otis started to speak, and Dean noticed it. "What were you going to say?"

"Nothing. Just thinking what an empire Laird Valley would be if one man owned it. The finest cattle range in the world, all hemmed in by mountains . . . like a world by itself!"

Armstrong was thoughtful. "You know," he said reflectively, "it would be one of the biggest cattle empires in the country. Probably the biggest."

Both men were silent on the way to Ma Boyle's. When they entered, the long table, still loaded with food at one end, was almost empty. Harran, who owned the Emporium, was there, and Doc Finerty. So was Powis.

Armstrong, pleased with himself at getting Otis to eat, sat down alongside Finerty. "How are you, Doc?" he asked. "Been out on the range?"

"Yeah, down to the Mains's place. She's ailing again." He sawed at his steak, then looked up. "Seen that durned Mexie Roberts down there. He was coyotin' down the range on that buckskin of his."

Marshal Pete Miller had come in. Miller was a lean, rangy man with a yellow mustache. A good officer in handling drunks and rowdy cowhands, he could do nothing about the rustlers. He overheard Doc's comment.

"Mexie, huh? He's a bad 'un. Nobody ain't never proved nothin' on him, but I always figgered he dry-gulched old Jack Hendry. Remember that?"

"I ought to!" Doc said. "Shot with a fifty-caliber Sharps! Never could rightly figure how that happened. No cover or tracks around there for almost a mile."

"A Sharps'll carry that far," Miller said. "Further, maybe. Them's a powerful shootin' gun."

"Sure," Doc agreed, "but who could hit a mark at that distance? That big old bullet's dropping *feet*, not just inches. That would take some shooting . . . and he was drilled right through the heart."

"They believed it was a stray bullet, didn't they?" Powis asked. "I remember that's what they decided."

Garfield Otis listened thoughtfully. During the period in question he had lived in Laird, but his memory of the details of Jack Hendry's death was sketchy at best. One factor in the idea interested him, however. He asked a question to which he knew the answer. "What became of Hendry's ranch?"

"Sam, that no-good son of his, sold it," Harran said. "You recall that Sam Hendry? Probably drunk it all up by now. He sold out to Pierce Logan and took off."

"Best thing ever happened to this town!" Powis said. "Logan's really done some good here. That livery stable and hotel never was any good until he bought 'em."

"That's right," Harran agreed. "The town's at least got a hotel a woman can stop in now."

Otis walked to the Longhorn beside Armstrong, and they stood at the bar together and talked of Nathaniel Hawthorne and Walt Whitman. Armstrong returned to his work, and Garfield Otis, fortified by a few extra dollars, proceeded to get very, very drunk.

He had been drunk many times, but when he was drunk he often remembered things he had otherwise forgotten. Perhaps it was the subject of discussion at supper, perhaps it was only the liquor. More likely it was a combination of the two and Otis's worry over Finn Mahone, for out of it all came a memory. At noon the next day, when he awakened in the haymow at the livery barn, he still remembered.

At first he had believed it was a nightmare. He had been drunk that night, too. He had walked out on a grassy slope across the wash that ran along behind the livery stable and the Longhorn. Lying on the grass, he had fallen into a drunken stupor.

Seemingly a long time after, he had opened his eyes and heard a mumble of voices, and then something that sounded like a blow. He had fallen asleep again, and when he awakened once more, he heard the sound of a shovel grating on gravel. Crawling closer, he had seen a big man digging in the earth, and nearby lay something that seemed to be a body.

Frightened, he had stayed where he was until long after the man had moved away. Then he returned to his original bed and slept the night through. It wasn't until afternoon the next day that he remembered, and then he shrugged it off as a dream. The thought returned now, and with it came another.

For the first time, things were dovetailing in his mind. As the pieces began to fit together, realization swept over him, but no course of action seemed plain. His brain was muddled by liquor, and that dulled the knowledge his reason brought him, so he did nothing.

Remy Kastelle awakened with a start. For an instant she stared around the unfamiliar room, trying to recall where she was and all that had happened.

Quietly, she dressed, and only then saw the folded

paper thrust under the door. She crossed the room and picked it up.

Had to take a run up to the next valley,
be back about eight. There's hot water over the fire,
and coffee in the pot.

When she had bathed and combed her hair, she poured a cup of coffee and went to the door.

She stopped dead still, her heart beating heavily and her eyes wide with wonder.

The stone cabin was on a ledge slightly above the valley, and she looked out across a valley of green, blowing grass toward a great, rust-red cliff scarred with white. It was crested with the deep green of cedars that at one place followed a ledge down across the face of the cliff for several hundred yards. Through the bottom of the valley ran Crystal Creek, silver and lovely under the bright morning sun. In all her life she had seen no place more beautiful than this.

Looking down the rippling green of the grasslands, she saw the enormous stone towers that marked the entrance, a division in the wall that could have been scarcely more than fifty feet wide. From out on the porch, she could look up the valley toward where Crystal Creek cut through another entrance, this one at least two hundred yards across, looking into a still larger valley. Scattered white-face cattle grazed in the bottoms along the stream. Not the rawboned half-fed range cows she knew, but fat, heavy cattle.

As she looked, she saw a horseman come through that upper opening, a big man riding at a fast canter on a black stallion. She watched him, and something stirred deeply within her. So much so that, disturbed, she wrenched her eyes away and walked back into the kitchen. Putting down her cup she went into the bed-room to get her hat. Only then did she see the picture.

There were three, two of them landscapes. It was the third that caught her eyes. It was a portrait of a girl with soft dark eyes and dark hair, her face demure and lovely. Remy walked up to it, and stared thoughtfully.

A sister? No. A wife? A sweetheart?

She looked at the picture first because of curiosity, and then her eyes became calculating, as with true feminine instinct she gauged this woman's beauty against her own. Was this the girl he loved? Was this the reason he preferred to live alone?

Memory of the cup and the warm coffee returned to her. Was he alone?

The sound of the arriving horse jerked her attention from the picture, and hat in hand she walked out to the porch.

"Hi!" Mahone called. "Had some coffee?"

Remy nodded. "If you'll show me the way, I'll start back now."

"Better let me show you the rest of the valley," he suggested. "This is beautiful, but the upper valley is even more so."

"No. I often stay away all night. Father's used to it. But I always head back early. I stay at the Brewsters' occasionally, and sometimes with the McInnis family. Once even at Judge Collins's ranch."

She laughed. "The judge was really nervous. I'm afraid he thought I was compromised and that he might have to marry me!"

Finn looked at her, his eyes curious. "You're right. And I think you'd better be sure somebody knows where you are from now on."

"You think there'll be trouble?"

"Uh-huh." He was deadly serious now. "That valley is

going to be on fire from one end to the other in a few weeks. Maybe even a few days. You mark my words."

Remy walked down to the corral while he roped Roxie and saddled her. "You know what they think, don't you?" she said.

"That I'm a rustler?" he asked. "Sure. I know that. But look around . . . why would I rustle? And if I did, how would I get them in here?"

"There isn't any other way?"

"Not from Laird. I've got all the cattle I want. As long as I keep the varmints down there's nothing to worry me here."

"If they accuse you, and try to make trouble, what will you do?" Remy asked as they neared the slate slide again.

He shrugged, and his face was grim. "What can I do? I'll fight if I have to. I never rustled a cow in my life, and I'm not going to take any pushing around."

She looked at Finn thoughtfully. "Texas Dowd doesn't think you're a rustler, but he warned me to stay away from you, that you were dangerous . . . to women."

Finn Mahone's head jerked around, and she could see the flare of anger in his eyes. "Oh, he did, did he? Yes, he would think that."

"Why did he say it?" she asked.

"Ask him," Finn replied bitterly. "He'll tell you. But he's wrong, and if he says that in public, I'll kill him!"

Remy tensed, and her eyes widened. There was something here she didn't understand. "Shall I tell him that, too?"

"Tell him anything you want to!" he snapped. "But tell him he's hunting the wrong man and he's a fool!"

"If there's trouble coming I'd like to think you were on our side," Remy said.

He looked at her cynically. "That cuts both ways, but

Dowd wouldn't stay with you if I was. Dowd wants to kill me, Remy."

"And what about you?"

For a moment, he did not answer, then he said simply, "No, I don't want to kill anybody."

He was silent, leading the way down to the slide. They made it now, by daylight, without mishap, but Remy kept her eyes away from the depths beyond the rim.

"You said," Finn suggested suddenly, "that you wanted me on your side. Who do you think is on the other side?"

They were fording the Laird, and she looked around at him. "I don't know," she protested. "That's what makes the whole situation so bad. Nobody seems to know."

She left him at the opening of the Notch and rode on toward home. She was well aware what the people of Laird would say if they knew she had spent the night in Crystal Valley. The ranch people who knew her would think little of it, for she came and went on the range as freely as a man. But, in town, those people would be another matter.

She was halfway to the Lazy K ranch when she met Texas Dowd. He was wearing his flat-brimmed black hat and a gray shirt. With him were Stub and Roolin, two of the hands.

"We was lookin' for you, ma'am," Dowd said. "All hell's busted loose!"

"What do you mean?" Remy reined the mare around, frightened at the grimness of their manner.

"Somebody shot Abe McInnis last night. He went off up the valley, with that cowhand named Tony. When they didn't get back, Roolin here, who was up that way waitin' for him, rode up after him with Nick James, that hand of Logan's.

"They found 'em back in a narrow canyon near a brandin' fire. Tony was dead, shot three times through the belly, once in the head. McInnis had been shot twice. Doc says he might live; he's in purty bad shape."

"Who did it? Who could have done it?"

"I don't know who done it," Roolin said suddenly, harshly, "but he took off through the mountains ridin' a black stallion. There was another man or two with him. Abe evidently come up on 'em, an' they went t' shootin'."

"People in Laird's some upset," Dowd said. "Miller's gone out that way to have a look. Abe's got him a lot of friends around."

"I'd like to have a talk with Mahone!" Roolin said. "I got my own ideas about him!"

She started to speak, then hesitated. "Just when did it happen?"

"Near's we can figger it was late yesterday afternoon," Roolin offered. "Could have been evenin', but probably was earlier."

That could have been before she met Mahone at the slide. Where had he been coming from then? He had offered no explanation. Was there a trail out through one of the narrow canyons that opened up near where she had first seen him? If there was, he could have ridden the distance without trouble.

Brewster was at the ranch when she got there, accompanied by Dowd. Her father had put his book aside and his face was grave. He was a quiet man, but she knew from past experience that when stirred he was hard, bitterly hard, and a man who would fight to the last shell and the last drop of blood.

Van Brewster was a burly man, deep-voiced and hard-bitten. His background was strictly pioneer. He had spent most of his life until now working in the plains country or the mountains, had soldiered, hunted, trapped, and fought Indians and rustlers.

"Abe was my friend!" he was saying as she entered, "and I aim to get the man responsible!"

Dowd drew back to one side of the room and thoughtfully rolled a cigarette. His eyes went from Kastelle to Brewster. He said nothing, invited nothing. A few minutes later, horses were heard in the ranch yard. "That'll be Logan an' Collins," Brewster said. "I told 'em we would meet here."

With them were Harran, the Emporium owner who ran a few cattle on the Collins range, and Dan Taggart, McInnis's foreman. All were grim and hard-faced, and all carried guns. "Miller's comin'," Taggart stated. "He's been on the range all day!"

"Find anything?" Harran asked.

"Some tracks," Taggart said, "mighty big hoss tracks. He thinks they were the tracks o' that stallion o' Mahone's!"

Dowd pushed away from the wall, his thumbs hooked in his belt. "Find 'em close to the body of either man? Or close to the fire?"

"Wal, no," Taggart admitted. "Not right close't. They was under some trees, maybe fifty yards away. The horse could've been tied there, though."

"It could have," Dowd admitted, "or he could have come up there and looked around and rode off, either before then, or later."

"If it was later, why didn't he report it?" Taggart demanded.

"Well," Collins interrupted, "if you recall, he's scarcely been welcomed around Laird. Probably didn't figure it was any of his business! Or maybe he didn't know what was goin' on."

"You defendin' him?" Taggart demanded. "You want t' remember my boss is a-lyin' home durned near dead!"

"I do not want any accusations without proof!" Judge Collins said sharply. "Just because one man's hurt and another's dead, that doesn't make Mahone guilty if he's innocent!"

"Well," Taggart said dryly, "if I see Finn Mahone on that place again, I'm goin' to shoot first and ask questions after!"

Dowd smiled without humor. "Better make sure it's first," he said, "or you won't live long. Finn Mahone's no man to drag iron on unless you intend to kill him."

"You sound like you know him," Brewster suggested.

Footsteps sounded on the porch, and the door opened. Alcorn was standing there, and with him Ike Hibby, Montana Kerr, and Ringer Cobb, all of Rawhide.

"I do," Dowd said, staring at the newcomers. "I know he's a man you hadn't better accuse of rustlin' unless you're ready to fill your hand."

Ringer Cobb was narrow-hipped and wide-shouldered; a build typical of the western rider. His guns were slung low and tied down. He glanced across at Dowd. "If you're talkin' about Mahone," he said casually, "I'll accuse him! All this talk of his bein' fast with a gun doesn't faze me none. I think he's rustlin'. He or his boys."

Judge Collins studied Cobb and pulled at his mustache. "What do you mean . . . his boys?" he asked. "I've understood Mahone played a lone hand."

"So have we all," Harran agreed, "but how do we know?"

That was it, Remy admitted, how did they know? How about that cup on the table, and the still-warm fire? Where had Mahone gone when he rode off that morning?

"How would he get cattle back into that country?" she asked. "Any of you ever tried to go through that Notch?"

"He does it," Cobb said. He looked at the girl, his eyes speculative. "An' for all we know, there may be another route. Nobody ever gets back into that wild country below the Rimrock."

"Nobody but the hombre that killed Tony," Taggart said grimly. "He was in there."

"All this is gettin' us nowhere," Brewster put in. "I've lost stock. It's been taken off my range without me ever guessin' until recent. I can't stand to lose no more."

"I think it's time we organized and did something," Alcorn spoke up.

"What?" Kastelle asked. He had been sitting back, idly shuffling cards and watching their faces as the men talked. His eyes returned several times to Pierce Logan. "What do you think, Logan?"

"I agree," Pierce said. He was immaculate today, perfectly groomed, and now his voice carried with a tone of decision, almost of command. "I think we should hire someone to handle this problem." He paused. "A range detective, and one who is good with a gun."

"That suits me!" Ike Hibby said emphatically. "That suits me right down t' the ground. If Mahone an' his boys are goin' t' work our cows, we got t' take steps!"

"You've said again that he has some men," Collins said. "Does anyone actually know that?"

"I do," Alcorn replied. "I seen him an' three others back in the Highbinders, two, three weeks ago. Strangers," he added.

Harran nodded. "He buys a powerful lot of ammunition. More than one man would use."

"Maybe," Kastelle suggested, smiling a little, "he's

heard some of this kind of talk and has been getting ready for trouble."

"It's more than one man would use," Harran insisted.

"What about this range detective?" Brewster asked. "Who could we get?"

"Why not Byrn Sonntag?" Hibby suggested. "He's in the country, and he's not busy runnin' cows like the rest of us."

"Sonntag?" Collins burst out. "Why, the man's a notorious killer!"

"What do you want?" Cobb said. "A preacher?"

"It takes a man like that!" Brewster stated dogmatically. "If he finds a man rustlin', why bother with a trial?"

Pierce Logan said nothing, but inside he was glowing. This couldn't be going better. . . .

"You're bein' quiet, Logan," Brewster said. "What do you think?"

"Well," Logan said, shrugging, "it's up to you boys, but if Miller can't cope with it, then perhaps Sonntag could."

"Mahone's supposed t' be a bad man with a gun," Cobb said, "or so Dowd tells us. Well, Sonntag can handle him."

Kastelle looked up. "By the way," he said, "has anyone ever seen Mahone rustling? Has he been caught with any stolen stock? Has he been seen riding on anybody's range? What evidence is there?"

"Well," Brewster said, uneasily, "not any, rightly, but we know—"

"We know nothing!" Collins said sharply. "Nothing at all! This suspicion stems from a lot of rumors. Nothing more."

"Where there's smoke there's fire!" Alcorn said. "I think Sonntag would be a good bet, myself."

"He could gather evidence," Logan admitted carefully. "We would then know what to do."

"You've not said what you think, ma'am." Taggart looked over at Remy. "Abe sets powerful store by what you think about stock. How do you figger this?"

"I don't believe Finn Mahone is a rustler," Remy said. "I think we should have plenty of evidence before we make any accusations. All we know is that we've missed stock and that Mahone keeps to himself."

Logan looked up, surprised. The feeling in Remy's voice aroused him, and he looked at her with new eyes. In the past few months he had taken his time with Remy, feeling he was the only man on the range at whom a girl of her type could look twice. Now, something in her voice made him suddenly alert.

"Well," Brewster said irritably, "what's it to be? Are we goin' to do something or just ride home no better off than when we came?"

"I'm for hirin' Sonntag," Alcorn said seriously.

"Me, too," Cobb said.

"Count me in on that," Ike Hibby said. He lighted his pipe. "I'm only running a few cattle, but I've lost too much stock!"

"Put it to a vote," Logan suggested. "That's the democratic way."

Judge Gardner Collins, Kastelle, Remy, and Texas Dowd voted against it. Alcorn, Hibby, Cobb, Brewster, and Taggart voted for Sonntag.

"How about it, Logan?" Collins said. "Where do you stand?"

"Well," he said with evident reluctance, "if it comes to a vote, I'm with the boys on Sonntag. That looks like action."

"Then it's settled!" Brewster said. He got to his feet. "I'm a-gittin' home."

"Mahone said something to me once," Remy said, in a puzzled tone. "He said the way to look for rustlers was with a pen and ink."

Ike Hibby jerked, and looked around hastily. Ringer Cobb's eyes narrowed, and strayed to Dowd. Texas Dowd was leaning against the wall again, and he looked back at Cobb, his eyes bright with malice.

Hibby shifted his feet. "Reckon I'll be headin' for home," he said. "Got a long ways t' go!"

Brewster picked up his hat and nodded good-bye to everyone. Alcorn and Ike glared at Remy, Alcorn licking his lips. "I don't figure I know what you mean, ma'am. But if anyone is accusin' anyone, it's us against Mahone. Not the other way around."

Slowly, they trooped out.

"Now what did I say?" Remy demanded, looking from her father to Dowd.

The tall Texan walked over and dropped into a chair. "You put your finger on the sore spot," he said grimly. "You blew the lid off the trouble in Laird!"

"Why, how do you mean?" she demanded, wide-eyed.

"Got a pen?" Texas said grimly.

She brought one out, and some paper. He looked up at her. "What's Abe's brand? A Spur, ain't it? Now look, an' I'll draw a Spur. Now what's Ike Hibby's brand? IH joined. Now just you take a look, ma'am . . ."

She looked at the rough drawing.

"You see what I mean? You take Abe's brand, add a mite more to the sides of the Spur to make it look like an I, then put a bar on the end of the Spur to make her look like the outside of the H."

Remy leaned over the table, excitedly. "But then, he could steal the Spur cattle and alter that brand without trouble!"

"Uh-huh, unless we caught him at it. Or unless we found some stock with altered brands. We ain't done either."

"You mean to say you've known this all the time?"

"I been thinkin' about it. But thinking something and havin' evidence ain't the same thing."

"But what about ours? The Lazy K?"

"It's probably made into a Box Diamond, and that's Ringer Cobb's brand. Brewster's Lazy S they change into a Lazy Eight."

"But then, that Rawhide crowd must be the rustlers!" Remy exclaimed.

"Uh-huh," Dowd agreed. "That's what I thought, but what can we prove?

"Something else, too," he added gravely. "Tonight the Rawhide bunch voted their own boss in as a paid, legal killer! Who's goin' to tell him where to stop? Or who he kills? Who will stop him once he's started?"

CHAPTER 4

Finn Mahone heard of the action of the Cattleman's Association when in Rico. He had made it a duty to visit Rico every so often, always hoping the man he had come west to find would show himself there again.

He had never seen the man for whom he was looking close up. He knew his name, that he had been a riverboat gambler, and that he was a wizard with cards and deadly with a pistol. He knew also that the man carried a derringer in his sleeve and was not above sneak-shooting a man.

Finn Mahone had trailed him from New Orleans to Natchez. All the time, the man had ridden a stolen steel-dust gelding. The man had ridden the big horse all the way to Santa Fe, where he traded it off for another animal. Mahone had bought the steel-dust from the new owner on a hunch and continued on.

Then he heard that a man answering the rough description had killed a man in Rico. But in Rico the trail was lost for good. Eventually, Finn had explored the Crystal Valley and settled down there. He was operating on a hunch that his man was somewhere around. He kept the big gelding, although he could not bring himself to ride it, and the horse grazed his upper pasture even now.

Ed Wheeling was in the Gold Spike Bar when he walked in. Wheeling greeted him with a smile. "How's it, Finn? Got any cattle? That last herd I bought from you was said to be the finest beef in Kansas City!"

"Thanks." Finn ordered a drink. "When do you want some? I reckon I can bring over a few. About a hundred head."

"That all you've got? I'll take them, and top prices any time you get them over here. What's this I hear about Sonntag being hired as a range detective?"

Mahone looked at him quickly. "Sonntag? That's bad."

"What I thought. The man's a killer. I saw him kill one man here in town only a few weeks ago. The man had an even break, if you can ever call it even when they go against him."

Finn turned his glass in his fingers. "Wheeling, what do you know about this rustling?"

Wheeling glanced right and left, then touched his tongue to his lips. "Nothing, if anybody asks. Me, I don't buy any doubtful beef, but there's others do. I'll tell you this much. There's been some queer-looking brands shipped out of here. Good jobs, but they looked burned over to me."

"Who buys 'em?"

"Well, don't go saying I told you. Jim Hoff bought 'em, but then, he'd buy anything he could get cheap."

"Thanks." He tossed off his drink. "This Sonntag deal is liable to be bad for those folks over to Laird. Sonntag is boss of that Rawhide bunch." He glanced at Wheeling. "They run the Lazy Eight, Box Diamond, and IH connected, if that means anything to you."

"It does," Wheeling replied. "It means plenty!"

Finn left the saloon. What Wheeling had told him only confirmed what he had believed. There was brand altering being done somewhere around. And some, at least, were being sold in Rico. They would move against him now, he had no doubt of that. The employing of Sonntag would give them a free rein. He wondered what the first move would be.

The noose was tightening now. Stopping in at the store he bought three hundred rounds of .44-caliber ammunition. His pistols had been modified to use the same ammunition as his Knight's Patent Winchester, which simplified things in that department.

He was just stowing it in his saddlebags when he saw Dean Armstrong. The newspaperman was coming toward him. "Howdy, Dean!" he said.

Armstrong's face was somber. "Watch yourself, Finn," he said. "I think Sonntag's gunning for you. I know Ringer Cobb is. He made his boast at the Cattleman's meeting that he would accuse you to your face."

"What happened at that meeting?"

"It was ramrodded, in a sense. Judge Collins, Kastelle, Remy, and Dowd voted against Sonntag. But Brewster and Taggart threw in with the Rawhide bunch."

"Taggart?"

"Abe McInnis's foreman. Abe was dry-gulched, wounded badly the same time they killed Tony Welt."

"Hadn't heard about that."

Armstrong looked at him quickly, worriedly. "Finn, they've got you pegged for that job. It happened in one of the canyons in the wild country south of the Rimrock. They found the tracks of a big horse, and some of them say they saw your stallion in there."

"I might have been there," Finn admitted, "but not when any shooting took place."

He dug his toe into the dust. "Remy voted against Sonntag, huh?"

"Yes. In fact, Finn, she spoke right out in the meeting and said she didn't believe you were a rustler."

"What did Dowd say?"

"He was against Sonntag. But on the whole, he didn't have much to say. I think Texas Dowd believes in killing his own beef."

"You're damned right he does," Mahone said sharply. "That man's got more cold-blooded nerve than any I ever saw!"

"What's between you two, anyway?" Dean demanded, looking curiously at Finn. "I'd think you two would be friends!"

Mahone shrugged. "That's the way things happen. We were friends once, Dean. For a long time. I know that man better than anyone in the world, and he should know me, but he's powerful set in his ways, and once he gets an idea in his head it's hell gettin' it out."

Finn Mahone headed across the plateau in sooty darkness. Dean's information and what he had learned from Wheeling put the problem fairly in his hands. The Rawhide bunch were evidently out to get him. Ringer Cobb had made his boast, and he was the type of man to back it up if he could.

From the beginning there had been an effort to hang the rustling on him. While his living alone would be suspicious to some, Finn had an idea that more than a little planting of ideas had been going on over the range. There was deliberate malice behind it. It was not Dowd's way to stoop to such tactics. Texas Dowd would say nothing. He would wait, patiently, and then one of them would die.

A roving, solitary man all his life, Finn had found but one man he cared to ride the river with. That man was Texas Dowd. They had ridden a lot of rivers, and their two guns had blasted their way out of more than one spot of trouble.

Had there been a chance of talking to Dowd, he would have done it, but there was too much chance the man would shoot on sight. Cold, gray, and quiet, Dowd was a man of chilled steel, the best of friends, but the most bitter of enemies.

One thing was now clear. It was up to him to prove his innocence. It might be a help to ride into town and see Lettie. She always knew what was going on, and was one of the few friends he had. She, and Garfield Otis.

What was it Dean had said about Otis? "Funny about Otis, Finn," he'd said. "He hasn't had a drink in almost a week. Got something on his mind, but he won't talk."

The trail dipped down into the Laird River Canyon, and the sound of rushing water lifted to his ears. Rushing water and the vague dampness that lifted from the trembling river. He should have told Ed Wheeling to say nothing about his bringing the cattle. Ed was a talkative man, and an admirer of those fat white-faced steers of Finn's.

This would be where they would wait for him, here in the canyon. A couple of good riflemen here could stop the passage of any herd of cattle, or of any man.

The cabin on the ledge was very quiet when he rode in. As he swung down from the stallion's back, he remembered the morning Remy Kastelle had stood on the steps waiting for him, and how her hair had shone in the bright morning sun.

The cabin seemed dark and lonely when he went inside, and after he had eaten he sat down to read, but now there was no comfort in his books. He got up and strode outside, all the old restlessness rising within him, that driving urge to be moving on, to be going. He knew what was coming, knew that in what happened there would be heartbreak and sudden death.

Aware of all the tides of western change, Finn Mahone could see behind the rustling in Laird Valley a deep and devious plan. It was unlike any rustling he had seen before. It was no owl-hoot gang suddenly charging out of the night on a wild raid, nor was it some restless cowhands who wanted money for a splurge across the border. This had been a careful, soundless, and trackless weeding of herds. Had it gone on undiscovered, it would have left the range drained of cattle, and the cattlemen broke.

He could see how skillfully the plan had been engineered. How careful the planning. As he studied what Dean had told him of the Cattleman's meeting, another thought occurred. The vote had been six to four to hire Sonntag. But what if McInnis had been there?

The dour New England Scotsman was not one for plunging into anything recklessly. He would never have accepted the hiring of Sonntag. Especially as Collins and the Kastelles had voted against it. This the leader of the rustlers must have figured. The shooting of McInnis had been deliberately planned and accomplished in cold blood.

Had McInnis been voting, Taggart either would not

have been there to vote, or would have followed Abe's lead. Brewster, hotheaded and impulsive as he was, would have been tempered by the McInnis coolness. Then the vote would have been against hiring Sonntag! At the worst, it would have been a tie, and no action.

That the meeting had been called before the shooting of Abraham McInnis, Mahone knew.

He sat down suddenly and wrote out a short note, a note that showed the vote had McInnis been present. He added, *Show this to the judge*. Then he enclosed it in an envelope, and decided he would send it to the newspaper office by Shoshone Charlie.

Carefully, he oiled his guns and checked his rifle. Then he made up several small packs of food and laid out some ammunition. He was going to be ready for trouble now, for it was coming. He could wait, and they might never get to him, but he preferred to strike first. Also, he had his cattle to deliver.

Mexie Roberts was not a man who hurried. Small, dark, and careful, he moved like an Indian in the hills. For several days now he had been studying the Lazy K from various vantage points. He had watched Texas Dowd carefully. Knowing the West as he did, he knew Dowd was a man whom one might never get a chance to shoot at twice. Mexie Roberts prided himself on never having to shoot more than once. His trade was killing, and he knew the tricks of his trade.

Lying on his belly in the dust among the clumps of greasewood, he watched every soul on the Lazy K. Shifting his glass from person to person, he soon began to learn their ways and their habits.

He was not worried about hitting Dowd, once he got

him in his sights. The Sharps .50 he carried was a gun he understood like the working of his own right hand.

There was no mercy in Mexie Roberts. Killing was born in him as it is in a weasel or a hawk. He killed, and killed in cold blood. It was his pride that he had never been arrested, never tried, never even accused. Some men had their suspicions, but no man could offer evidence.

He had been given the job of killing Dowd, and there was in the job a measure of personal pride as well as the money. Texas Dowd was to Mexie Roberts what a Bengal tiger is to a big-game hunter. He was the final test. Hunting Dowd was hunting death in its most virulent form.

In a few days now, perhaps a few hours, he would be ready. Then Dowd would die, and when he died, there would be no one near to see where the shot came from, and Mexie Roberts would have his hideaway carefully chosen.

All over Laird Valley tides of trouble and danger were rising. Men moved along the streets of Laird with cautious eyes, scanning each newcomer, watching, waiting.

In his office beside the barbershop, Judge Gardner Collins moved a man into the king row and crowned him. Doc Finerty rubbed his jaw and studied the board with thoughtful eyes. Neither man had his mind on the game.

"It was my fault," Collins said. "I should have stopped it. Don't know why I didn't realize how Brewster and Taggart would vote."

Dean Armstrong came in, glanced at the board, then placed a slip of paper on the checkerboard between them. "Found this under my door this morning," he said. "It's Mahone's handwriting."

For	*Against*
Ike Hibby	Collins
Ringer Cobb	Kastelle
Alcorn	R. Kastelle
Taggart	Dowd
Logan	
Brewster	

Had Abe McInnis been there:

Ike Hibby	Collins
Ringer Cobb	Kastelle
Alcorn	R. Kastelle
Logan	Dowd
Brewster (?)	McInnis
	Taggart (?)

Show this to the judge.

Collins studied it thoughtfully. "I reckon he's got it figured proper," he said. "That would make it at worst a tie vote. Taggart would have gone along with his boss, I know that. Dan's hotheaded, but Abe always sort of calms him down and keeps him thinking straight."

"You see what it implies, don't you?" Dean indicated. "That Abe McInnis was dry-gulched on purpose!"

"Uh-huh," Finerty agreed, "it does. I agree."

"Let's call another meeting," Armstrong suggested, "and vote him out. You've got some stock running with the judge, haven't you, Doc? Enough to vote?"

"It wouldn't do," Collins said. "The Rawhide bunch wouldn't meet. We couldn't get a quorum now. No, he's in, and we might as well make the best of it. What's he been doing, Dean?"

"Riding all over the range so far. That's all."

.   .   .

Pierce Logan sat in his office. He wore a neatly pressed dark gray suit and a white vest. His white hat lay atop the safe nearby. As he sat, he fingered his mustache thoughtfully.

It had been a long wait, and hard work, but now he was there. Only a few more weeks and he would be in possession of all he had hoped for. They would be shaky, dangerous weeks, but the danger would be of the sort he understood best.

He had come out of the carpetbag riots in New Orleans with money. Enough to come west in obvious prosperity. The little affair near New Orleans, one of those times when the ingrown rapacity of the man had let go like an explosion, had passed over without trouble. Since arriving in Laird he had bided his time. Now he was ready.

He was not worried about Texas Dowd. Sonntag had set something up, and it would be taken care of soon. Sonntag was range detective, and any killings he might commit would have a semblance of legality. There was opposition here in town, he knew. Judge Collins would be against him, but the judge was no longer young. Finerty could not stand against him, and as for Armstrong . . . Logan didn't like Armstrong. At the first hint of trouble from *The Branding Iron,* he would have to have the presses smashed up.

His eyes shifted out the window, and suddenly, he stiffened.

A man was walking slowly along the sandy hillside beyond the livery barn and corrals. He was walking along as though studying the ground. Now and then he would halt, kneel down, and study it carefully, then he would rise and move on. Occasionally he would sift a little dirt through his fingers.

The man was Garfield Otis.

Pierce Logan put a hand to his brow. He was sweating. His heart pounding, he slid a hand in a drawer for a gun. Then drew it back. No, that wasn't the way.

But what could the old fool be looking for? Why would he be examining that hillside, of all places?

It had been years ago. Certainly, Otis could know nothing. Yet he watched him, and Logan knew for the first time what it meant to fear.

If he was discovered now, he was ruined. Not even the Rawhide bunch could save him. It was only his power and money that held them together, and if the lid blew off this—!

Garfield Otis was wandering back down the wash now. He would be in the saloon in a few minutes. But no, Otis hadn't been drinking lately. And Otis was a friend of Mahone's.

Whatever was done must be done at once, and Logan knew there was only one thing that could be done. He got up and walked out into the street.

Finn Mahone had taken an old game trail east from the entrance to Crystal Valley. It led him down, and across a corner of the lava beds, then into the wild country of the Highbinders north of the Lazy K.

His stallion walked slowly, and Finn kept one hand near his walnut gun butt. The chance of seeing an enemy here was slight, although he had decided against trying the Notch. If anyone were to lie in wait for him, that would be the ideal spot.

The country in which he now rode was country where few horsemen ever went. The hillsides of the Highbinders were too grassless to draw cattle away from the fertile bottoms of the Lazy K range. This was a broken, partly timbered, and very rocky country that offered nothing to any man. Sheep or goats might have lived there; cattle could not.

Yet, when he was almost due north of the Lazy K ranch buildings, he stopped and swung down.

Coming out of the woods and turning into the small trail he followed were the recent tracks of a horse!

Finn loosened his gun in its holster and walked on, leading Fury. On second thought, he turned off the trail and chose a way under the pines, avoiding the dust where his tracks would be seen. When he had gone a little way further, he smelled smoke.

At first, it was just a faint suggestion, then he got a stronger whiff. Tying the stallion to a low branch, he worked his way cautiously through the brush. He had gone almost a hundred yards when he saw a faint blue haze rising from a hollow among the rocks.

Crawling out on a flat-topped rock that ended in a clump of manzanita, he lay on his belly and stared down into the hollow.

A fire, small and carefully built, burned among some stones. A coffeepot sat on the stones, being warmed. A buckskin horse was tethered nearby, and not far away, a grulla packhorse.

There was one man, and Finn watched him curiously. The man was small and dark, and at the moment Finn spotted him, he was fastening a long narrow piece of white cloth to a tree trunk. Peering at it, Finn could see that it had a cross printed on it near the top, and then graduated markings running down its length. At the bottom was a weight so that the strip would hang straight down.

When it was fastened, the small man carefully paced

off a certain distance and marked the spot, then he picked up his rifle, a Sharps buffalo gun. Finn's brow furrowed.

Puzzled, Mahone watched the man carry his Sharps to the mark on the ground and rest the muzzle in the crotch of a forked stick he carried. Laying prone, the little man carefully aimed at the cloth strip and then proceeded to work the screw-adjustable peep sight that was fitted to the big gun up and down, making minute adjustments until it was lined up with one of the marks on the cloth.

"Well, I'll be forever damned!" Finn Mahone muttered. "That's a new one on me!" The dark man was calibrating his sights for a long shot over a previously measured distance.

When he was satisfied, the man left the rifle where it was and returned to his fire. He drank coffee, ate a little, and took a hurried look around. Then he put out his fire, scattered it, and carefully wiped out all footprints with a pine bough. For a half hour he worked until every mark of the camp had been obliterated.

Only then did he take his rifle. Mounting the buckskin, which with the packhorse had been led into the trail, he held his rifle with great care, then he moved off, walking the horse.

Finn Mahone got up quietly and walked back to his own horse. Moving carefully, he followed the strange rider. The man's every action gave evidence that he had no intention of riding far, and the only place close to them was the Lazy K ranch!

Who, then, was the killer after? For Finn had no doubts about the man's intentions. Remy? That would serve no purpose, Frenchy Kastelle? Probably not.

Who, of all the men on this range, would be most dangerous to successful rustling? Texas Dowd. Who, on this range, might match guns with Sonntag or Ringer Cobb or

Montana Kerr? Only, aside from himself, Texas Dowd. All of which meant that this man intended to kill Dowd.

His conclusion might be mistaken, but Finn could think of no logical alternative.

When they drew near the edge of the timber, Finn tied the stallion in a concealed position among the trees and, rifle in hand, moved out after the unknown sharpshooter.

The man had tied his horses with a slip knot and had vanished into the brush. Finn started to follow, then hesitated and walked back to the horses. Untying them, he retied the knot, and lashed it hard and fast. The man who rode these horses wasn't going to be getting away in a hurry!

Then, working with infinite care, Finn Mahone worked down along the marksman's trail.

He lost the trail on the edge of the brush. Here the man had moved into a gully, and whether he had gone up or down, Finn could not tell. Yet from where he lay on the side of the bluff Finn had an excellent view of the grassy field between the Lazy K ranch buildings and the position he occupied. The sharpshooter would have to move out into position from here, and get into place to fire on the buildings.

Suddenly, Finn saw the man. He had come out of the gully and was snaking along the ground, keeping low in the grass, still handling his rifle with utmost care. When the man reached the top of a low knoll, his position would be excellent.

Only then did Mahone realize how carefully this had been planned. The way to the knoll was completely covered from observation from anywhere but this bluff. The man could never have been seen from the ranch.

The Sharps rifle, known to kill at distances up to a thousand yards, had occasionally been effective at even greater distances, as Billy Dixon had proved at the Battle of Adobe Wells. It used the most powerful black powder cartridges ever made, and fired up to 550 grains of lead with terrific force and remarkable accuracy.

With the distance deliberately paced off, probably late at night when all were asleep, the unknown marksman would know exactly how much his bullet would drop, and now the finely machined sight was set for precisely that range. One shot would be all he'd get at a target like Dowd, but as Finn correctly surmised, the man had no intention of firing more than one shot.

Mahone lost him, then found him again, and when he next sighted him he was on the crest of the knoll and settling into position. Finn eased his own rifle up, and waited.

There was little movement around the Lazy K. Occasionally someone appeared, then vanished. The man below lay perfectly still. Had Finn not known he was there, he could never have picked him out on the grassy, boulder-strewn knoll.

Then the ranch house door opened, and Finn lifted his head. Remy was walking down to the corrals. A hand led her white mare out, and the girl swung into the saddle and galloped away over the plains, riding west.

Finn's eyes followed her. How beautifully she rode! He had never seen a woman ride with such grace. Angry with himself, he wrenched his eyes away.

A man had come from the ranch house and was walking down to the corral. He wore an old black hat, but even at that distance Finn could recognize the straight carriage, the easy movement of the shoulders. Texas Dowd was a man difficult to forget and easy to pick out.

Mahone's eyes dropped. The man below was waiting for some particular thing, Finn could see that. All men are creatures of habit to some extent, and the marksman had evidently studied Dowd until he knew his every move.

No one else was in sight. The cowhand who led out Remy's horse had vanished, and the ranch lay hot in the glare of the sun. Dowd led out his horse and tied it to a rail of the corral fence. Then he brought out the saddle, and threw it on the horse's back. Dowd was standing with his back squarely to the sharpshooter now, but the man waited. Then, slowly he eased his rifle up and Finn, even at this distance, could almost see the man settling his cheek against the stock ready for his shot.

Finn lifted his rifle and triggered three fast shots at the figure below. Even as he fired, he heard the big rifle boom from the knoll, but his first shot must have come close, for the rifleman threw himself to one side.

Finn got a hasty glimpse of Dowd's horse rearing, but already his eyes were searching the grass below for the killer. The man had vanished as if he had dropped into the earth itself!

Riveting his eyes on the grass, Finn began to search it with infinite care, taking it section by section, but he could see nothing of the man. He suddenly realized this was no place for him. If Dowd was to find him here he would be sure it was Finn who had fired, and the sharpshooter was certainly making his getaway.

Scrambling through the brush, he started back to the horses. Somehow in his rush he took a wrong turn, and though delayed only a minute or two longer than he had expected, he reached the horses just as the marksman appeared. The fellow rushed to the horses and jerked at the slip knot. It stuck, and then Finn said, "All right, turn around and throw up your hands!"

Mexie Roberts wheeled like a cornered rat and his hand flashed for his pistol. Finn's rifle blasted and Roberts staggered back, coughing, his eyes wide and staring.

He blinked once, very slowly, then sat down and rolled over, drawing his knees up tightly, and died.

Mahone wheeled and raced for his horse. Then he was in the saddle and heading down range as fast as he could ride. He had no desire to see Dowd now. The Texan would see what had happened from the tracks.

Meanwhile, there was business in town. If Sonntag was there, and looking for him, he could find him. Laird, he felt, was the center of things. Knowing as little as he did about all the people there, Finn had only a few ideas. He intended to learn what he could, and there were two sources on which he could rely: Lettie Mason and Otis.

Remy Kastelle, riding west, heard the sharp cracking report of the Winchester, followed by the heavy boom of the Sharps, then the Winchester twice again. She wheeled her horse and started back on a dead run. She was just reaching the ranch house when she saw Texas Dowd, gun in hand, leave the ranch at a gallop.

Swinging alongside she disregarded his motions to stay back, and rode on. Suddenly, he seemed to sight something in the grass, and wheeled, riding over to the knoll. He swung down from the horse and picked it up. It was Roberts's Sharps rifle.

He looked up at the girl, then removed his hat. The Sharps had torn a ragged gash in the brim. "Somebody shot at him," Dowd said, "or he'd a had me sure! I heard that first shot and jerked. This came next."

The grass was pressed down where Mexie had crushed it in his retreat. The route by which he had approached was not the return route. Mexie had been too cagey for that. Yet his return had been a flight, and Dowd followed, riding his horse until he came to the two horses and Roberts's body.

He rolled the man over, and Remy drew back, her face pale. "Who . . . who is it?" she asked.

"I've seen him around. Name of Roberts. Shot twice, right through the heart." He looked up at her. His face was bleak and hard. "Not many men shoot like that!"

Texas stepped over the body and looked at the knot. "No hombre expectin' to leave in a hurry ever tied a horse like that!" he said. "Whoever shot him knew these horses were here. He tied that knot so if he was slow gettin' back, this hombre wouldn't get away!"

Carefully, Dowd went through his pockets. There was some ninety dollars in bills. One, a twenty, was pasted together with a piece of pink paper. Dowd put them in his shirt pocket. Scouting around, he found the bush where the black stallion had been tied. His face stiffened as he looked. Then he lifted his eyes to the girl. "It's him, damn his soul!" he said bitterly.

"Who?"

"Finn Mahone! He seen this hombre cat-footin' around the hills. He followed him, an' when he saw what he was up to, he scared him out of there. Then he got back here, an' this hombre tried to shoot it out with him."

"Finn Mahone!" Remy stared at Dowd. "Then he saved your life, Tex!"

"Yeah." Tex stared at the tracks of the big horse. "That's the third time!"

"Tex," Remy said quickly, "what's between you and Mahone?"

Texas Dowd raised his eyes and looked at her. "He murdered my sister," he said coldly.

CHAPTER 5

Dan Taggart loped his sorrel pony toward the McInnis ranch. At the time Mexie Roberts was lying in wait for his shot at Dowd, Taggart had been inspecting cattle far to the south.

Taggart was a man of nearly forty who looked ten years older. Rarely clean shaven, he was grim, hard, and loyal. He was one of those riders who were the backbone of the cattle business. When he rode, he rode, in the parlance of the cattle country, "for the brand." In other words, his loyalty was not a thing to be taken lightly.

He was a man without imagination. Hardworking, ready to fight if need be, never hesitating at long hours or miserable conditions. Abe McInnis, who knew a good man when he saw one, had made Taggart foreman. It was the first position of responsibility Dan Taggart had ever held. He took it seriously, and he did more work than any two of his cowhands.

That day he had seen a heifer with a fresh brand. He got a loop on her, and inspected the brand. It was P Slash L, the Logan brand. There was nothing surprising about it, as the cattle of the two ranches grazed the same land in this area, and had done so without question for some time.

Nick James, who had formerly ridden for McInnis, saw Taggart pull down the heifer and rode over. He grinned at the older man. "Figger we're rustlin', Dan?"

"Nope." Taggart released the heifer and got up. "Just havin' a look. That Kastelle girl said somethin' the other day. Bothers me some."

"What was that?" James asked. He rolled a smoke and sat his horse, waiting.

Taggart rolled his quid and spat. "Said somethin'

about this here Mahone feller sayin' if we was to hunt rustlers we should do it with a pen an' ink."

Nick looked at Taggart quickly, his eyes shrewd. "Yeah," he said, carefully, "not a bad idea. You got that Spur brand, Dan. Feller could make that over into a lot of things."

"Uh-huh," Taggart agreed. He picked up a bit of dead mesquite root. "Like an IH connected?"

Nick James's face was expressionless. He lighted his smoke. "Yeah," he said again, "you can do purty well with a Lazy K, too."

Taggart looked up. "Nick, I wouldn't say this to many people, but I reckon I got stampeded into doin' somethin' foolish the other night. First time I ever went to one of them Cattleman's meetin's, though." He looked up again. "I voted for Sonntag."

"Heard about it," Nick said gravely. "You seen *The Branding Iron*?"

"No, why?" Taggart looked up at Nick.

The P Slash L cowhand dug into his saddlebag. "Take a look then."

SONNTAG CHOSEN FOR RANGE INVESTIGATION

By a vote of six to four, the Cattleman's Association voted to appoint Byrn Sonntag as range detective to investigate and deal with rustling activities. Abraham McInnis, popular cattleman of the Spur Ranch, was unable to be present. There has been considerable wonder about how the vote would have gone had McInnis not been confined to his bed due to the mysterious shooting in the canyon below Rimrock. McInnis, seriously wounded in a yet unexplained shooting, is believed by many of his friends to be opposed to any such action as the hiring of a notorious gunman.

Dan Taggart, foreman of the Spur, voted for Sonntag in McInnis's place. Had he voted against Sonntag the question would have been dropped for the time being.

"Looks kind of bad," Taggart admitted. "I wished that girl had spoke up before I voted. Minute she said that, I began seein' pictures in my head of all them brands."

"Yeah," Nick agreed. "Know how you feel."

"Well," Taggart said. "P Slash L's in the clear on that, even if Logan did vote for Sonntag. No brand in the valley can be made into a P Slash L."

"That's right," Nick James glanced off across the prairie. "It's too right."

Taggart looked up, scowling. "Huh? What did you say?"

"Dan," Nick said, "we lost some cows about a month ago. Maybe twenty head. I'd been workin' back in Sage Canyon up until the day before, then Pierce told me to start breakin' a couple of broncs we got."

"What about it?"

"Those broncs could have been broke any time, Dan."

Dan Taggart got into the saddle and watched Nick James riding away. The more he thought about it, the surer he was that his vote had been a bad thing. He wished that McInnis was conscious so he could talk to him. He was worried, and had no idea what course was best.

Clouds were bunching up over the Highbinders to the north. He dug his slicker out of his saddlebags and rode on with it lying conveniently across the saddle in front of him.

. . .

It was already pouring rain when Finn Mahone rode into Laird. On a hunch, he had returned to Crystal Valley and thrown a hackamore on the old steel-dust gelding and brought it with him down into town. If push came to shove in the trouble with Texas Dowd the steel-dust might, just might, get him a fair hearing. In the past his pride had kept him from asking for understanding from the man who once had been his friend. But the situation was now different. He had just saved Dowd's life, and they were both older and wiser. Heavy clouds loomed over the town and rain was falling in sheets. Not knowing what sort of reception he could expect, he avoided the livery stable and rode down a back street until he came to Doc Finerty's. He led the stallion and gelding inside the doctor's barn, rubbed them dry, and got feed from the bin.

Splashing through the gathering pools of rain, he went to the back door of Lettie's place. Turning the knob, it gave under his hand and he stepped within, loosening the buttons on his slicker to have his guns available. He was standing there, dripping water in the light that reflected from over the stairway, when Lettie came into the hall.

"Finn!" she exclaimed. "Oh, it's good to see you."

She was a small woman, beautifully shaped, and Finn was always surprised to find her in such a business. She wore beautiful but conservative clothing, and always looked smart and attractive. He knew enough of her story to admire her for her determination and her fine independence of spirit. Nor could he blame her for choosing this business, for when left a widow there had been only the choice between running a gambling house or slowly falling into a pauper's life. She had not hesitated to make her decision, heedless of her reputation.

One of those unaccountable movements that swept the tide of drifting mankind into some of the farthest and most unusual backwaters had brought her to Laird.

"It's good to see you again, too, Lettie." He nodded toward the parlor. "Who's in?"

"Nobody, right now. I guess the rain's keeping them home. Finn, what's been happening? I hear Sonntag is gunning for you."

Mahone shrugged. "I haven't seen him. He in town?"

"No, but Ringer Cobb is. Be careful."

"Sure. Is Otis around?"

"No, he isn't. He's wanting to see you, though. He's been acting very strange. Stopped drinking all of a sudden, and seems to have something on his mind. You'd better see him."

"I will. Right now I want to look up Judge Collins." Lightning flashed almost without cessation, and the rain had risen to a thundering roar. "Hombre tried to kill Tex today," he told her. "Slim, wiry, dark fellow."

"Mexie Roberts. He comes and goes, Finn, always by himself."

"Know why he would want to kill Dowd?"

"For money. Roberts never killed anybody unless he got paid. If he tried to kill Texas, somebody was paying him."

Mahone looked down at her. "Who d'you think, Lettie?"

She hesitated, then she looked up quickly. He could see doubt and worry in her eyes. "I don't know, Finn. I would be wrong if I said Sonntag or Salter . . . it feels like someone is playing with everyone like they were puppets!"

"I agree, but that doesn't help me know who it is. Well, I'm going over to see Collins. Armstrong, too."

"Be careful of Cobb!" she warned.

He went out the front door, gathering his slicker about him but not fastening the buttons. At this time of night, Judge Collins might be in the Longhorn, as there was no light at Doc's. Or the judge might be at Ma Boyle's for coffee. At the thought of coffee, Finn suddenly realized he was hungry.

He slopped down the street in the pelting rain, and went on past the lights of the Longhorn. There was loud talk from within, and he hesitated while rain ran down his slicker and dribbled off on the walk. Otis might be in there. Collins, too. On the other hand, Ringer Cobb was almost sure to be. For an instant longer he hesitated, half in mind to go in and end it right then. But when he saw Ringer, if it ended in a fight he might have to get out of town, and he had things he needed to do. He went on down the street.

There was a light burning at *The Branding Iron*. He hesitated, then pushed open the door and walked in. When he had the door closed, he looked around. "Hey, Dean?"

There was no answer. "Dean!" he called again, louder. When there was still no answer, he walked around the high counter toward the trays of type and the desk.

Dean Anderson was lying facedown on the floor, his head bloody. Quickly, Finn bent over him. He was alive. Hurrying to the back door he filled a wash pan from the water bucket, grabbed up the towel that Dean kept hanging there, and hurried back.

Lifting him, he cradled Dean's head on his arm while he put the cold towel on his head. Gently, he sponged away the blood. It was a cut, a very nasty cut.

There was another, higher and in his hair. He sponged

that off, too, and then Armstrong began to stir and mutter. "Hold still!" Finn commanded.

When Armstrong's eyes opened, they stared about in confusion. At this moment, without his dignity, he looked strangely young. Then he looked up and saw Mahone.

"Finn!" he said. "Man, I'm glad to see you!"

"What happened?" Mahone demanded.

"Cobb pistol-whipped me. Came in here about six, just after the rain started. Started in half joking about what I'd said in the paper, then he hit me over the eye with a pistol barrel."

"You mean that item about Sonntag?"

Dean shook his head, then gasped and caught it with both hands. "No, the piece I had in today. I put out an extra edition." He looked up. "It's on the table there."

APPOINTMENT OF SONNTAG A MISTAKE
The appointment of Byrn Sonntag, notorious gunman, to investigate the cattle rustling was a mistake. If the election was to be held again tomorrow, the result would be against him. Since arriving in the Laird Valley country, Sonntag has killed at least three men, and his associates at Rawhide can scarcely be classed as good citizens. There are those on the range who declare it is more than a coincidence that certain brands belonging to Rawhide ranchers are very easily developed from brands already on this range. If Byrn Sonntag is to investigate rustling, it might be a good idea to begin in his own home town.

Finn Mahone looked up, grinning. "Dean," he said, "it took guts to write that, but if I were you, I'd start packing a gun. Your paper gets around. Whoever is behind all this doesn't have a chance of making it work if the news gets outside of Laird Valley."

"That's what I thought, and that's what I wrote!" Dean said firmly. He crawled to his feet and clutched the desk for support. "What good is a newspaper unless it tells the truth and fights for the rights of the people?"

Mahone shrugged. "A lot of them should ask that question of themselves," he said dryly. "I'd better get Doc for you," he said. "You'll need some stitches in that head!"

"He's at Ma Boyle's," Dean said. "Or was starting for there just before Cobb showed up."

"What are you going to do now?" Mahone asked, curiously.

"Do?" Dean demanded. "I'll tell you what I'm going to do! I'm going to print what just happened, call it the cowardly attack it was, and tell who did it and why!"

"Then you'd better pack a gun," Finn advised. "This business is turning bad and I don't like it. I've already killed one man today."

"You have?" Armstrong stared at him. "Who?"

"Fellow named Roberts. He tried to dry-gulch Texas Dowd."

Finn pulled his slicker around him and walked outside. Rain was still pouring down, and the street was dark and empty. The blare of music came from the Longhorn, and he heard shouts there, and once a yell. It sounded like Ringer Cobb.

He pushed open the door and stepped into Mother Boyle's in a gust of wind and water. When he had the door closed, he turned his back to it and stood there, looking at the room, a big, somber figure with his rain-soaked hat, his dark slicker, and his green eyes taking the room in with one measuring glance.

Ma Boyle was standing beside Doc Finerty with a pot

of coffee, and Judge Collins had turned as he entered. Nick James was there, the first time Mahone had seen him since the day of the fight. James looked up, quickly and with interest. He had one of those young-old faces, merry and friendly at times, then grave and serious. He was scarcely more than a boy, but had been doing a man's work since he was eleven.

"Doc," Finn said, "better go have a look at Armstrong. Cobb pistol-whipped him."

"I was afraid of that!" Doc said. He got up and reached for his slicker. "Keep some coffee on, Ma!"

Finn sat down at the end of the table, between James and Collins. Collins was concerned. "When Sonntag came in, I knew trouble was coming!"

Finn had hung his slicker and hat near the stove. He dished up some food and poured the coffee. Briefly, and quickly, he outlined the trouble at the Lazy K, and the outcome.

"Roberts is a paid killer." Judge Collins was puzzled. "Doesn't seem like Sonntag would hire any killing done."

"He wouldn't," Mahone said, speaking past half a slice of bread and butter. "Not him."

Nick James stirred his coffee and looked from one to the other. "You ever think maybe something else was behind this?"

Judge Collins turned his head and looked at Nick. This man was shrewd, the Judge knew. James had ridden for him, and for McInnis. He was one of the best hands in the valley. "What are you thinking, Nick?"

The young puncher shrugged, and gulped a swallow of coffee. "Ain't made up my mind. Some things sure look funny, though."

Finn Mahone put his coffee down carefully. Suddenly he was remembering the tall, powerfully built man who was standing behind Remy that day he fought Leibman. "Any rustlin' out your way?" he asked, casually.

Nick nodded. "A little, here and there. Never when anybody's around." He stirred his coffee again. "I think I'll quit," he said suddenly.

"You can always have a job with me," Collins said. "You were the best hand I had, Nick."

"Or with me," Mahone suggested, looking up.

Their eyes met across the table. "Didn't know you hired any hands," Nick said. "Heard you played it alone."

"I have, but I've got some work ahead and could use help. I'd want a hand that would sling a gun if he had to . . . but not unless he had to."

"I'll get my stuff tomorrow," James agreed. His face tightened. "An' collect my time." Then he glanced at Mahone again. "How do I get there? They tell me a man can't go through the Notch unless he knows the way."

"That's right, and don't try it alone. You get your gear, an' if I don't see you, go up and camp in the Notch. There's good water, and plenty of grass. I'll be along."

The door slammed open then, and wind and rain swept into the room. The newcomer struggled to get the door closed, then turned. It was Ringer Cobb.

Finn knew at once the man had been drinking and was in a killing mood. He was not the type who staggered and floundered when drunk. Liquor brought out all the innate cruelty in the man, and if anything, steadied him and made him colder.

His eyes fastened on Mahone's and a light danced in them, an ugly, dangerous light. "You're Finn Mahone," he said, standing just inside the door, his slicker hanging around him, his hands dangling.

Nick James pushed back gently, out of the way. Finn lifted the coffeepot and calmly filled his cup. "That's right," Mahone replied. "An' you're Ringer Cobb. You're the man who walked into the newspaper office and slapped a defenseless man with a Colt. Makes you a pretty bad boy, doesn't it?" Cobb glared at Mahone, his teeth half bared. "What's the matter?" Mahone said. "Don't you like the sound of the truth?"

"You should be ashamed!" Ma Boyle glared at Cobb.

"I've heard about you." Cobb took a step nearer and tried to change the subject back to the one he had in mind. "Heard you're pretty fast with a gun. That right?"

"I do all right." Finn lifted the cup and sipped a little coffee. "Better sit down and have a cup of coffee. Do you good."

"Huh?" Ringer was puzzled. Then his eyes sharpened. "Scared, huh? Think yuh can talk me out of it."

"No," Mahone replied, and his voice hardened, "I'm just trying to talk you out of Boot Hill, because if you reach for that gun . . . *I'll kill you!*"

Ringer Cobb took a long breath through his nose, and his fingers widened. Finn sat perfectly still, just looking at him, and Cobb's eyes wavered. He looked at Finn, and started to speak, but Mahone seemed to have lost interest, and he remarked to Collins, "Hand me that cup, Judge, and I'll pour this man some coffee." He looked over at Cobb. "If you're not going to shoot me you might as well have some coffee."

He took the cup and filled it. "Better have some of that cake Ma bakes, too, Ringer. She's plenty good."

Ringer Cobb swayed a little, staring around uncertainly. Then he slumped on the bench, and he was trembling with tension. He took the cup, and started to lift it, but some of the coffee slopped over.

Mahone turned back to Nick. "My place is some of the best range in the world," he said, "most of it subirrigated by water off the Highbinders. Not much erosion in there, an' I don't run enough cattle to keep it fed down. I don't aim to get rich, just to make enough to get along pretty well."

"Sounds all right," Nick said.

None of them seemed to notice Cobb. Several times he started to say something, but Finn Mahone continued to talk, calmly, easily.

Suddenly, Ringer got up, jerking to his feet so hard he tipped over his almost empty cup. Then he wheeled and rammed through the door and was gone. Finn reached across the table and straightened the fallen cup.

Judge Collins looked at Nick James, and James mopped the sweat from his brow. "You backed him down!" Nick said. "Just outnerved him!"

"Better than a shootin', don't you think?"

"Awful close to a shooting, Finn," the judge said. "Awful close."

Finn filled a cup, took the cake, and, holding both under his slicker, went out the door and headed for the print shop.

Nick James looked at Collins. "Judge," he said, "how could anybody ever figger him for a rustler?" Then his eyes widened a little. "Suppose he an' Sonntag . . . ?"

"Don't get anxious, son," the judge said. "I'm sure Finn's good, but you don't want to be out of a job, right? If those two fight, very likely both of them will die!"

Dan Taggart was a slow-thinking man. He sat in the bunkhouse on the Spur and smoked his pipe. The other hands had turned in, but Dan sat there, all through the pounding rain. On his return he had gone in to see Abe, but McInnis was still unconscious, although better. Mrs. McInnis had her sister with her now. Her sister was Mrs. Harran, wife of the storekeeper.

Unable to ask the advice of his boss, the foreman had gone back to the bunkhouse and stayed there except for a few minutes to eat. He was vastly disturbed, afraid he had done wrong, and wanting desperately to repair the damage he had done.

That the fault was not his alone he did not see. Brewster had voted as he had, and so had Logan. When Logan's name came into his mind he remembered Nick's peculiar attitude. What was it Nick said? That they had lost some cows after he had been ordered out of Sage Canyon? That didn't make sense. Would Logan have his own cows rustled? Taggart stirred uneasily, afraid he was out of his depth, but worried and uncertain of what to do.

He glanced around at the sleeping hands, but there was none of them he could turn to, nor who would have been able to give the advice he wanted. Taggart felt the need of advice from a superior, of leadership. His job as foreman was still too new. Only one thing he knew: The voting-in of Sonntag as range detective had been a bad thing. It had put the rustlers in the saddle.

He got up and pulled off his shirt, his pipe still in his mouth. Then he stood for a moment, scratching his stomach. He would ride over to Kastelle's in the morning. Abe McInnis set powerful store by Texas Dowd's opinion, and that of Remy Kastelle.

Pierce Logan was sitting at his desk in a bright, rain-washed world when the door opened and Byrn Sonntag walked in.

He had seen the man fifty times, talked with him nearly as many, and yet the man always did something to him, something he didn't like. There was something in Sonntag's very physical presence, his enormous vitality, the brash, raw health of him, and his deep, somewhat overpowering voice that made Logan feel less than he liked to feel.

Sonntag was in rare form this morning. He stamped into the office and threw his big body into a chair. He tossed his hat to the wide, low windowsill, and stared across at Logan.

He was a big man, weighing all of two hundred and forty pounds, with a leonine head covered with thick, dull red hair. His sleeves were rolled up, and red hair curled on his brawny and powerful forearms.

"Heard the news?" he demanded. His voice was harsh and rang with authority.

Logan looked at him carefully. "What news?"

"Roberts is dead. Somebody killed him when he tried to git Dowd. It wasn't Dowd. Range folks figger it was Finn Mahone. Dowd ain't talkin'. Mahone must've spotted Roberts an' trailed him down. Anyway, he got two slugs through the heart."

Logan scowled. He had been depending on Roberts to do another job for him, too. A job on a man much closer, and eventually more dangerous than Texas Dowd.

"Anything else?"

"Yeah, Cobb went over to that paper an' pistol-whipped Armstrong last night. That was my order. Then he went into the eatin' house, an' Mahone was there."

"Mahone? In town?" Pierce Logan was incredulous. "Where were you?"

"I was busy. I can't be everywhere!" Sonntag growled. "Anyway, Ringer wanted him, an' he went after him."

"Yes?" Logan leaned forward, eagerly.

"An' nothin' happened. Mahone made a fool out of him. Bluffed him out of it. Told him to set down an' have some coffee, an' if he drew a gun he'd kill him. Ringer sat down an' drank the coffee!"

"The devil!" Logan got up angrily. "Only two men blocking this thing and your men muff both of them! I tell you, Sonntag, those men *have* to be out of this!"

"Don't get riled up," Sonntag replied deliberately. "We'll take care of them. Anyway," he added, "it's all in the open now, anyway. That girl of Kastelle's spilled the whole thing. Started people thinkin'. I knowed it was too plain—you could fool 'em only so long as they didn't know there was any rustlin' goin' on."

"Get Dowd and Mahone out of the picture, and I don't care how wild you go," Logan said. "I mean that. You can run off every cow on the range!"

Sonntag sat up and his eyes gleamed suddenly. "Say! That's all right! The boys would like that!" He looked up at Logan who was pacing the floor. "By the way, Mahone was over to Rico. He promised Ed Wheeling a shipment of cattle."

"Good! That's the only good news you've given me! Get some altered brands among them, I don't care whose or how. Nobody will see them over here, anyway. All we want is the story of some funny brands!"

"Fine with me." Sonntag got up to go. "Got any money? I gave Roberts three hundred out of my own pocket."

Logan hesitated, then drew out a billfold and handed over several bills.

"Better make it four hundred," Sonntag said. "I can use it!"

Pierce Logan looked up, but Sonntag wasn't even looking at him. Logan's eyes were ugly when he counted out the other hundred.

Sonntag was getting too big for his boots, Logan decided. Yet, he needed the man. Only Sonntag could keep the Rawhide bunch in line. Ringer Cobb's failure irritated him, and he got to his feet and paced the length of the office. He would have to do some of these jobs himself.

What had frightened Cobb? The man was reputedly dangerous, and he could sling a gun, but he had backed down cold for Mahone. Roberts was dead. That meant something would have to be done about Dowd immediately. Too bad they couldn't all do their jobs as neatly as he did. He, Pierce Logan, would do the job on Dowd, if necessary.

He turned and walked out of his office and down the street toward the Longhorn. Judge Collins sat on his step, tilted back against the wall. He waved casually at Logan. "Old fool!" Logan muttered. "I'll have all that self-importance out of him in a few days!"

Impatience was driving him, and he realized its danger. Yet inefficiency always irritated him, and he wanted this over and done with.

He saw a roan horse at the hitching rail, and Logan stared at it. What was James doing in town? There was plenty for him to do out on the range.

Logan pushed open the door and strode into the Longhorn. Nick looked up when he came in, and shoved his hat back. "Howdy," he said briefly.

"How are you, James?" Logan said. "Got a message for me?"

"No," James said, "only that I'm quittin'."

"Quitting?" Pierce Logan turned his head to look at Nick again. "Why?"

"No partic'lar reason. I never stay on one job too long. Sort of get off my feed if I do."

"Sorry to lose you." Logan poured a drink from the bottle. "Going to work right away?"

"Uh-huh." Nick's voice was elaborately casual. "For

Finn Mahone." Logan put the bottle back on the bar. There might be more in this than was immediately apparent. Nick James was smart. Maybe he was too smart. "I see," he lifted his drink, "but I didn't know Mahone used any hands?"

"Changed his mind, I guess."

The door pushed open and Texas Dowd walked into the room. With him was Van Brewster. "Where's Sonntag?"

Logan turned. "Haven't seen him. What's the trouble?"

"Plenty!" Dowd's eyes were chill. "Mex Roberts tried to dry-gulch me the other day. When I went through his pockets, I found nearly a hundred dollars. That's a lot of money for a range tramp. One o' the bills was stuck together with pink paper. Brewster here recognized it as one he lost in a poker game to Sonntag."

"Sonntag's the type who does his own killing," Logan suggested. "You're on the wrong track, Dowd."

"I'll make up my mind about that!" Dowd's voice was sharp. "If Sonntag hired Roberts to kill me, he did it on orders. I want to know whose orders!"

Logan almost asked him who he believed had given the orders when he caught himself. If he asked that question Dowd might give the right answer, and if he did, it would mean a shooting. This was neither the time nor the place for that.

"That's an angle I hadn't thought of. Sonntag's out on the range somewhere, and I imagine he'll be in town tonight."

"All right." Dowd turned abruptly. "Then tell him I want to see him. If he's got an explanation, I want it!"

Dowd strode out and Logan poured another drink. He was jumpy. That damned fool Sonntag! Why did he have to use a marked bill? This whole thing was going to bust wide open, and unless he was mistaken, Sonntag was down at Lettie Mason's right now.

Pierce Logan returned to his office and seated himself at his desk. Abe McInnis was down in bed and in no shape for anything. Van Brewster was a hotheaded fool. Remy Kastelle was a mere girl, and her father a lazy ex-gambler who would rather read books than work. Judge Collins was too old, and Finerty was not a gunfighter. Dean Armstrong could be taken care of at leisure.

It all boiled down to two men, and it always came back to them, to Dowd and Mahone. Dan Taggart, the foreman at the Spur, was rough and ready and a fighter if he ever made up his mind, but that was a process that ran as slow as molasses in January. There were only a few moves left; Logan just had to make those moves pay off.

It was time he rode out to the Lazy K and had a talk with Remy. Once they were married, he could have Dowd discharged, and the man would leave the range— if Sonntag didn't kill him first. The time for waiting had passed, but definitely.

Pierce Logan went to his stable and threw a saddle on his horse. As he rode out of town, he saw a horseman far ahead. It was Nick James, on his way to the Notch.

Far ahead of Pierce Logan and already on Lazy K range, Banty Hull, Frank Salter, and Montana Kerr rode side by side. They had their orders from Sonntag, and immediately they moved out. They were after a bunch of Lazy K cattle. At the same time, far to the north and east of them, Ike Hibby, Alcorn, Leibman, and Ringer Cobb were moving down on one of Brewster's small herds.

With two hundred head, they started for Rawhide. This was no matter of altering brands, it was an outright, daylight steal.

Montana Kerr saw the rider first, and jerked his head at him. "Who the hell is that?"

Hull rode up a little, peering under his pulled-down hat brim. "Looks like Dan Taggart. Headed for the Lazy K, I reckon."

"He's seen us."

"Yeah." Montana's voice was flat. "I never liked him anyway."

Taggart's route intersected theirs within two miles. He glanced from one to the other, and his heart began to pound. He had never seen Rawhide riders on this range before. Something in their eyes warned him, but Dan Taggart was not the man to back up, and even had he been, he would not have had a chance.

"Howdy, boys." His eyes shifted from one to the other. Their faces were all grim, hostile. Some sixth sense told him what was coming. "What's up?"

"Your number," Hull said.

"Huh?" Taggart knew he was no match for these men. If he could get some cover, with his rifle, he might . . . but there was no chance of that. It was here and now. "You boys off your range, ain't you?"

"This is all our range," Salter said harshly. "Startin' t'day."

"I reckon other folks'll disagree," Taggart said. "Tex Dowd for instance."

"Dowd!" Salter spat the word. "I reckon I know him. I know him from Missouri, and I'd like t'hang his hide on a fence!"

Taggart shrugged. "Your business," he told them. "You boys go your way, an' I'll go mine. I reckon I'll be ridin' on."

He had his hand in his lap, only inches from his gun, but he knew Montana Kerr, knew the man was a killer, and knew that even leaving the others out, he wouldn't have a chance. He started his horse and rode on. For a moment, he thought he would get away with it. Then Kerr yelled at him.

Dan Taggart turned in his saddle and Kerr's hand flashed with incredible speed. Taggart grabbed for his gun, but two slugs hit him and he went down, hitting the ground in a heap, and dead before he hit it.

All three men emptied their guns into his body. "That'll be a lesson to 'em!" Salter's face was vicious as he spoke. "No use to botch the job like we did on McInnis."

They swung wide and headed around the Lazy K, driving cattle ahead of them.

Behind them Dan Taggart lay sprawled in the thin prairie grass, his shirt darkly stained with blood, and the grass beneath him red. His gun was still in its worn holster.

His horse, after running away when Taggart's body fell from it, watched the three riders trot their horses from the scene of the killing. Curious, and lonely without its master, the cow horse walked back.

Taggart lay on the ground and the horse drew nearer. At the smell of blood, it shied violently, rolling its eyes, but impelled by a curiosity greater than its sense of danger, moved closer. The smell of blood was too much for it, and jerking its head away, it trotted off a little distance.

On the crest of a rise it stopped briefly, looking back. Then, turning away, it trotted toward home, pausing from time to time to crop a mouthful of grass.

CHAPTER 6

Remy Kastelle sat on the cowhide-covered settee in the great, high-ceilinged living room of the Lazy K ranch house. The room as always was cool and still, and for this very reason she had always loved it. There was something of a cathedral hush in the great room, and the longer she lived in the house, the more she understood why her father had built the room so large.

Kastelle had put his book aside and was idly riffling a deck of cards through his fingers. He had never cared for his onetime profession, and had no longing to return to it. Yet his life had taught him the uncertainty of things if no more, and he felt the necessity of retaining all his old skill.

The silence in the big room was unbroken save for the ripple and snap of the cards. Kastelle shuffled the deck quickly, ran his thumb over the edges, and in a few rapid, easy movements, all apparently part of his shuffling, he had selected the proper cards and run up a couple of good hands.

He in-jogged the top card, took off the bottom and shuffled off, then, locating the break with a finger, he shuffled off again and with a neat throw had his stack on top. Then he cut the deck, shifted the cut back, and dealt the hands, three fives showing up in his imaginary opponent's hand, three jacks in his own.

From time to time he glanced at Remy, but said nothing. Her beauty always came to him with something of a shock. The fact that he had seen her grow from a long-legged, coltish girl, who lived only to ride, into a beautiful woman did nothing to detract from her beauty. Her mother had been lovely, and his own mother had been a beautiful woman, but neither of them could compare to the vivid loveliness that was his daughter.

He had never worried about her. Growing up beside him she had grown up singularly independent, choosing her own way always, and if guided by him, the guiding was so slight that neither of them were ever conscious of it.

Their relationship had always been more than that of father and daughter. They understood each other as people. She knew her father's pride in his appearance, his love of horses, his sensitive response to beauty. She knew what his life had been before he bought the first ranch back in Texas. She had never been ashamed that her father was a professional gambler. She knew what had led to it, and knew how he felt.

The war with Mexico had ended, and Kastelle, a major in the cavalry, had found himself discharged in a foreign country with no prospects except an agile mind and a willingness to embrace the future. He had no possessions other than the horse he rode and the clothes he wore. Gold had recently been discovered in the foothills of the California Sierras, and so like hundreds of other veterans he sold his horse and bought passage on a windjammer headed to San Francisco.

Within months the town was swarming with sailors, treasure seekers, merchants, mining speculators, and revolution plotters from Latin America. Many of them had money. Kastelle, from then on known as Frenchy, became a habitué of the cafés and gambling houses.

A skillful horseman and an excellent shot, he possessed only one other skill. He knew how to handle cards. Swiftly, in the months that followed, he learned more by applying his skill. For a professional gambler he possessed perfect equipment. Cold nerve, an unreadable face, skillful fingers, and a shy, scholarly manner that was deceptive. Best of all, he possessed no gambling instinct. He played cards to win.

A few years before the nation tore itself apart with the war against the Confederate States, Frenchy was briefly married. An outbreak of cholera carried off his young wife, along with thousands of others, and left him with a baby daughter to care for.

With no other attachments in his life, he was with Remy much of the time. They talked a lot, and he made no attempt to spare her the details of his career. He told her of the men and women he met, sketching them coldly with words as an artist might with a brush. It was not long until all these people lived and breathed for her.

Remy's conception of what was right and wrong, or when men and women were at their best and worst, came entirely from these accounts of her father's. His instinct for people was almost infallible, and she acquired much of it, growing up with a precocious knowledge of the world and the facts of life such as few children ever have.

No matter what her troubles, she always turned to him, and she had never found him lacking in understanding. He rarely reproved her. A suggestion from him, or his unspoken approval or disapproval, was all she needed. Gradually, as she grew older, she came more and more to handle her own problems.

On this day, Kastelle sensed that something was troubling her. Remy was restless, uneasy. Several times he thought he detected tears in her eyes, but he was not certain.

Remy had attracted men to her from the time she was fourteen. She was accustomed to their interest, and she knew how to handle them. The men she met had rarely attracted or interested her. Dowd seemed like an uncle or a friend, and it wasn't until she met Pierce Logan that love and marriage entered her mind.

Tall, handsome, and an interesting conversationalist,

he had gone riding with her several times, and she had entertained him at home a bit more. Occasionally, when in town, she had eaten with him at Ma Boyle's. He was exciting and fascinating, but she had never discussed him with her father, nor he with her. Always, she had been a little hesitant about bringing the matter up.

Then had come the morning she walked into Ma Boyle's and asked about the black stallion. She had lifted her eyes and found herself looking at Finn Mahone.

She never forgot that moment. She remembered how imperiously she had swept into the room, her riding crop in her hand, so filled with the picture of that magnificent black stallion that she could think of nothing else.

His calm assurance nettled her, and she was actually pleased when she thought Leibman would whip him. Only Dowd had as much assurance as that, and knowing Dowd's abilities, she had never been put off by his manner.

The fight in the street, the ride across those awful slides, and the night in the cabin, all had served to increase her interest. Carried away by the excitement of the ride across the slate, and by the necessity for getting somewhere, Remy had not fully realized that she was trapped, that she must stay alone in the cabin with him.

She was not too disturbed by it. She carried a .41 derringer that her father had given her, and would not have hesitated to use it. She fully expected to have to warn him away, and then he hadn't even come near her door. She had never decided whether she was pleased or angry about that.

Texas Dowd's disclosure of his reason for hating Mahone shocked her. She wanted to know if the picture of the beautiful woman that she had seen in Finn's bedroom had been Dowd's sister, but his dour and forbidding reaction denied any possibility of further talk.

His statement seemed utterly at variance with every conception she had formed of the character of Finn Mahone. Murder of any kind seemed beyond him, and murder of a woman was unthinkable. Killing, yes. Childhood familiarity with war and sudden death allowed her to accept that. To kill in defense was one thing, however; murder was another. Yet the statement had been made, and there was something in the flat finality of it that had her believing, even while she refused to admit to herself that it was true.

Staring out the door where the shadow of the porch cut a sharp line across the brightness of the morning, Remy tried to analyze her feelings for Finn, and could find no answer. She was nineteen, a young lady by all the standards of her time, and her own mother had been married well before that age. Yet Remy had had no serious romantic dealings with boys or men. The idea of love, while always in her mind, had never become quite real to her.

Kastelle riffled his cards and waited. Sensitive to all the nuances of Remy's feelings, he knew she was going to talk to him, that she was troubled. It was the first time in almost two years that she had come to him with a problem, and the interval made the silence harder to break.

She picked up a book, then put it down. She got up and crossed to the fireplace and idly toed a stick back off the hearthstone. She looked out the door again, then back to him. "Did Dowd ever tell you about his sister being murdered?"

Kastelle nodded. "Why, yes, he did. It was a long time ago."

"Tell me about it."

He shrugged and put the cards aside. "There is very

little I can tell you. Louisiana was in bad shape right then; the whole South was in a turmoil. Carpetbaggers were coming in, the freed slaves were wandering about, uncertain of what to do, and there were renegade soldiers from both armies on the loose.

"Riots and outbreaks were common in New Orleans, houses were burned on plantations, and there was a lot of looting going on. More than one man decided it was a good chance to get rich, and they weren't all carpetbaggers by a long shot. Renegade southerners were just as bad in many cases.

"Dowd was living with his sister, who was about as old as you are now, on a farm just out of New Orleans. It had belonged to his uncle, and wasn't a large place, at all.

"It was on a bayou, and was quite lovely. He didn't tell me much about it, but it seems there was a friend living there with him, a chap he had met in Mexico right before the war. They had both fought in revolutions down there, and had become friends.

"Dowd went to New Orleans on business, and while he was gone one of those riots broke out, and he was overdue in getting home. When he did get back, his sister had been murdered. From what he said it was pretty ugly.

"He found a button in her hand that had come off a coat this friend was wearing, and the friend was nowhere around. The house had been thoroughly looted. Three men who lived nearby swore they saw the friend riding away on a horse, and he was, they said, bloody as could be.

"Dowd started after his friend, and swore he would kill him on sight. The chase followed clear to Mexico, and Dowd lost him there, was nearly killed by some old enemies, and returned to Texas. That was when I met him."

"He told me the friend was Finn Mahone," she said.

Kastelle looked at her quickly. Her eyes were wide and she was staring out the door.

So that was it! He had noticed how different Remy had been acting of late, and had wondered about it. He recalled, then, how Remy had stood up for Mahone at the Cattleman's meeting.

"I didn't know." Remy had grown up, he realized that with a pang. He had known she would, and had known that when she did, she would fall in love. Now it had to be with this man . . . a murderer.

"You've met Mahone?"

"Yes." Without taking her eyes from the door, she told all that had transpired. He listened attentively, and realized when she had finished that his pipe had gone out. He refilled and lit it.

Kastelle stared at the floor. He never knew what to say at a time like this because there simply wasn't anything he could say. He raised his eyes to look at Remy, and found she was gone. She had walked out of the room and he had not noticed.

He got up and walked to the door. Remy was walking dejectedly toward the corrals. Kastelle shook his head, unaware of any way he could help her except to listen and try to be a strong and stable presence.

Two cowhands were sitting on the steps of the bunkhouse, and one of them had a rifle across his knees. Kastelle walked down to them. They grinned as he came up.

"Howdy!" Jody Carson said. "Dowd told us to stick around today."

Kastelle nodded. He left the ranch business strictly up to the man from Texas. "Is he expecting trouble?"

"Yeah." Carson leaned his elbows on the top step. "Pete was crossin' the Laird trail yesterday an' run into

Nick James. Nick's headin' for the Notch. He's goin' to work for Mahone."

"Mahone's hiring hands?"

"Uh-huh. Anyway, Nick said Mahone ran a blazer on Ringer Cobb in Ma Boyle's place an' made him back down. Story's all over town about Roberts tryin' to kill Dowd, too."

"Where's Marshal Miller?"

"Over to the McInnis place, waitin' for Abe to talk, I reckon." He sat up suddenly. "Hey! What's all this?"

They turned, and Kastelle's heart gave a leap. Texas Dowd was coming in with a body across a saddle. His face was hard. He reined in and swung down. "It's Dan Taggart," he said, "killed down on our south range."

Carson and Pete helped him remove the body from the saddle, and they looked at it. Kastelle's eyes hardened as he looked. He had known and liked Taggart, as these men had. The man was literally riddled with holes.

Dowd's face was grim when he looked up. "This is the beginning," he said. "God knows where it'll end." He looked at Jody. "You an' Pete stick right here. Don't you get off this place on no account. An' watch for that Rawhide bunch!"

Jody Carson had his own opinion of the men from Rawhide. That opinion had been bolstered by what he'd heard from Nick James. His eyes found Dowd's. "Nick told Pete that Taggart was sorry he voted for Sonntag. He wanted to do something about it powerful bad."

"Maybe Sonntag done this?" Pete suggested.

Dowd shook his head. "No, this was more than one man. Sonntag wouldn't have wasted shots, either. I scouted around. There were three men, cutting north toward the Highbinders. Happened several hours ago, I reckon."

Dowd stared at the bloody, shot-up body, and his lips

tightened. Yet he was thinking now of Finn. If only Mahone were riding with him! These men . . . they meant well, and they would try, but in the end they were not hard enough, not fast enough. Byrn Sonntag was a bear with lightning in his hands, and he had men like Frank Salter and Montana Kerr riding with him.

Getting that bunch would be a job for men to do, not boys. He stood there, lonely and bitter, remembering the time in Mexico that he and Mahone had been informed by a soldier sent out from town that they must bring themselves to the commandant at once.

They were carrying ten thousand dollars in gold, their payment for fighting. They well knew what would happen to their ten thousand if it ever got in the clutches of that commandant. Mahone had looked up, and he had said in that easy, tough voice of his, "Tell the commandant that Finn Mahone an' Tex Dowd are ridin' down the main street of his town, an' if he wants us, or our gold, tell him to come an' get us!"

And an hour later, after a leisurely meal, they had mounted up and ridden through the little Mexican town . . . and there was not a soul in sight.

Dowd knew he had to kill Mahone. Whenever he thought of that brutal murder, a tide of fierce anger rose within him. Yet somehow, something held him back. It was not only that he had not had the chance to meet Mahone since that time, nor was it that there was no way across the slides. Something in him refused to admit that what had happened had happened.

The dust of the same roads had pounded into their faces, and the powder smoke of the same battles had burned their nostrils. He shook his head, and looked up. He turned then and walked into the bunkhouse.

Resolutely, he put aside all thought of Mahone. There was planning to be done.

He had, as it was a slack time, just four hands on the ranch. With the Negro cook, and Kastelle and himself, there were seven. The cook was a tough man and loyal, but he was as old as Frenchy Kastelle and not in as good shape.

What was coming now was open warfare. He knew without further evidence that this was the beginning. Or rather, Roberts's shot at him had been the beginning. Had Mahone not killed Mexie Roberts, Dowd would be dead now. Abe McInnis was in bed, seriously wounded. Taggart killed. On top of that, if they had killed Dowd the range would have been open to do what they pleased.

He got up and paced the floor. Desperately, he needed someone to side him. This was no longer a lone-wolf job. He couldn't be everywhere, and there was still Sonntag. He was out on the range somewhere, and wherever he was, death would soon follow. Texas Dowd knew without doubt that Sonntag would be gunning for him, and that meant he had to kill Sonntag.

It would settle nothing. Someone else was behind this, someone who had ordered his death.

Mahone?

Dowd shook his head. Finn would do his own killing. Suddenly, he remembered he had two men out on the range. They were riding alone . . . and the killers of Taggart had been headed north!

He lunged from the house and ran for his horse. "Stay here!" he yelled at the men by the bunkhouse. He hit the saddle and was gone.

Frenchy Kastelle walked back into the house. Coolly, he got down from their rack his new Winchester '73 and the Sharps .50. Then he checked their loads and put them within easy reach of his hand. He went into his bedroom and got his .44 and belted it on.

Kastelle snapped to with a start. Remy! Where was *she*? He turned and stepped to the door and saw Jody Carson staring out over the range. "Where's Remy?" he called.

Jody ran around the corner of the bunkhouse and stared at the corral. "Her mare's gone!" he yelled. "She must've headed out."

Kastelle stood an instant in indecision. Carson's face was a picture of worry. "Gosh, Boss! I never give her a thought, we're so used to her comin' an' goin'!"

"I know," he said. He held himself still and tried to think where she could have gone. Perhaps just for a ride, to ride away her own doubts and bitterness. If so, she might have gone in any direction. Kastelle stood there, his mind curiously alert. He tried to think of everything, tried to decide what was best to do. "We would be foolish to look for her," he said finally. "We'll have to wait."

"Well, nobody's goin' to come up to her on that mare. That Roxie can outrun anything on this range, unless it's that black of Mahone's."

"Dowd's out now," Carson said, "an' Bovetas an' Rifenbark are still out there. I reckon Dowd figgered they might run into them Rawhide hands that killed Taggart."

Kastelle sat down on the porch, his Winchester close at his hand. Carson stood for a minute, waiting, then walked back to the bunkhouse. Pete Goodale looked up. "The boss wears those guns like he could use 'em," he said. "Never seen him wear one before."

The day drew along slowly, and the sun reached the meridian, then started its long slide toward the distant Rimrock, a high red bulwark against the green range.

Texas Dowd kept his horse at a canter to save it, and headed back up range. He saw few cattle, and this area had been covered with them a fortnight ago. His face drew down in hard lines. He had waited too long. He should have gone to Rawhide and killed Sonntag. If Sonntag was gone, the rest of them would fall apart . . . but again he recalled his belief that behind Sonntag was another, unknown person.

He was almost to the edge of the Highbinders when he heard a faint yell. He reined in his horse and shaded his eyes against the glare of the sun. Someone was waving a hat. He jacked a shell into the chamber of his Winchester and rode ahead, his eyes studying the ground. When he got a little closer, a man got up out of the grass. It was Rifenbark.

"What happened?" Rif's head was bloody and he was limping.

"Three of them Rawhide hands. I seen 'em drivin' some cattle ahead, so I started down range. I was a ways off. Bovetas, he seen 'em before I did, an' he rode down on 'em."

Rifenbark's eyes were bleak. "They never give him a chance. I seen it, an' I also seen I wasn't goin' to do much good agin' three of 'em on a hoss. I hit dirt, an' when they got close enough, I opened up with my rifle.

"Never did no good, though. Never even winged one. They just waved at me an' rode on, then two of 'em circled back, an' one got in this here shot that cut my scalp. I shot again, but didn't get neither one, although I burned 'em up some."

"Where's your horse?"

"Yonder in them trees. I seen him movin' there a minute ago."

Dowd wheeled his horse and started for the trees. He would get Rif mounted, and then they would cut along toward Brewster's. They might come up with the herd again.

. . .

Far away to the east, two separate riders were headed toward Brewster's as toward the apex of a triangle. One of these was Remy Kastelle; the other was Pierce Logan.

Pierce Logan rode rapidly. He was heading for Rawhide, and he had a few plans he wanted to put into execution, and he was looking for a man to replace Mex Roberts. Despite himself, he was worried. He could think of no particular reason why he should be, although he had planned to have Dowd out of the way before things came to a head.

He had chosen Roberts to kill Sonntag when the time came, and now that chance was gone. If Sonntag were to be killed, he must find someone else . . . or do it himself. It might come to that.

A vast impatience lay upon him. Cool planning had been his best hand, but now movement had taken the place of thinking. He knew and approved of what the Rawhide crowd were doing today. Before nightfall, fear would be alive on the range. As long as he had the chance to place the blame on Mahone or his "gang" it would be all right . . . but that was touch and go so far, because they had not had a chance to mix any altered brands into the cattle he was selling.

Pierce Logan had ridden out of town after his meeting with Dowd, and he had stayed the night in a line shack on Brewster's range. He would stay out of sight as much as possible. At all costs, he wished to avoid being forced to show his colors.

He reached the Brewster ranch to find the house in flames and the stock driven off. There was no sign of anyone around the place. Yet he had scarcely ridden into the yard when he heard a low moan. He swung his horse, and his pistol flashed into his hand.

The groan sounded again, and he swung down and walked toward the barn. It had been left standing due to the amount of feed stored there, and some valuable saddles. Logan had been cold-blooded about that. "Might as well keep it, Byrn," he said dryly. "We can use that stuff, and the feed will be good for our horses."

"Logan?" Pierce turned his head to the voice and saw a hand wave feebly from under a pile of sacking. "Help!" The voice was weak.

In two strides he was beside the sacking and jerked it back. Van Brewster, his shirt covered with blood, lay on the barn floor. His lids fluttered and he tried to speak again. Coolly, Logan lifted his pistol. They'd botched the job, but he might as well finish it.

Then he heard a horse's hooves. Wheeling, he saw Remy Kastelle ride into the ranch yard on her white mare. Thrusting his gun into the holster, he called to her. "Come here! Brewster's hurt!"

Remy dismounted and ran to him. He took her elbow and showed her the wounded man. Then, cursing under his breath, he picked up a bucket and went for water while she unfastened the man's rough shirt. Van Brewster was badly wounded, she could see that at a glance. If he lived it would be more luck than anything they could do. If only they had Doc Finerty!

"Logan . . . started . . ." Brewster's mutter faded, then his eyes opened again, ". . . shoot me," he ended.

The words made no sense. Obviously he was delirious, and she thought no more of what he had said. An hour later, with the wounds bathed and bandaged from some supplies she carried in her saddlebags, she stood facing Logan.

"He can't be moved, Pierce." Her voice was worried. "I'm going to stay here with him. Why don't you ride for Doc? That horse of yours will get to him faster than anyone else."

"Leave me with him," Logan suggested. "Your mare is fast, and you'd be safer in town than here."

She hesitated. "No, I'll stay. Ever since this started I've been carrying a few things with me. If he should need help, I could give it to him. I'll be all right."

"Well . . ." He hesitated. She was here, alone. Why not now? In a few days . . . ? Then he told himself not to be a fool. He wanted the Lazy K. He could get a clearer title by marriage, and besides, she would be an asset. There was plenty of time. He told himself that coolly, while he avoided her glance. She was the loveliest girl he had ever seen. Only one had been nearly so beautiful.

"All right, I'll go. Be careful," he advised, "and stay out of sight." This would prevent him from going on to Rawhide, but that could wait. He would appear to be doing more good this way. Finerty would remember it, and Brewster, if he lived. Had Brewster seen him lift that pistol? He doubted it. Mounting, he waved good-bye and started the bay horse at a fast canter.

Remy looked after him, wondering about him again as she often had in these last few days. He sat his horse splendidly. He was a man a woman could be proud of. But . . .

She walked back to the barn and gathered more sacks to make Brewster more comfortable. Time and again she walked to the door, but it would be hours before Logan could return.

Pierce Logan was in no hurry. He was going for Finerty, but he was hoping that Brewster would die before the doctor could reach him to help. Hurrying would only increase the chances for Brewster to live. Still, if he did live he would be ill for a long time, and by that time the whole trouble would be settled, one way or another.

Now that he was away from her, he was glad he had not molested Remy Kastelle. There was something about being alone with a woman like that that always fired him with some strange, burning desire. Yet, he could wait. All this, and her, would soon be his. Only three obstacles remained. Texas Dowd, the plan against Finn Mahone, and Byrn Sonntag.

The Rawhide gunman was his man, but he was too powerful a force for Logan to leave in the field. Sonntag had started changing Logan's policy when the Rawhide boys began their outright theft. Sonntag controlled the men doing the rustling. So Logan had no choice but to go along with it or be sidelined. As soon as the events in the Laird Valley came to a head, Logan and Sonntag were going to have to find out who was boss. Yet it was a simple choice . . . only one would be alive.

North of him the clans were gathering in Rawhide. Byrn Sonntag had been sitting at a table waiting for them. Montana Kerr came in, dusty from his long ride. Briefly, he reported. Sonntag fingered his glass. Dan Taggart was dead. That was good, for the man had fight in him. Bovetas was dead. That was unimportant, but it was another gun eliminated. Brewster was dead, or so the report came in. The Brewster and McInnis operations were out of the fight, and the bulk of their cattle were on the move. There remained only the Lazy K.

Logan was soft on hitting the Kastelle ranch. He had some plan of his own, for he had always told Sonntag to go easy. The reason he gave was the watchfulness of

Texas Dowd, but Sonntag suspected it had more to do with the girl. The thought of Dowd irritated Sonntag. The man was good with a gun. But how good?

He knew Dowd slightly. Finn Mahone was still only a name to him, once or twice their trails had crossed, but always at a distance.

Ike Hibby, Ringer Cobb, Banty Hull, and the rest of them had ridden in from the range. The war was on, and the Rawhide riders had struck fast and hard.

He was not worried about Laird. Its citizens would have little effect outside the town. There would be resistance, but a resistance of spirit rather than physical power. Byrn Sonntag had nothing but contempt for resistance of the spirit. Such resistance is of avail only so long as one's enemy is aware of things of the spirit, and aware of public opinion. Sonntag knew that Logan wanted to keep the war bottled up in Laird Valley. Sonntag could see the advantage in that. Yet Pierce Logan disturbed him. Why, he couldn't say.

Logan, he was well aware, was in the clear. At no point was Logan obviously involved. His skirts were clean, and there was nothing for him to worry about if the plan failed. Sometimes Sonntag wondered if he needed Logan. Yet, he had to admit, he was better heeled now than any time in his life, fear of reprisals was almost nonexistent, and it looked like his men were riding to complete dominance of the valley.

Texas Dowd, sided by Rifenbark, made a wide sweep of the Lazy K range. Mile by mile, bitterness welled up within him. The range had been swept of cattle. Back in the brakes there would be some, of course, but all those in sight had been driven off. Open war had been declared, and the attack was all to the advantage of the enemy.

Distant smoke warned him of fire at Brewster's, so the two rode on. When still some distance away, he recognized Remy's mare and put his horse to a gallop.

Remy ran from the barn to greet him. "It was the Rawhide bunch! If Logan and I hadn't got here—!"

Dowd's interruption was quick. "Logan here? Who got here first, you or him?"

"Why, he did . . . why?"

Dowd's face was expressionless. "Just wondering. This is a long ways from P Slash L range, and a long way from Laird."

"Surely you don't suspect Pierce?" Remy was incredulous.

"I suspect everybody!" Dowd replied shortly. "Hell's broke loose! Taggart's been murdered, an' so's Bovetas!"

Remy's face went white. Dan Taggart she knew well, and Bovie . . . why, he was one of their own boys! Tex went on to tell her about the missing cattle.

While Rif kept watch, Dowd swung down and went inside. Van Brewster was lying on the sacks, breathing hoarsely. His face was wet with sweat and he looked bad. Texas Dowd was familiar with the look of wounded men, and he wouldn't have given a plugged peso for the cattleman's chances.

Without saying anything further to Remy he walked outside. A study of the earth, where it wasn't packed too hard by sun and rain, showed him it was the same lot from Rawhide. The fact that Rawhide was not many miles away made him no happier. They were in no position to defend themselves if attacked. The barn was a flimsy structure, and outnumbered as they might be, there would be almost no chance for them.

That the Kastelle ranch was in the hands of few men was bad. Dowd was a practical fighting man, and he knew such a division of forces was often fatal. Now, when they lacked so much in strength and were encumbered by a dying man, it was infinitely worse. He made his decision quickly.

"Remy," he said, "get on your horse, and you and Rif head for the ranch. I'll stay with Brewster. There's nothing more you or anybody can do until the doctor comes."

Remy shook her head. "No, we'll stay. What if they come back?"

Dowd's face was like ice. "You'll do as I say, Remy. Never since you was a little girl have I given you an order. I'm givin' you one now! Your father's probably worried to death by now. He's alone with just the hands at the ranch, and that's the next place they'll hit. They've wrecked McInnis and Brewster. Believe me, if they tackle the ranch he'll need all the help he can get. You two start back, and don't loaf on the way."

An instant longer she hesitated, but there was a cold logic in what Dowd said. The ranch must not be lost, and their fighting power must be kept intact. "All right, I'll go."

She walked out and swung into the saddle. Rifenbark hesitated, rubbing his grizzled jaw. "Gosh, Tex, I—"

"Get along," Dowd said. "I'll be all right."

When they had ridden away he stood there in front of the barn. Brewster's house was a heap of charred ruins, still smoking. The barn was a crude building of logs, but most of them were mere poles. It was nothing for defense. Nor was there a good spot around. If he was tackled here . . . well, he would have a damned slim chance. And Brewster could not be moved.

He hunted around until he found Brewster's rifle; luckily, it was in the scabbard on his saddle. With it was an ammunition belt. He brought it back into the barn, and then got some sacks and filled them with sand.

These he piled against the wall. There were some grain-filled sacks, and he added them.

Twilight came, and then night. He sat back against the sacks and listened to the hoarse breathing of the wounded man. Outside, little stars of red twinkled and sparked among the black of the dying fire.

Pierce Logan had been here. Why? The thought got into his mind and stuck there. This part of the range held nothing for Logan. He had made no practice of visiting surrounding ranches. There was no reason for his being here, and the thought nettled Dowd. He liked to have a reason for things. He stared into the night, and then let his eyes shift to the ruins of the house.

At that moment he heard the sound of horses' hooves. He sat still, listening.

They were drawing nearer, coming from the direction of Rawhide, and there were a good-sized bunch of them. Texas Dowd got to his feet and walked to the door of the barn. He loosened his six-guns in their holsters and picked up a rifle. His gray eyes worked at the night, striving to see them when they first appeared.

They were talking. He distinguished a voice as the hard, nasal twang of Frank Salter. "You git that Brewster? Was he dead, Al?"

"You was here. Why didn't you look?" Alcorn demanded querulously. "Of course I killed him!"

Texas Dowd had no illusions, nor any compunctions when it came to fighting outlaws and killers. He lifted his rifle, leveled at the voice of Alcorn, and fired.

As though a bolt of lightning had struck among them, riders scattered in every direction, and several of them fired. Dowd saw the flame stab the night, but he was watching his target. Alcorn slid from his horse and fell loosely, heavily into the dust and lay still.

Tex dropped to the ground and lay quiet, listening to the shouting and swearing among the Rawhiders. Then several shots rang out and Dowd heard a bullet strike the log wall. He lay quiet, ignoring it. He had no intention of wasting ammunition on the night air.

He could hear their argument, for their voices carried in the clear, still air. "Like hell Brewster's dead! He got Al!"

"That wasn't him," Montana said. "Brewster might not of been dead, but he was far gone when I last seen him! Somebody else has moved in!"

The voices seemed to be centering around one group of trees, so Dowd lifted his rifle and fired four times, rapid fire. Curses rang out, then silence. He chuckled to himself. "That will make them more careful!" he said.

Texas Dowd settled down behind the sandbags. It was lighter out there, and he could see any movement if an attempt was made to cross the ranch yard. Beside him Brewster stirred, and when Dowd looked down he saw the man's face was gray and his breathing more labored. Van Brewster was going to die.

Dowd whispered to him, "Who shot you, Van?"

He was repeating the question a third time when Brewster's lips stirred. After a moment, the words came. "Bant . . . y Hull, Alcorn . . . an' them."

"I got Alcorn," Dowd told him. "I'll get Hull for you, too."

Brewster's eyes fought their way open and he caught at Dowd's shirtfront. "Watch . . . Logan. He start . . . ed to shoot me."

Pierce Logan? Dowd's mind accepted the thought and turned it over. Logan, the innocent bystander, the man on the sidelines. Why not him?

.   .   .

Over in the dark brush, Montana Kerr was growing irritable. "Let's rush the place! Let's dig him out of there, whoever he is!"

"Wait!" Hull suggested. "I have a better plan. We'll try fire!"

CHAPTER 7

It was Pierce Logan himself, coming for Doc Finerty, who brought the first word of the range war to Laird. As Doc threw a few necessary articles into his saddlebags, Logan gave a brief account of what he wanted them to know. Brewster was badly wounded, perhaps dead, and his ranch house had been burned.

The second bit of news came from Nick James. He was almost at the opposite side of the Lazy K range, heading for the Notch, when he heard the shots fired by the rustlers at Bovetas and Rifenbark. Leaving his packhorse, he turned back, riding warily. So it was that he arrived at the Lazy K just in time to meet Remy as she returned from Brewster's.

Nick James headed for Laird on a fresh horse. His news, added to that brought by Logan, had the town on its ear. The cattle had been driven off the Lazy K and Brewster's spread in one sweep. Bovetas was dead. Taggart was dead. Brewster was wounded. Rifenbark had recognized the Rawhide crowd.

While the streets filled with talking, excited men, Finn Mahone rolled off the bed in the back of Ma Boyle's and pulled on his boots. There were voices in the hall and a sudden pounding on his door. Springing to his feet, gun in hand, he opened it wide. Lettie Mason was standing there.

"Finn!" she cried. "Come quickly! I've just found Otis and he's badly wounded. He's been lying out in the brush where he was left for dead. He wants to see you."

On the way to her place, Lettie told him the news. Finn's mind leaped over the gaps and saw the situation just as it was. Dowd had stayed at Brewster's with the dying man, so he would be there alone. A dangerous position if the rustlers came back. Finn was prepared to find Texas and explain himself. If his plan worked . . . At the thought of riding beside his old comrade again, his heart gave a leap.

Garfield Otis, his face gray and ghastly with the proximity of death, was fully conscious when they came in. A messenger from Lettie had caught Finerty as he was leaving town. Logan had not been with him, for Pierce had no intention of returning to Brewster's. If Finerty was killed, it would be one more out of the way.

"Don't talk long," Finerty warned, "but it will do him good to get it off his chest, whatever it is!"

Otis put out a hand to stop Finerty from leaving, and then he whispered hoarsely, "Logan shot me . . . he's hand in glove with Sonntag. I've seen him talking with him, more than once. One time I was drunk an' seen . . . Logan kill a . . . man. He's . . . he's . . . buried on the hill back of the liv . . . ery stable. It's Sam . . . Hendry!"

"Hendry?" Finerty grabbed Finn's arm. "Logan must have bought the ranch from Hendry, then stole his money back. We figured Sam went off and blew it in, but he never got away! What do you know about that?"

"Old man Hendry was killed by a dry-gulcher," Lettie suggested. "Probably it was Mex Roberts, so maybe we can guess who hired him?"

"Looks like Logan, all right," Mahone admitted. "I think I'll have a talk with him."

"Finn," Lettie interrupted, "there's something else I'd better tell you. Pierce Logan came from New Orleans. I recognized him and I've heard him talk about it. He used another name then, Cashman . . . I don't remember the first name."

Mahone turned square around. "When did Logan first come into this country? About six months or so before I did?"

"Maybe a little less," Finerty said. He looked from Lettie to Finn. "You know something?"

Finn Mahone ignored the question, his heart racing. Pierce Logan was in town, but what was suddenly more imperative was seeing Texas Dowd. After all these years Finn found himself choosing friendship over vengeance. Now, more than ever, he had to see Dowd. The past could wait!

"Let's go, Doc!" he said. "I'm riding with you. Lettie, you said Nick had come back into town? Tell him to keep an eye on Pierce Logan. Not to get into any fight, just keep watch. I'm coming back for him!"

He saddled the black, grabbed up the gelding, and they headed out.

When they had come most of the way, Finn turned to Finerty. "Doc, I don't like the look of that glow in the sky! You come along as fast as you can."

The black stretched his legs. Finn, crouching forward, kept his attention focused tightly on riding, one hand on the reins, the other gripping the gelding's lead rope as lightly as he dared. He didn't want to lose the horse, especially now, but if it misstepped he would have to let go before he was jerked from the saddle. Finn's eyes were riveted on the glow against the night sky. If they had fired that old pole barn, Dowd would be finished.

After the horses had covered a couple of miles, he slowed them for a breather, and then let them out again.

Now he could see the fire, and it was partly the glow from the burned house, and partly the flames from a huge haystack nearby, fired by the rustlers to give them a better shooting light.

Mahone slowed to a canter, and then to a walk. He unlimbered his rifle and moved closer, and when he did, he could see what the outlaws were about.

They had a hayrack piled high with hay, and they were shoving it toward the embattled defender of the barn, obviously planning to set it afire once it was against the pole side of the crude structure. Whether the barn burned or not—and it would—anyone inside would be baked by the awful heat.

Finn watched one of the dark figures moving, and then he lifted his rifle, took careful aim, and fired!

The man screamed and fell over on the ground, and the rustlers, shocked by the sudden attack, broke and ran for cover. Finn got in another shot as they ran, and saw a man stumble. Dowd must be alive, for a rifle barked from the barn as the attackers fled.

Riding swiftly, Mahone rounded the ranch yard, keeping out of the glow of the fire, and then emptied his Winchester into the grove of trees where the outlaws had gone. Swiftly, and still moving, he reloaded his rifle and checked his six-guns.

Yet even as he moved in for another attack, he heard the gallop of fast-moving horses, and saw the dark band of rustlers sweep off across country. They had abandoned the field for the moment, and were probably headed for an attack upon the Lazy K. Finn rode close, then swung to the ground.

"Tex!" he yelled. "I want to talk, Tex! Peace talk!"

Dowd's voice rang loud over the firelit yard. "I've nothing to say to you, Mahone!"

"Tex, you're a damned, bullheaded fool!" Finn roared back at him. "You got what you thought was evidence and jumped to conclusions. I wasn't anywhere near the plantation when it happened!"

Silence held for several minutes, and then Dowd yelled back. "Is Finerty comin'? Brewster's in a bad way!"

"Be here in a minute. I'm coming in, Tex! You hold your fire!"

Leaving the stallion standing ground-hitched, Finn walked out into the firelight. With quick, resolute steps he crossed the hard-packed earth toward the barn. Dowd, hatless, his face grimy, was waiting for him.

"The man who killed Honey is in Laird," Finn said, halting, "and I've got some proof."

Dowd's face did not change. Suspicion was still hard in every line of it. "Who?" he demanded.

"Pierce Logan."

"Logan?" Dowd took a step nearer. "What do you mean, Finn? How could that be?"

"I trailed him, Tex. I got home before you did, and I found her. She was still alive then, and she grabbed me. That's how she got that button. She gave me the name of the man, for he had come by the place before. When the riots started and the country was full of fighting and burning, he came back. He went crazy . . . Well, I trailed him. I lost him, finally, in Rico.

"Now I hear Pierce Logan hit Rico and killed a man there about that time, and then came on over here. Lettie Mason can tell you that he's from New Orleans and the name he was using back then."

"You said Honey knew his name—what was it?"

"Cashman—remember? He was a renegade southerner who tied up with the carpetbaggers and some of the tough crowd around New Orleans. He lived on the Vickers place a few miles west of you for a while."

Texas Dowd stared at Finn, his bitterness ebbing. This was the one man he had loved like a brother. "How do I know you're not lyin'?"

Finn whistled between pinched fingers. Fury trotted up into the firelight, the steel-dust gelding following. Dowd looked from the horses to Mahone, eyes narrowing.

"What's this?"

"Look closely. That's Vickers's gelding. You chased me quite a ways—did I take two horses?"

"No."

"The only time I ever saw Cashman, it was off across a field, and he'd borrowed that horse to go into town. When he fled, he stole it from Vickers. He left the horse in Santa Fe. I bought him a couple of months later." Finn examined Dowd. "I figured that someday I might get the chance to show him to you."

"I never seen Cashman. Heard of him, though."

"I'm told he's a bad man with a gun, Dowd."

"I'll find out." Dowd's expression was grim. His wind-darkened face was tight and still. Then he turned to Mahone. "Thanks for getting Roberts. He would have killed me sure."

"Ask Lettie, Tex. She can tell you his name, too."

"I'd like to believe all this."

"Then believe it."

Doc Finerty rode up and swung down. Tex wheeled and guided him to Van Brewster. Finn stared after Texas, and then a slow grin swept his face and he followed them until Tex looked up. "Dowd, let's leave Doc and go to Rawhide. Let's burn that rathole around their ears, just you and me."

Texas Dowd held himself thoughtfully for a moment, and then he grinned. "You always were one for raisin' hob," he said. "All right, let's go!"

The two riders covered the distance to Rawhide at a rapid gallop. Byrn Sonntag had ridden out a few minutes after the others had started back into Laird Valley, so except for a few of the followers of the Rawhide crowd, few people were around. As the two horsemen clattered down the street, a shot was fired from a window. Dowd wheeled, putting a bullet through it, and then sprang from his horse and went into the barroom. "Get out!" he said to the fat-faced bartender. "Get out and quick! I'm burnin' this place down!"

"Like hell!" The bartender swung and grabbed for his shotgun, but a bullet smashed his hand into a bloody wreck.

"Get out!" Dowd yelled. "You get the next one in your belly!"

The bartender scuttled for the door, and Dowd kicked a heap of papers together and broke an oil lamp in them, then dropped a match. Down the street there was shooting, and he rode out to find Finn Mahone standing in the street with his Winchester in his hand. Finn looked up, a dark streak of soot along his jaw, and an angry red burn. "Someone damn near checked me out."

"You get him?"

"Right between the eyes."

The flames inside the saloon were eating at the floor now, and creeping along the bar. The frame buildings, dry as ancient parchment, would go up like tinder in a high wind.

Both men swung into their saddles, and lighting some sacks, raced from door to door, scattering the fire. The wind caught the flames, and in a matter of minutes the outlaw town was one great, roaring, crackling inferno. "That will kill a lot of rats!" Finn yelled above the sound of the flames. "Let's ride out of here!"

Away from the town, Finn glanced at the tall Texan. "It's like old times, Dowd!"

"Sure is." The Texan stared bleakly down the road. "I'm an awful fool, Finn."

"Forget it. How could you know any different? Honey had that button . . . and it was Logan, all right. It checks too close not to be him. My trail petered out in Rico, but I never knew much about Logan, and never paid much attention to him until the day I saw him on the street with Remy Kastelle."

They rode on, heading toward Laird. Neither of them were much worried about the Lazy K. Jody Carson, Rifenbark, and Pete Goodale were there, and aside from them there was the cook and Kastelle himself. As for Remy, she could handle a rifle better than most men.

The two rode on, side by side, looking toward the town of Laird. Texas Dowd eased himself in the saddle. "I want Logan," he said carefully.

"He's yours."

Doc Finerty was standing beside the pole barn when they rode up, and there was already a graying light in the east. "Van's in a bad way, but he's got a chance," Doc said. He glanced from one to the other. "Where you been?"

"We burned Rawhide," Finn said. "Now we're scalp-hunting. Dowd wants Logan."

"Logan! Well, you look out for Sonntag. He's danger-ous, Finn. He's the worst of them all."

Mahone gestured at Brewster. "Would he make it to Laird in a buckboard?"

"He might," Doc said dubiously. "I've been studying

about it. He would have better care there. Lettie, she'll take him in, and she's a good nurse, the best around here."

Finn got the buckboard from behind the pole barn and they roped a couple of horses and got them hitched. The ride to town was slow and careful, and as daylight came, the buckboard creaked to a stop outside of Lettie Mason's. Finn rounded the stallion and faced down the street. There was no one in sight, for it was barely rising time for the people of Laird. Smoke was beginning to lift from a couple of chimneys.

When Brewster was inside in the care of Lettie, and Doc was sitting over coffee, Finn and Dowd walked outside. "Nick James was to keep an eye on him. Let's walk up to Ma Boyle's."

Laird was quiet in the early morning light, and the dusty street was very still. Somewhere a door slammed, and then a pump began to creak, and afterward they heard a heavy stream of water gushing into a wooden bucket.

The two men walked up the street, then stepped on the boardwalk. Suddenly, Finn saw that the saloon was open. He pushed through the doors. Red Eason looked up, his face growing suddenly still, watchful as he saw who his visitors were.

"Two, and make them both rye," Finn said.

Red poured the drinks and put the bottle on the bar. He glanced from one to the other, and he swallowed. He laid his hands on the bar in plain sight.

"Nice in California, Red," Mahone said suddenly. "You'll enjoy it there."

"Listen," Red Eason said quickly, "I never made any trouble for you fellows. I can't leave. I . . ." His voice dwindled away as they both looked at him.

"Red," Finn leaned his forearms on the bar, "I like this town. I feel at home here. Dowd likes it, too. We've some mighty fine folks around here, and we want to see the town clean and keep it a nice place for people to live. Not like that Rawhide. If this place got as bad as Rawhide, we might have to burn it, *too*."

"We don't want to do that," Dowd said gently, "so Finn and me, we sort of decided to weed out the undesirable elements, as they say. We sort of figure you come under that particular handle."

Eason's face was stiff. He was frightened, but there was still fight in him. "You can't get away with it!" His voice was thick. "Pierce won't stand for it!"

"Don't call him that, Red," Finn said. "Call him Cashman. That's what Dowd's going to call him when he sees him. Cashman's the name of a murderer. The murderer of Tex's sister. He killed Sam Hendry, too. Had him drunk and then killed him and buried him out back of the livery stable. Otis saw it."

Both men tossed off their drinks, then turned toward the doors. At the doors, Finn looked back. "It's nice in California, Red. You should be able to get a lot of miles between you and here before sundown . . . if you start now!"

Ma Boyle was bustling about, putting food on the table and pouring coffee when the two men walked in the door together. Judge Collins looked up, smiling. "How are you, Finn? Hello, Dowd!"

"We brought Brewster to town," Mahone said. "He may pull through. Logan started to kill him when he found him dying. Remy got there and scared Logan off."

Powis was at the table, staring at them, his eyes large.

"Logan, was it?" Collins avoided looking at Powis, and although he was disgusted with himself for it, he felt a little glow of satisfaction that Powis was there to hear it, for the man's abject worship of authority and the power of Pierce Logan had always irritated him.

"Seen the Rawhide bunch?"

"Alcorn's dead. So is Ike Hibby. They attacked Dowd at Brewster's place. The rest of them are off on the range, somewhere."

"You won't have to worry about Rawhide," Texas drawled. "It ain't there anymore."

The door pushed open suddenly, and Nick James came in. He glanced quickly from Dowd to Mahone. "Finn," he said quickly, "Pierce Logan's stayed close to his place all night. He's getting ready to come out."

"Thanks." Mahone glanced over at Texas Dowd. "All right," he said, "are you going to take him or am I?"

Dowd turned. "I am."

Powis put his cup down. It rattled nervously in his saucer. He pushed back in his chair and cleared his throat. "Well," he said, simulating heartiness, "time I got to work."

"Sit down, Powis." Gardner Collins looked less the judge and more the cowhand and cattleman at that moment. "You stay right here. Dowd will tell Logan he wants him."

Texas turned his eyes toward the barber, and the man's face paled. Finn lifted his cup. "He's a friend of Logan's?"

"Sort of," Collins agreed. "Seems to think he's king."

"Well," Finn said, "times are changing around here." He put his cup down. "Powis, Red Eason is headin' for California and expects to make a lot of distance before sundown. He might like a traveling companion."

The barber stared from one to the other. "But my business!" he protested. "Everything I've got is here!"

Finn Mahone looked at him levelly. "You don't need anything you can't carry. Start traveling."

Nick James had been standing by the window, holding the cup of coffee he had poured. "Logan just came out," he said.

Dowd finished his cup, and got to his feet. "Ma," he said, "that sure is good coffee." The sound of his boot heels echoed on the floor.

They sat very still, and the slam of the screen door made them all jump a little.

Pierce Logan was crossing the street to Ma Boyle's when a door slammed, and he looked up. Texas Dowd, tall in his blue jeans and gray shirt, was standing on the step in front of Ma Boyle's. Instantly, Logan was apprehensive, for there was something in Dowd's whole appearance that warned him of trouble.

As he stood there on the step before his office, looking diagonally across the street at Texas Dowd, a peculiar awareness of life came over him. Somehow, he had never seemed to think of the sun's easy warmth, the gray dust in the street, the worn, sun-warped and wind-battered frame buildings. He had never thought much of the signs along the streets of Laird, their paint cracked and old. Now, he seemed aware of them all, but mostly he was aware of the tall, still figure standing over there, looking up the street at him.

Then, the feeling passed. After all, there was no way his part in all this could be known. He was simply getting jumpy, that was all. He was being foolish. After he had his morning coffee, he would feel better. Why should just the appearance of Dowd startle him so?

"Cashman!"

The voice rang like a great bell in the silent, empty street, and Logan jerked as though stabbed.

"Cashman! Start remembering before I kill you! Start

remembering a girl on a plantation in Louisiana! That girl was my sister!''

Pierce Logan stood very still. This alone he had not expected. This past was over. It was gone. That girl . . . Dowd's *sister*? He shook his head suddenly, remembering that awful, bloody afternoon. His lips tightened and a kind of panic came over him, but he stiffened suddenly. That finished it, then. It finished it all, unless he could kill Dowd. His hand flashed for a gun and he drew in a single, sweeping movement, and fired as his gun came level.

His face gray, he crouched in the street, knowing he had missed, and the tall Texan in the gray shirt walked toward him, his long lantern jaw and his face very still, only his cold gray eyes level and hard. In a surge of panic, Logan fired two quick shots. One of them kicked up dust at Dowd's feet, and the other plucked at his sleeve.

Texas Dowd stopped, no more than a dozen feet away, and fired. The sound of his gun was like the roll of a drum, and at each shot, Logan jerked as if struck by a fist. Then, slowly, he sank to the dust, the pistol dribbling from his fingers.

Feeding shells into his gun, Texas Dowd backed slowly away from the fallen man, then turned and walked back to Ma Boyle's. Judge Gardner Collins cleared his throat as Dowd came in, and Finn Mahone poured a fresh cup of coffee. At no time had he risen from the table. He didn't have to. He knew Dowd.

CHAPTER 8

Finn Mahone and Texas Dowd reached the Lazy K, riding slowly for the last few miles. Both men rode with rifles ready, uncertain as to whether they would find the ranch safe, or besieged. As they drew near, the two men let a gap widen between them and rode warily up to the ranch. Jody Carson was the first person they saw.

"Howdy," he said, grinning at them. "You two missed the fun."

"We had some our ownselves. What happened here?"

"That Rawhide bunch bit off more'n they could chew. Montana Kerr, Ringer Cobb, Banty Hull, and Leibman rode in here this mornin' about sunup. They were loaded for bear an' looked plumb salty, an' I reckon they was."

"Was?"

"That's what I said." Jody put a hand on Finn's saddle horn. "You know, I never rightly had the boss figured. He lazed around up there to the house, takin' it easy, an' lettin' Texas here an' Remy run the whole shebang, but when we heard the place was liable to be attacked, he r'ared up on his hind legs, strapped on some guns, an' then he told us what was what.

"Well, sir! You should have seen them hardcases. They rode in here big as life an' tough as all get-out. You could see it stickin' out all over them. They was just a-takin' this here spread over, an' right now. Dowd was gone, an' he was the salty one of the crowd, they reckoned. Well, I reckoned so, too.

"When they rode up they swung down and started for the house, but the boss, he stepped out on the porch. 'Howdy, boys,' he says, big as life an' slick as a whistle, 'lookin' for somethin'?'

" 'Well, I reckon!' Kerr tells him, 'we've come to take over this here place, an' if you don't want no trouble, you stay the hell out of the way!'

" 'But s'posin' I want trouble?' the boss says, an' he says it so nice that they don't take him very serious.

" 'Don't you be foolish,' Kerr says, 'you can come out of this alive if you're smart!'

" 'That's what I was fixin' to tell you,' Kastelle says, 'you boys crawl back in those saddles an' light out of here, an' you can go your way. We'll just make like it never happened,' he says.

"Montana, he still can't figure Frenchy Kastelle makin' any fuss. Never guessed he was the fightin' type. He starts to say somethin' when Cobb opens his big face. 'Let's get 'em, Monty. Why stand here palaverin'?' Then he went for his gun . . .

"It was a bad thing to do, Tex. Too bad them boys couldn't have lived long enough to know their mistake. I tell you, we had our orders, an' we were a-layin' there all set with our rifles an' shotguns. There was Pete, Rif, Wash, an' me, with Remy up to the house. Cobb, he reached, but he was a mite slow. The boss shot him so fast I didn't even know what happened. He'd told us aforetime. He says, 'If they ride off, let 'em go. If they fire one shot . . . wipe 'em out!'

"Mister, we wiped 'em! When Cobb went for his gun, the boss drilled him, an' then the whole passel of ours cut loose on 'em an' I don't think they ever knowed what hit 'em. They must have figured we was either gone, or so skeered we wouldn't fight none.

"Pete, he and Rif are out back now, diggin' graves for the lot of them."

"Anybody hurt?"

Jody chuckled. "Nary a one! They never had a chance! Hell, if this don't scare all the outlaws out of Laird Valley, they just ain't the smart folks we figure 'em for."

He looked up at Finn, then at Tex. "What happened to you-all?"

Dowd explained briefly about the fight at the Brewster

ranch, the killing of Alcorn and Hibby, and the subsequent raid upon Rawhide and how it had been left in flames. Mahone went on from there to tell about the killing of Pierce Logan, and how Eason and Powis had left town.

Carson chuckled. "Well, now! Ain't that somethin'? This will sure make believers out of those bad hombres! This will be a place to leave alone!" Suddenly, he frowned. "What about Sonntag?"

Mahone shrugged. "Neither Sonntag nor Frank Salter have shown up. Sonntag is plenty bad, and Salter is a fit partner for him. The two of them are poison, and while they may have left the range, I doubt it. They'll stick around."

Finn Mahone's eyes had been straying toward the ranch house. Finally, he shoved his hat back on his head, and his face flushed as he suggested, "I expect I'd better go up and tell Frenchy what happened."

Dowd chuckled. "Sure. You might tell Remy, too!"

As Finn trotted the stallion toward the house, he heard them both laughing at him, and he grinned in spite of himself.

Remy Kastelle came out the door as he mounted the steps. "Finn! Oh, it's you! And Tex is back! What happened?"

Frenchy had come into the doorway behind her, and Mahone explained the situation as quickly as possible.

It was Remy who repeated the question. "What about Sonntag?"

"Neither he nor Salter have been heard from, but they may show up yet. I've got to get back to my place and move some cattle. Ed Wheeling over at Rico wants to buy some stock from me."

Hours later, on the road back to Crystal Valley, Finn

Mahone rode swiftly. Nick James had left that morning and was to meet him at the Notch, and they would go on to the valley together. With James and Shoshone Charlie, he could manage the drive all right. Dowd had offered him a hand, but Mahone refused.

He said nothing to them of his worries, but he had his own ideas about what had become of Byrn Sonntag. The big redheaded gunman was probably in Rico. It would be like him to go there, for he knew the place and they knew him. Jim Hoff, the buyer of stolen cattle, was there; Sonntag would need money and he could sell some of the rustled cattle to Hoff.

The following day, Finn Mahone pushed his own herd of cattle through the upper canyon of the Laird. He had his sale to make, and he had the sense that the last act of the Laird Valley cattle war was going to play itself out in Rico.

Finn knew there would be rustling and robbery in the Laird Valley as long as Byrn Sonntag and Frank Salter were at large. Now that he was no longer being set up to be a scapegoat, the rustlers would have no compunction about taking his cattle along with those of everyone else. Texas Dowd had said little, but Mahone knew that he felt the same.

Nick James rode by. Mopping sweat and dust from his brow, he grinned at Mahone. The white-faced cattle moved briskly ahead, bawling and frisking, occasionally stopping to crop disinterestedly at the sparse desert growth. Soon they were mounting the trail to the plateau on which Rico stood.

The scattered shacks that lay around Rico appeared, and then the stockyards. A couple of hands rode up and helped them to corral the stock. Finn left Shoshone Charlie and Nick James to drown their thirst, and headed for the Gold Spike to see Wheeling.

When the stock buyer saw him, he almost dropped his glass. "Mahone, you'd better be careful. Sonntag is in town selling cattle. If he sees you around, he'll think you've come after him."

"I wouldn't want to disappoint the man," Mahone commented, grimly.

"Well, that Salter is with him, and he's mean as a burro jack and that isn't all! Frenchy Kastelle hit town about noon, rode over from the ranch with his daughter and Texas Dowd. They're trying to figure out where their missing stock got to. Jim Hoff saw them, and I know he's said something to Sonntag."

Finn Mahone thought quickly. Byrn Sonntag would be trying to cash in on Logan's rustling scheme. He and Salter had hundreds, if not thousands, of stolen cattle to sell and that meant the stakes were high enough to kill for. If the Kastelle outfit was in town asking questions, there was a good chance they would run afoul of Sonntag and Salter. No doubt Remy's father was as fast as Carson had assured them, and surely Texas Dowd was as tough as they came, but in a match with a gunman of Sonntag's caliber anyone involved was bound to get hurt.

Mahone turned and walked swiftly to the door. He glanced sharply up and down the street, then pushed outside. Almost the first man he saw was Jim Hoff. The fat, sloppy buyer was coming up the boardwalk toward him, but when he saw Finn, he started to cross the street. "Hoff! Hold on a minute!"

Reluctantly, the man stopped, staring uneasily at Finn. "Where's Sonntag? Tell me, and quick!"

"I don't know," Hoff protested.

Mahone did not wait. He slapped the buyer of stolen stock across the mouth, hard enough to rattle his teeth. "Next time you get a pistol barrel! Where is he?"

"Down to his shack! An' I hope he kills you!" Hoff pointed further down the street to a tarpaper cabin half concealed by brush.

Shoshone Charlie had come out of the saloon. "Charlie," Finn said, "keep your eye on this hombre. If he makes a move toward a gun or to communicate with anybody, skin him alive."

The Indian moved nearer Hoff, and the cattle buyer backed away. The Indian might not be young, but he was wiry and tough, and his knife was good steel.

Nick James moved up. "What is it, Boss?"

"Sonntag and me, when I find him!"

Door by door, Finn worked down the street. Sonntag might be at the shack, but he might not be. Mahone also went down the street, only a glance was needed to tell him who was in each place he visited. When he stopped at the stock corrals, and stared down the road, he could see the dark frame shack where Sonntag lived when in Rico. It was an ugly place to approach.

The square little house stood on a mesquite-dotted lot with nothing near it but the crowded corrals and a small stable, not unlike the flimsy structure at the Brewster ranch.

The road approaching it was flat and offered no cover. He could wait until Sonntag started for town, but Finn was in no mood for waiting now. If Kastelle and Remy were in town there was every chance of them getting hurt, for the town was small, and Sonntag was not about to be thwarted at the last minute.

Finn stepped out from the corrals and started down the path, walking fast.

.   .   .

Ed Wheeling walked to the door of the Gold Spike and stared after Mahone, then stepped out on the boardwalk. Slowly, the word had swept the town. Finn Mahone was going after Sonntag and Salter.

Remy was in the general store when she heard it, and she straightened, feeling the blood drain from her face. She turned and started for the door. Her father, seeing her go, was startled by her face. He followed swiftly down the road.

The door of the square house opened, and Byrn Sonntag stepped out.

He had pulled the door closed behind him before he saw Finn Mahone. He squared around, staring at him to make sure he saw aright. Then, stepping carefully, he started toward him.

Neither man spoke.

Seventy feet apart, they halted, as at a signal. Finn Mahone felt a queer leaping excitement within him as he stared across the hot stretch of desert at Byrn Sonntag. Ever since he could recall wearing a gun, he seemed to have been hearing of Sonntag, and always his name had been spoken in awe.

Standing there, his features were frozen and hard now, and his eyes seemed to blaze with a white light.

Sweat trickled down Mahone's cheek. He could smell the sage, and the tarlike smell of creosote bush. The sun was very warm and the air was still. Somewhere, far off, a train whistled.

"Heard you're sellin' cattle, Sonntag."

"Just a few critters, here an' there."

"We may have to skin a few, check the brands."

"No, you're not. I'm goin' to kill you, Mahone."

Finn Mahone drew a deep breath. There was no way

around this. "All right, when that train whistles again, Sonntag, you can have it."

They waited, and the silence hung heavy in the desert air. Salter was out there somewhere but Finn knew he couldn't fight both of them, so he put the old guerrilla out of his mind and focused on Sonntag. Sweat trickled down Mahone's brow, and he felt it along his body under his shirt, and then he saw the big gunman drop into a half crouch, his body tense with listening. When the whistle came, both men moved. In a blur of blinding speed, Finn Mahone saw Sonntag's gun sweeping up, saw flame stab toward him, and felt a hammer blow in his stomach, but his own gun was belching fire, and he was walking toward Sonntag, hammering bullets into the big redhead, one after another.

He went to his knees, and sweat came up into his face, and then his face was in the sand, and he looked up, still clutching his guns, then he dug his elbows into the sand, and dragged himself nearer.

Somewhere through the red haze before him he could hear the low bitter cursing of Sonntag, and he fired at the sound. The voice caught, and gagged, and then Finn got his feet under him, and swayed erect only to have his knees crumple under him. In a sitting position, he could see Sonntag down, but the man was not finished. Mahone triggered his gun, but it clicked on an empty chamber.

Sonntag fired, and the bullet plucked at Finn's trouser leg. Finn dug shells from his belt and began to feed them into the chambers of his six-gun. Off to his left there was a rattle of pistol fire and the dull boom of the Spencer that Frank Salter carried. Someone was helping Mahone out.

Sonntag was getting up, his thick shirt heavy with blood, his face half shot away. What enormous vitality forced the man to his feet, Mahone could never imagine, but there he was, big as a barn, seemingly indestructible.

Mahone got to his feet, and twenty feet apart they stared at each other. Finn brought his gun up slowly.

"You're a good . . . man, Mahone," Sonntag said, "but I'll kill you an' live to spit on your grave!"

His own gun swung up swiftly, and blasted with flame, but the shot went wild, and Finn Mahone fired three times, slowly, methodically.

Sonntag staggered, and started to fall, then pitched over on his face. He squeezed off another shot, but it plowed a furrow in the sand.

It was awfully hot. Finn stared down at the fallen man, and felt his own gun slip from his fingers. He started to stoop to retrieve it, and the next thing he knew was the sound of singing in a low, lovely voice.

His lids fluttered back and he was lying on his back and Remy was bending over him. The singing stopped. "Oh, you're awake? Don't try to talk now, you must rest."

"How long have I been here?"

"A week tomorrow."

"A *week?* What happened to Sonntag?"

"He's dead . . ."

"And Salter?"

"When you're better you can thank my father."

"I thought Sonntag was going to kill me," Finn said thoughtfully.

"Don't think about it now," Remy advised. "You'll be well soon."

He caught her hand. "I'll be going back to the valley, then. It's never been the same since that morning when you were waiting on the steps for me. I think you should come back, and stay."

"Why not?" Remy wrinkled her nose at him. "That's probably the only way I'll ever get that black stallion!"

He caught her with his good arm and pulled her close. "Wait! That's not the way a wounded man should act!" she protested.

Then their lips met, and she protested no longer.

THE SKULL
AND THE
ARROW

Heavy clouds hung above the iron-colored peaks, and lancets of lightning flashed and probed. Thunder rolled like a distant avalanche in the mountain valleys. . . . The man on the rocky slope was alone.

He stumbled, staggering beneath the driving rain, his face hammered and raw. Upon his skull a wound gaped wide, upon his cheek the white bone showed through. It was the end. He was finished, and so were they all . . . they were through.

Far-off pines made a dark etching along the skyline, and that horizon marked a crossing. Beyond it was security, a life outside the reach of his enemies, who now believed him dead. Yet, in this storm, he knew he could go no further. Hail laid a volley of musketry against the rock where he leaned, so he started on, falling at times.

He had never been a man to quit, but now he had. They had beaten him, not man to man but a dozen to one. With fists and clubs and gun barrels they had beaten him . . . and now he was through. Yes, he would quit. They had taught him how to quit.

The clouds hung like dark, blowing tapestries in the gaps of the hills. The man went on until he saw the dark opening of a cave. He turned to it for shelter then, as men have always done. Though there are tents and wickiups, halls and palaces, in his direst need man always returns to the cave.

He was out of the rain but it was cold within. Shivering, he gathered sticks and some blown leaves. Among the rags of his wet and muddy clothing, he found a match, and from the match, a flame. The leaves caught, the blaze stretched tentative, exploring fingers and found food to its liking.

He added fuel; the fire took hold, crackled, and gave off heat. The man moved closer, feeling the warmth upon his hands, his body. Firelight played shadow games upon the blackened walls where the smoke from many fires had etched their memories . . . for how many generations of men?

This time he was finished. There was no use going back. His enemies were sure he was dead, and his friends would accept it as true. So he was free. He had done his best, so now a little rest, a little healing, and then over the pine-clad ridge and into the sunlight. Yet in freedom there is not always contentment.

He found fuel again, and came upon a piece of ancient pottery. Dipping water from a pool, he rinsed the pot, then filled it and brought it back to heat. He squeezed rain from the folds of his garments, then huddled between the fire and the cave wall, holding tight against the cold.

There was no end to the rain . . . gusts of wind whipped at the cave mouth and dimmed the fire. It was insanity to think of returning. He had been beaten beyond limit. When he was down they had taken turns kicking him. They had broken ribs . . . he could feel them under the cold, a raw pain in his side.

Long after he had lain inert and helpless, they had bruised and battered and worried at him. Yet he was a tough man, and he could not even find the relief of unconsciousness. He felt every blow, every kick. When they were tired from beating him, they went away.

He had not moved for hours, and only the coming of night and the rain revived him. He moved, agony in every muscle, anguish in his side, a mighty throbbing inside his skull, but somehow he managed distance. He crawled, walked, staggered, fell. He fainted, then revived, lay for a time mouth open to the rain, eyes blank and empty.

By now his friends believed him dead. . . . Well, he was not dead, but he was not going back. After all, it was their fight, had always been their fight. Each of them fought for a home, perhaps for a wife, children, parents. He had fought for a principle, and because it was his nature to fight.

With the hot water he bathed his head and face, eased the pain of his bruises, washed the blood from his hair, bathed possible poison from his cuts. He felt better then, and the cave grew warmer. He leaned against the wall and relaxed. Peace came to his muscles. After a while he heated more water and drank some of it.

Lightning revealed the frayed trees outside the cave, revealed the gray rain before the cave mouth. He would need more fuel. He got up and rummaged in the further darkness of the cave. He found more sticks and carried them back to his fire. And then he found the skull.

He believed its whiteness to be a stick, imbedded as it was in the sandy floor. He tugged to get it loose, becoming more curious as its enormous size became obvious. It was the skull of a gigantic bear, without doubt from prehistoric times. From the size of the skull, the creature must have weighed well over a ton.

Crouching by the firelight he examined it. Wedged in an eye socket was a bit of flint. He broke it free, needing all his strength. It was a finely chipped arrowhead.

The arrow could not have killed the bear. Blinded him, yes, enraged him, but not killed him. Yet the bear had been killed. Probably by a blow from a stone ax, for there was a crack in the skull, and at another place, a spot near the ear where the bone was crushed.

Using a bit of stick he dug around, finding more bones. One was a shattered foreleg of the monster, the bone fractured by a blow. And then he found the head of a stone ax. But nowhere did he find the bones of the man.

Despite the throbbing in his skull and the raw pain in his side, he was excited. Within the cave, thousands of years ago, a lone man fought a battle to the death against impossible odds . . . and won.

Fought for what? Surely there was easier game? And with the bear half blinded the man could have escaped, for the cave mouth was wide. In the whirling fury of the fight there must have been opportunities. Yet he had not fled. He had fought on against the overwhelming strength of the wounded beast, pitting against it only his lesser strength, his primitive weapons, and his man-cunning.

Venturing outside the cave for more fuel, he dragged a log within, although the effort made him gasp with agony. He drew the log along the back edge of his fire so that it was at once fuel and reflector of heat.

Burrowing a little in the now warm sand of the cave floor, he was soon asleep.

· · ·

For three weeks he lived in the cave, finding berries and nuts, snaring small game, always conscious of the presence of the pine-clad ridge, yet also aware of the skull and the arrowhead. In all that time he saw no man, either near or far . . . there was, then, no search for him.

Finally it was time to move. Now he could go over the ridge to safety. Much of his natural strength had returned; he felt better. It was a relief to know that his fight was over.

At noon of the following day he stood in the middle of a heat-baked street and faced his enemies again. Behind him were silent ranks of simple men.

"We've come back," he said quietly. "We're going to stay. You had me beaten a few weeks ago. You may beat us today, but some of you will die. And we'll be back. We'll always be back."

There was silence in the dusty street, and then the line before them wavered, and from behind it a man was walking away, and then another, and their leader looked at him and said, "You're insane. Completely insane!" And then he, too, turned away and the street before them was empty.

And the quiet men stood in the street with the light of victory in their eyes, and the man with the battered face tossed something and caught it again, something that gleamed for a moment in the sun.

"What was that?" someone asked.

"An arrowhead," the man said. "Only an arrowhead."

AFTERWORD

I n the Foreword to *West of Dodge* (Bantam, spring 1996)
I told about finding a box of my father's unpublished
manuscripts, lost for some time in the confusion of ma-
terials that my father left behind. Here again I have
dipped into that box and collected a group of stories that
I think make up one of the most interesting books of
short stories we have ever published.

To some of you a few of these tales will seem familiar,
and that is the fascinating thing about this particular
book: five of these stories were the genesis of later novels.
But unlike the novellas collected in *The Trail to Crazy Man*
and *The Rider of the Ruby Hills*, these are not simply a
shorter version of the later novels; they are early experi-
ments in characterization and plot that were altered sub-
stantially when they were enlarged to book form. Since
Dad almost never did any rewriting, this is also one of
the very few occasions any of us will have to see an early
or "first" draft of a book by Louis L'Amour. In compar-
ing the short stories to the novels you can see the ways
the stories evolved as they were developed into a longer
form. I've put together a few notes here that might be of

interest regarding the evolution of the stories in this collection.

"Caprock Rancher" was expanded in 1971 to become *Tucker*. The hero's first name was changed (the reason known only to my father) and the theme was also altered; in the short story Edwin Tucker grows into manhood by learning the truth about his juvenile delinquent buddies and cementing the relationship with his father. In the novel, however, Shell Tucker's father dies while they are chasing after the stolen money. Shell is then both after the money and out to get revenge on his onetime friends who have caused his father's death. He eventually learns that killing is not an answer he can live with, and comes up with a way to make his enemies destroy one another. Finally he finds that he cannot allow even this vengeance to control him, and decides to go on with his life.

After "Desperate Men" was written it had a strange half-life during which, even though unpublished, it was purchased by a motion picture company and eventually produced as *Kid Rodelo*. Louis took this opportunity to expand it into novel form, and the book was released around the same time as the movie. In doing so he added two major elements to the story. One, a woman named Nora Paxton who is taken along with the convicts on their trip into the desert. The other, the fact that Rodelo has served his time but needs to return the stolen gold to prove that he was innocent of the robbery. These two elements are actually quite well integrated into the plot of the novel, but the version in this collection has the Spartan purity that is deeply important in a good short story. Here Dan Rodelo is not innocent of the crime he was imprisoned for; he's simply a tough kid in a bad spot. There is no woman and no complicated agendas. It is just the men, the gold, and the desert.

"End of the Drive" became *Kiowa Trail*. The two characters who are the hero and heroine of *Kiowa Trail* were added to the basic idea of "End of the Drive." Tom Gavagan, "End of the Drive's" young romantic, becomes Tom Lundy in the novel, a minor character who gets killed when he violates the city ordinance forbidding trail drivers north of the town's main street. His death is the catalyst that causes the rest of the outfit to wreak a unique revenge on the town. *Kiowa Trail* is also one of a handful of my father's stories to take place partly in Europe.

"The Skull and the Arrow" is a good example of the incredible length of time it can take for a story to work its way through a writer's creative processes. The story was written sometime in the mid-1950s and through an odd series of circumstances became, surprisingly enough, *Last of the Breed*. About ten years later Dad wanted to write a book about a reconnaissance pilot much like Gary Powers who, instead of being captured, escapes. It was a cold-war fantasy but one that originated in the days of Eisenhower rather than Reagan. When Louis was planning the book, twenty years before he started writing, it was going to be called *The Skull and the Arrow* and based in part on this story. At a critical moment, when the hero is on the verge of giving up to either the Siberian cold or the Soviet soldiers, he takes refuge in a cave and, just like the nameless character in this book, discovers the evidence of a prehistoric battle between a huge bear and a man armed only with primitive weapons. The pilot is encouraged because the man seems to have survived this encounter with a Russian bear, and decides to press on. I have no idea why this sequence was not included in the novel *Last of the Breed*, but when the manuscript was finally finished it was not included.

"The Lonesome Gods" is another good example of

how a brief examination of a theme can evolve into a novel. Like *The Skull and the Arrow*, it shares no part of the characters or plot of the novel; it simply explores the idea that the gods of ancient peoples may respond to the attention of a person from another time and another culture. That theme and the title are the only similarities.

"The Courting of Griselda" did not develop into a novel, but its hero, Tell Sackett, is well known to many readers. It is with great sadness that I bid this character farewell, as there are no more stories about him left to publish.

"Elisha Comes to Red Horse" is a sort of sequel to the novel *Fallon*. The town of Red Horse is again the setting of a confidence game, this time of biblical proportions. Macon Fallon has disappeared from the scene but Brennen, the saloon owner, and a couple of the other original characters remain. At one time Dad intended to turn this story into a full-length novel and wrote several versions of the first chapter without going any further. The earliest versions do not include references to the characters from *Fallon* and I think it was only later that he noticed the town had the same name and that they were both stories about con artists, and played up the similarities.

"Rustler Roundup" is unrelated to any of Dad's other work, but this collection is a good place to put it. It was originally written in December 1947 and was submitted to *Standard* magazine's editor, Leo Margulies. He returned it for some minor revisions, but Dad seems to have never gotten around to sending it back.

In the next collection of stories there will be a never-before-published Kilkenny novella, another story about Utah Blaine, and the last remaining tale of the Talon family, along with six other stories. The title of that book will be *Monument Rock* and the stories in it will finish off the mysterious box that I discovered several years ago. *Mon-*

ument Rock will be published in the spring of 1998, and following its release we will go back to bringing out books containing the rest of the Louis L'Amour short stories that were previously published back in the pulp magazine days. I think we have enough books to get us well past the millennium.

In the back of *West of Dodge* we published a list of people I was trying to locate in regard to the biography of my father that I am writing. I want to include a special thanks here to the old friends and acquaintances of Louis L'Amour who have contacted me for all the help they have offered me in my research.

The following is an updated list of the people I am trying to contact. If you find your name on the list, I would be very grateful if you would write to me. Some of these people may have known Louis as Duke LaMoore or Michael "Micky" Moore, as Louis occasionally used those names. Many of the people on this list may be dead. If you were a family member (or were a very good friend) of anyone on the list who has passed away, I would like to hear from you, too. Some of the names I have marked with an asterisk (*); if there is anyone out there who knows anything at all about these people, I would like to hear it. The address to write to is:

Louis L'Amour Biography Project
P.O. Box 41183
Pasadena, CA 91114-9183

Marian Payne—Married a man named Duane. Louis said in 1938 that he had known her for five years. She moved to New York for a while; she may have lived in Wichita at some point.

Chaplain Phillips—Louis first met him at Fort Sill, then again in Paris at the Place de Saint Augustine officer's mess. The first meeting was in 1942, the second in 1945.

Anne Mary Bentley—Friend of Louis's from Oklahoma in the 1930s. Possibly a musician. Lived in Denver for a time.

Betty Brown—Woman that Louis corresponded with extensively while in Choctaw in the late 1930s. Later she moved to New York.

Jacques Chambrun*—Louis's agent from the late 1930s through the late 1950s.

Des—His first name. Chambrun's assistant in the late 1940s or early 1950s.

Friscia*—Joe, possibly from Boston. One of two men that Louis met in jail in Phoenix in the mid-1920s. They joined the Hagenbeck & Wallace Circus together. They rode freights across Texas and spent a couple of nights in the Star of Hope mission in Houston.

Pete Boering*—Shipmate of Louis's on the *S.S. Steadfast.* Born in the late 1890s. Came from Amsterdam, Holland. His father may have been a ship's captain. Louis and Pete sailed from Galveston together in the mid-1920s.

Harry "Shorty" Warren*—Shipmate of Louis's on the *S.S. Steadfast* in the mid-1920s. They sailed from Galveston to England and back. Harry may have been an Australian.

Joe Hollinger*—Louis met him while with the Hagenbeck & Wallace Circus, where he ran the "privilege car." A couple of months later he shipped out on the *S.S. Steadfast* with Louis. This was in the mid-1920s.

Captain Douglas*—Captain of the ship in Indonesia that Louis served on. A three-masted auxiliary schooner.

Joe Hildebrand*—Louis met him on the docks in New Orleans in the mid-1920s, then ran into him later in Indonesia. Joe may have been the first mate and Louis second mate on a schooner operated by Captain Douglas. This would have been in the East Indies in the late 1920s or early 1930s. Joe may have been an aircraft pilot and flown for Pan Am in the early 1930s.

Turk Madden*—Louis knew him in Indonesia in the late 1920s or early 1930s. They may have spent some time around the old Straits Hotel and the Maypole Bar in Singapore. Later on, in the States, Louis traveled around with him putting on boxing exhibitions. Madden worked at an airfield near Denver as a mechanic in the early 1930s. Louis eventually used his name for a fictional character.

"Cockney" Joe Hagen*—Louis knew him in Indonesia in the late 1920s or early 1930s. He may have been part of the Straits Hotel-Maypole Bar crowd in Singapore.

Mason or Milton*—Don't know which was his real name. He was a munitions dealer in Shanghai in the late 1920s or early 1930s. He was killed while Louis was there.

Singapore Charlie*—Louis knew him in Singapore and served with him on Douglas's schooner in the East Indies. Louis was second mate and Charlie was bos'n. He was a stocky man of indeterminate race and if I remember correctly Dad told me he had quite a few tattoos. In the early 1930s Louis helped get him a job on a ship in San Pedro, California, that was owned by a movie studio.

Renee Semich—She was born in Vienna (I think) and was going to a New York art school when Louis met her. This was just before World War II. Her father's family was from Yugoslavia or Italy, her mother from Austria. They lived in New York, where her aunt had an apartment overlooking Central Park. For awhile she worked for a company in Waterbury, Connecticut.

Ann Steeley/Cathy O'Donnell*—A friend of Louis's in Oklahoma in the late 1930s (Ann Steeley was her real name), she later went to Hollywood and had a career in the movies.

Enoch Lusk—Owner of Lusk Publishing Company in 1939, original publisher of Louis's *Smoke From This Altar*. Also associated with the National Printing Company, Oklahoma City.

Helen Turner*—Louis knew her in the late 1920s in Los Angeles. Once a showgirl with Jack Fine's *Follies.*

Frank Moran—Louis met him in Ventura when Louis was a "club second" for fighters in the late 1920s. They also may have known each other in Los Angeles or Kingman in the mid-1920s. Louis ran into him again on Hollywood Boulevard late in 1946.

Jud and Red Rasco*—Brothers, cowboys; Louis met them in Tucumcari, New Mexico. Also saw them in Santa Rosa, New Mexico. This was in the early to mid-1920s.

Olga Santiago—Friend of Louis's from the late 1940s in Los Angeles. Last saw her at a book signing in Thousand Oaks, California.

Jose Craig Berry—A writer friend of Louis's from Oklahoma City in the late 1930s. First person to review *Smoke From This Altar*. She worked for a paper called the *Black Dispatch*.

Evelyn Smith Colt—She knew Louis in Kingman at one point, probably the late 1920s. Louis saw her again much later at a Paso Robles book signing.

Kathlyn Beucler Hays—Friend from Choctaw, taught school there in the 1930s. Louis saw her much later at a book signing in San Diego.

Floyd Bolton—Came to Choctaw and talked to Louis about doing a movie in the Dutch East Indies. This was in the late 1930s.

Lisa Cohn—Reference librarian in Portland; family owned Cohn Bros. Furniture Store. Louis knew her in the late 1920s or early 1930s.

Mary Claire Collingsworth—Friend and correspondent from Oklahoma in the 1930s.

C.A. Donnell—Rented Louis a typewriter in Oklahoma City in the early 1930s.

Duks*—I think this was his last name, probably a shortened version of the original family name. First mate on the *S.S. Steel Worker* in the mid-1920s. I think he was a U.S. citizen, but he was originally a Russian.

Maudee Harris—My Aunt Chynne's sister.

Parker LaMoore and Chynne Harris LaMoore*—Louis's eldest brother and his wife. Parker was secretary to the governor of Oklahoma for a while, then he worked for the Scripps-Howard newspaper chain. He also worked with Ambassador Pat Hurley. He died in the early 1950s, and although we know most of the positions he held in his professional life, we have very little information about him personally. Chynne was his wife and she lived longer than he did, but I don't know where she lived after his death.

Haig*—His last name. Louis described him as a Scotsman, once an officer in the British-Indian army. Louis says he was "an officer in one of the Scottish regiments." Louis knew him in Shanghai in the 1930s, but we don't know how old he would have been at the time. He may have been involved in some kind of intelligence work. For a while, he and Louis shared an apartment that seems to have been located just off Avenue King Edward VII.

Joe Davenport—Louis heard of him in China. In the early to mid-1930s he was to deliver a shipment of guns and ammunition to General Ma but was killed before he could make the connection. He was once a U.S. Marine.

Milligan—A pilot in China in the mid-1930s. A friend of Haig's. We think that he saved Louis's life by getting him out of the country. Born in Texas, once a U.S. Marine.

Lola LaCorne—Along with her sister and mother, was a friend of Louis's in Paris during World War II. She later taught literature at the Sorbonne, and had (hopefully still has) a husband named Christopher.

Dean Kirby—Pal from Oklahoma City in the late 1930s who seems to have been a copywriter or something of the sort. Might have worked for Lusk Publishing.

Bunny Yeager—Girlfriend of Dean Kirby's from Oklahoma City.

Virginia McElroy—Girl with whom Louis went to school in Jamestown.

Eleanor and Geraldine "Jeri" Medsker—Sisters from Shawnee, Oklahoma. Louis knew them in the late 1930s. Louis last saw Eleanor at a book signing in Thousand Oaks, California.

George Russell—Friend of Louis's from Kingman in the late 1920s, married one of the Von Biela sisters.

Any of the Von Biela sisters—Louis knew them in, you guessed it, Kingman, Arizona.

Arleen Weston Sherman—Friend of Louis's from Jamestown, when he was thirteen or fourteen. I think her family visited the LaMoores in Choctaw in the 1930s.

Her older sister's name was Mary; parents' names were Ralph and Lil; Ralph was a railroad conductor.

Merle Templeton—A man Louis knew from Kingman. He ran a rodeo for Bill Bonelli in Los Angeles. Bonelli was a political figure of some sort.

Harry Bigelow—Louis knew him in Ventura. He had a picture taken with Louis's mother, Emily LaMoore, at a place named Berkeley Springs around 1929. Louis may have known him at the Katherine Mine, near Kingman, Arizona, or in Oregon.

Tommy Pinto—Boxer from Portland; got Louis a job at Portland Manufacturing.

Percy E. "Steve" Stephens—Louis knew him in Kingman; he was married to Alice Von Biela. Louis saw him again at a book signing in Escondido in 1983.

Nancy Carroll*—An actress as of 1933. Louis knew her from the chorus of a show at the Winter Garden in New York and a cabaret in New Jersey where she and her sister danced occasionally, probably during the mid- to late 1920s.

Judith Wood—Actress. Louis knew her in Hollywood in the late 1920s.

Stanley George—The George family relocated from Kingman, Arizona, to Ventura, California, possibly in the late 1920s.

Anyone familiar with Singapore in the late 1920s, the *old* Straits Hotel and/or the Maypole Bar.

Anyone who is very knowledgeable in the military history and/or politics of western (Shansi, Kansu, and Sinkiang Provinces) China in 1935-37.

Anyone who served on the *S.S. Steel Worker* between 1925 and 1930.

Anyone who served on the lumber schooner *Catherine G. Sudden* between 1925 and 1936.

Anyone who served on the *S.S. Steadfast* between 1924 and 1930.

Anyone who served on the *Annandale* between 1920 and 1926.

Anyone who served on the *Randsberg*, a German freighter, between 1925 and 1937.

Anyone familiar with the Royal Government Experimental Hospital in Calcutta, India.

About
Louis L'Amour

"I think of myself in the oral tradition—as a troubadour, a village tale-teller, the man in the shadows of the campfire. That's the way I'd like to be remembered—as a storyteller. A good storyteller."

It is doubtful that any author could be as at home in the world re-created in his novels as Louis Dearborn L'Amour. Not only could he physically fill the boots of the rugged characters he wrote about, but he literally "walked the land my characters walk." His personal experiences as well as his lifelong devotion to historical research combined to give Mr. L'Amour the unique knowledge and understanding of people, events, and the challenge of the American frontier that became the hallmarks of his popularity.

Of French-Irish descent, Mr. L'Amour could trace his own family in North America back to the early 1600s and follow their steady progression westward, "always on the frontier." As a boy growing up in Jamestown, North Dakota, he absorbed all he could about his family's frontier heritage, including the story of his great-grandfather who was scalped by Sioux warriors.

Spurred by an eager curiosity and desire to broaden his horizons, Mr. L'Amour left home at the age of fifteen and enjoyed a wide variety of jobs including seaman, lumberjack, elephant handler, skinner of dead cattle, miner, and an officer in the transportation corps during World War II. During his "yondering" days he also circled the world on a freighter, sailed a dhow on the Red Sea, was shipwrecked in the West Indies and stranded in the Mojave Desert. He won fifty-one of fifty-nine fights as a professional boxer and worked as a journalist and lecturer. He was a voracious reader and collector of rare books. His personal library contained 17,000 volumes.

Mr. L'Amour "wanted to write almost from the time I could talk." After developing a widespread following for his many frontier and adventure stories written for fiction magazines, Mr. L'Amour published his first full-length novel, *Hondo*, in the United States in 1953. Every one of his more than 100 books is in print; there are nearly 230 million copies of his books in print worldwide, making him one of the bestselling authors in modern literary history. His books have been translated into twenty languages, and more than forty-five of his novels and stories have been made into feature films and television movies.

His hardcover bestsellers include *The Lonesome Gods*, *The Walking Drum* (his twelfth-century historical novel), *Jubal Sackett, Last of the Breed,* and *The Haunted Mesa.* His memoir, *Education of a Wandering Man,* was a leading bestseller in 1989. Audio dramatizations and adaptations of many L'Amour stories are available on cassette tapes from Bantam Audio publishing.

The recipient of many great honors and awards, in 1983 Mr. L'Amour became the first novelist ever to be awarded the Congressional Gold Medal by the United States Congress in honor of his life's work. In 1984 he was also awarded the Medal of Freedom by President Reagan.

Louis L'Amour died on June 10, 1988. His wife, Kathy, and their two children, Beau and Angelique, carry the L'Amour tradition forward with new books written by the author during his lifetime to be published by Bantam.